KRIMSON SURGE

KRIMSON EMPIRE BOOK 3

JULIA HUNI

KRIMSON SURGE

KRIMSON EMPIRE
BOOK 3

JULIA HUNI

Krimson Surge Copyright © 2020 by Julia Huni

All rights reserved

All names, settings, characters, and incidents in this book are fictional. Any resemblance to someone or something you know or have read about, living or dead, is purely coincidental. This is fiction. They're all made up.

The distribution of this book without permission is a theft of the author's intellectual property. If you would like permission to use material from the book (other than a short excerpt for review purposes), please contact info@juliahuni.com. Thank you for your support of the author's rights.

Cover by Deranged Doctor Designs

Originally published by Craig Martelle, Inc.

Published by
IPH Media, LLC
PO Box 62
Sisters, Oregon 97759

Second US edition, August, 2023

For my Kickstarter backers:

Alice Hickcox
AM Scott
Andy fytczyk
Angelica Quiggle
B. Plaga
Barb Collishaw
Brenton Held
Bridget Horn
Buzz
C. Gockel
Carl Blakemore
Carl Walter
Carol Van Natta
Cate Dean
Chicomedallas123
Christian Meyer
Clark 'the dragon' Willis
Clive Green
Craig Shapcott
Daniel Nicholls
Danielle Menon

Dave Arrington
David Haskins
Debbie Adler
Diana Dupre
Don Bartenstein
Donna J. Berkley
E. C. Eklund
Edgar Middel
Elizabeth Chaldekas
Erudessa Gentian
fred oelrich
Gary Olsen
GhostCat
Ginger Booth
Giovanni Colina
Greg Levick
Heiko Koenig
Hope Terrell
Ian Bannon
Isaac 'Will It Work' Dansicker
Jack Green
Jacquelin Baumann
Jade Paterson
James Parks
James Vink
Jane
Jeff
Jim Gotaas
John Idlor
John Listorti
John Wollenbecker
K. R. Stone
Karl Hakimian

Kate Harvey
Kate Sheeran Swed
Katy Board
Kevin Black
Klint Demetrio
Laura Rainbow Dragon
Laura Waggoner
Laury Hutt
Liliana E.
Luke Italiano
M. E. Grauel
Mandy
Marc Sangalli
Marie Devey
Mark Parish
Martin
Mel
Michael Carter
Michael Ditlefsen
Michael L. Whitt
Michelle Ackerman
Michelle Hughes
Mick Buckley
Mike W.
Moe Naguib
Niall Gordon
Nik W
Norm Coots
Patrick Dempsey
Patrick Hay
Paul
Pauline Baird Jones
Peggy Hall

Peter Foote
Peter J.
Peter Warnock
Ranel Stephenson Capron
Regina Dowling
Rich Trieu
Robert D. Stewart
Robert Parker
Rodney Johnson
Roger M
Rosheen Halstead
Ross Bernheim
Sarah Heile
Sheryl A Knowles
Stephen Ballentine
Steve Huth
Steven Whysong
Susan Nakaba
Sven Lugar
Ted
(The other) Ted
Ted M. Young
Terry Twyford
The Creative Fund by BackerKit
Thomas Monaghan
Timothy Greenshields
Tom Kam
Trent
Tricia Babinski
Valerie Fetsch
Vic Tapscott
walshjk
wayne

werelord
Wesley Dawes
William Andrew Campbell (WAC)
Wolf Pack Entertainment
Yvette

CHAPTER 1

QUINN DUCKED. A foot slashed through the air over her head, narrowly missing her temple. She swept her leg out, but her opponent avoided it. She leaped back to give herself breathing room, but the attacker pushed forward.

She ducked behind the couch, but the other woman surged over the furniture, clearing it easily. Quinn backpedaled, threw a choppy punch, and ran across the room. Breathing heavily, she spun, hands up and crouching. The attacker launched a flurry of jabs and kicks. Quinn backed away, blocking, trying to maintain her balance. She spun, catching the other in the gut with a lucky back-kick. Spinning again, she followed the kick with a couple low punches. Feeling fingers scrabbling over her shirt, she broke away.

Her assailant grabbed the collar and yanked her back. She spun around, closer to the attacker, loosening the fabric biting into her throat. At close quarters, she slammed her rigid hand toward the neck. The attacker deflected the blow, grabbing her hand and whipping her around into a headlock.

Quinn yanked at the arm locked around her throat, slowly cutting off her air. "Look, Elvis!" she croaked.

The arm dropped away. "You're supposed to tap out, not invoke an ancient deity." Francine released her and stepped back.

Quinn swung around and lunged, but Francine easily blocked the attack.

"And pretending to surrender then attacking is not fair play."

"If I'm fighting for my life, I'm not playing fair," Quinn gasped, her lungs heaving. She leaned over, hands on knees. "How are you not even winded?"

"My heart rate is up," Francine said. "But I've been doing this a lot longer than you have. You got in some good hits."

"You said you haven't done any sparring in a year." Quinn staggered across the room to grab a bottle of water. "Want one?"

Francine caught the bottle Quinn tossed and opened it. "I haven't done any sparring, but I've worked out. Gotta keep the speed and flexibility. You never know when you might need it." She sipped then closed the lid. "You're doing very well, for a beginner."

Quinn shook her head. "I shouldn't be a beginner. I used to do this stuff. Well, not quite this style, but I learned a little hand-to-hand when I was on active duty."

"That was a long time ago," Francine said. "If you don't use it, you lose it. Ready to go again?"

Quinn nodded. "I'm not getting any younger. Let's do this."

By the end of the hour, both women were breathing heavily. Quinn wiped the sweat from her forehead and bowed to Francine. "Thank you."

Francine ruined her own bow with a shrug midway. "It's good for me, too. Passes the time. When do we arrive at Sendarine?"

Quinn picked up her comtab. "In about four hours. I guess we'd better put things back." She tucked the device into her pocket and grabbed the end of the couch. "Gimme a hand with this."

They slid the couch to its usual position and latched the clamps, then unfolded the table and locked it into place.

"Leave the chairs stowed." Maerk strode into the room. "We

won't need them until later, and they're safer tucked away. How was the workout?"

Francine grinned. "She's getting better. But don't fall for her Elvis routine."

Maerk's face scrunched in confusion. "I don't know what that means."

"Neither does she," Quinn said. "Elvis was an ancient Earth philosopher, not a deity."

"Depends on who you ask," Francine retorted. "I'm hitting the shower." She jumped onto the bench at the back of the room and pulled down the folding ladder. "You should probably do a little stretching before you come up. Don't want to get stiff."

Quinn pulled a mat out of the cupboard under the bench Francine had just vacated, then glanced at Maerk. "Did you need something?"

He shook his head. "Checking the cargo. Liz checked in with Sendarine Station, in orbit above Sendarine. We don't have to stop there, so we'll land in an hour."

"Guess I'd better get warmed down and cleaned up," Quinn said. "Have you seen Ellianne?"

"She's up front with Liz," Maerk said. "She's picking up the flying thing as fast as Dareen did. That girl's going to be a force to reckon with in the next few years."

Quinn's lips twitched. "She's already a force to be reckoned with. She's eight going on eighteen."

Maerk clapped her on the shoulder. "You'll get through it. The nice thing about raising kids on a ship is you have a whole crew to keep you from murdering them." He winked and sauntered out of the lounge.

"LUCAS LARAINE, I am going to strangle you with this charging cable and feed you to the space whales!" Lou Marconi yelled through the intercom. She ran frustrated fingers through her messy gray hair, making it stand on end. "You can hide, but I will find you! I know this ship better than anyone else."

Her grandson, End Whiting, chuckled. "You might find him, but that kid is wiry. He can probably squirm into places you couldn't possibly reach. What did he do this time?"

"He changed the orientation on all my screens," Lou spat. "Look at that! Everything is sideways."

"Gramma, I showed you how to fix that before." End leaned over her shoulder and swiped at the view. "It's right here, under settings." With a flick and a swipe, he fixed the display. "That probably wasn't Lucas, though. Not sophisticated enough. That looks like something Dareen might do."

"She knows better than to mess with my navigation screens," Lou grumbled. "I finally got you two trained up to be halfway decent crew members instead of pesky kids, and they give me another one. I can't believe I agreed to let him fly with us."

"I didn't do it, Lou," Lucas' voice came through the intercom. "Whatever it was. I've been working with Stene for the last four hours." His voice cracked then dropped into a lower register. "I've been busy!"

"He's been with me," Stene agreed.

End's lips twitched again. Just because Lucas wasn't on the bridge didn't mean he was innocent. He remembered pulling that kind of remote prank himself not too many years ago.

"Fine," Lou said, her eyes narrow. "Whoever it was, you'd better not do it again." She slapped the intercom icon, cutting the connection. "I need more—better—security."

"You have all the passwords and biometrics, Gramma," End said. The problem was, she tended to wander away, leaving the system unlocked. It was a small ship, and they all knew better than to do anything dangerous, so internal security wasn't a high priority. "I can set the auto-lock to a shorter—"

"Not now. Dammit, I forgot to make my announcement." Lou

swiped the screen again and the intercom icon lit up green. "We're in our parking orbit. Anyone who wants to go dirtside, be at the shuttle in twenty. Out." She flicked something, and the screen went sideways. "End!"

He smothered a laugh. "I'll take care of this, Gramma. You can get ready to drop."

After Lou stomped off the bridge, he called Lucas again. "Nice job. Using the adaptive tech with a voice prompt—genius."

The boy snickered, then fell silent. "I don't know what you're talking about."

"Good one, kid," End said. "I have trained you well."

END FLEW "HIS" shuttle, the *Screaming Eagle,* to the Sendarine landing field with Dareen riding co-pilot. He parked on the apron and started the shutdown sequence.

"Field payment processed," Dareen said. "We're cleared to unload."

Kert and Lou unbuckled their restraints and climbed out of the jump seats behind the pilots. "You're getting better," Lou said. "Almost as smooth as Dareen."

Dareen grinned and punched her brother's arm. "Almost."

"That landing was flawless," End protested.

"The landing was good," Lou said. "You hit a few bumps on the taxi."

"I can't help it if they don't maintain their strip," End grumbled.

"It's called steering." Dareen rotated her wrist as if using joystick. "You drive *around* the bumps."

He rolled his eyes. "Whatever." He pushed past his sister and followed Lou to the cargo hold. Kert went to the rear to lower the ramp. Lucas clutched the cargo tablet, ready to shift the pallets of equipment they'd brought to Sendarine.

Dareen trailed behind. "The buyer says he's running late." She poked at her comtab. "But we can start unloading. Just stack it there. He's got his own equipment."

Under Kert's direction, Lucas used the cargo arm to move the pallets from the ship to the apron. The buyer arrived a few minutes later, and they helped transfer the goods to his truck. Dareen completed the financial transaction.

"Textbook," Kert said.

"I wish they all went that smoothly," Lou grumbled. "I wonder what Liz has us picking up?"

"Me, for one thing." Tony strode to the ship.

"Tony!" The next few minutes involved rounds of hugs, backslapping, and general merriment.

"Liz hasn't landed yet?" Tony asked.

"They're on final right now." Dareen waved her comtab. She squinted into the distance. "There they are!"

They watched the *Swan of the Night* land smoothly on the runway, then taxi toward them. About halfway down the apron, the ship curved to the right, then returned to the centerline. "Your mother knows how to avoid the bumps," Lou said.

End shook his head but couldn't hide his grin. He hadn't seen his parents since they'd left Lunesco three weeks before. Lou's ship had made a side trip to pick up the cargo they'd just unloaded, while the *Swan* had stayed behind to get the latest sugar gourd harvest. Three pallets of sugar gourds should put a tidy sum in the family coffers.

As the *Swan* taxied toward them, a boxy, unmarked vehicle drove onto the apron from the opposite direction. It parked a few hundred meters away, and three beefy men climbed out. Two of them held weapons, while the third carried a comtab.

"You think that's their buyer?" Lou asked. She jerked her head toward the shuttle. Kert disappeared inside

"Probably," Tony said. "Frentzen Enterprises is known for its security."

Kert returned with four blast rifles. He handed them out. "Don't want to look weak in front of the buyers. If that's what they are."

While the others watched the *Swan* taxi toward them, End kept his eyes on the Frentzen truck. Something about it didn't feel right. He noticed Tony doing the same. "Has anyone checked with Mom?" End asked. "To ID that truck?"

Lou grunted. "She says it's them."

A flicker of movement at the corner of the nearest building caught his eye. He nudged Tony. "You see that?"

Tony handed his rifle back to Kert and reached into his pocket. "I saw *something*." He flicked his comtab, and one of his tiny drones buzzed into the air.

End glanced at Tony's screen as the drone approached the corner. The screen flashed and went blank. "What was that?"

"Something not good," Tony said. "Everyone inside. We don't need to be exposed while Liz does business. Kert, shut the back ramp to three-quarters so we can see over it. We'll provide backup." As he spoke, he hurried the family up the ramp.

The men by the truck swung toward the building, their guns pointed at the corner where Tony's drone had been fried.

"Liz, get back to the runway," Lou called into her comtab as they scrambled up the ramp. "I don't care if your buyer is mad, we've got hostiles. Wait at the launch point until we figure out what's going on."

"I'm sending another drone," Tony said. "Keeping it out of range this time." The tiny mechanical thing buzzed away from his hand and through the closing gap between the ramp and the top of the ship.

Kert stopped the ramp at shoulder height. End, Dareen, and Kert rested their rifles on the top edge of the door, pointed at the building. Tony leaned against the ramp to watch the Frentzen truck through the triangular gap.

Lou grumbled, then dragged a crate to the rear ramp. "Lucas, get over here." She handed the boy her rifle. "How good a shot are you?"

Lucas grinned. "I'm an expert in *Mad Rush Four*."

"Have you ever shot a gun in real life?" Lou demanded.

He nodded. "My dad took me to the firing range at Hadriana. I'm not quite as good IRL."

"Okay, climb up on that box and keep watch on the building. Don't shoot anything. I'm putting the safety on." She flicked a switch before handing him the weapon. "Look formidable. I'm going up front to start the launch checklist." She slapped her comtab as she ran across the cargo bay. "Liz, status!"

"Our neighbors are looking nervous," Tony said. "I think they're getting ready to bolt."

"Anything from the drone?" End asked.

"Just reached the corner," Tony said. He squinted at the device. "Ah, crap. It's a bunch of kids with air rifles! Kert, drop the ramp. I'm going to give those kids—"

"Leave it," Kert said. "Buzz 'em with the drone, if you want, but it's not worth the risk. There could be real danger out there."

"If no one has picked me up in the five days I've been here, I doubt they'd come for me now," Tony said.

"That isn't what you seemed to think a few minutes ago," Dareen replied. "Besides, you aren't the only one people are looking for." She jerked her head at Lucas.

Tony heaved a sigh. "You're right. I'm recalling the drone. We'll hold off on the family reunion until we're back in orbit. You got the inter-ship airlock working?"

"Yeah," Kert said as the others pulled their rifles in and he shut the ramp. "Worked great with the shuttle last week."

Tony swiped his comtab. "Lou, false alarm—it was just kids. But let's stay buttoned up and launch as soon as Liz is unloaded. No point in having all the Marconi potatoes in one basket."

CHAPTER 2

QUINN PACED across the *Swan's* lounge, trying to work out her frustration and her sore muscles at the same time. Sashelle, the Eliminator of Vermin, leaped off the back of the couch and tangled around her feet, tripping her up. She grabbed the corner of the table to keep from falling and glared at the caat. "You ignore me ninety percent of the time," she grumbled, "and mess with me the other ten."

Ellianne skipped across the lounge to scoop up the huge caat. "Sassy isn't messing with you, Mom. She's being friendly."

"Friendly?" Quinn laughed. "With friends like that... What is taking so long?"

Ellianne plopped down on the couch with the caat in her lap. "Good kitty," she cooed as she scratched behind the animal's ears. The caat purred, staring at Quinn with narrowed eyes.

Quinn glared back.

The hatch to the cockpit opened and Maerk stuck his head through. "We're good to unload. Just have to taxi over to the landing space. But Lou and company don't want to wait. They had a bit of a dustup. They'll guard our six from inside the ship, then we'll meet them upstairs." He pointed his thumb upward. "She said something about potatoes."

"Potatoes? In one basket?" Quinn asked. When he nodded, she shrugged. "Probably a safer plan. Do you need help unloading?"

Maerk shook his head. "Only three crates, remember? Francine's already got 'em on the loading panel. We'll transfer them to the buyer and off we go. We won't even shut down the engines. You two stay here."

He disappeared into the cockpit again, then returned. As he walked between Quinn and Ellianne, he slid a mini blaster into her hand. "Just in case." Then he disappeared through the hatch to the cargo bay.

"What's just in case?" Ellianne asked. "Shouldn't we have guns if there might be bad guys?"

Quinn laughed. "There aren't any bad guys here." She pushed the mini blaster into her jacket pocket and felt something hard. "What's this?" She pulled a small, flat rectangle out, trying to remember the last time she'd worn this jacket.

"Looks like a data-card," Ellianne said. "My tablet has a slot for that size."

"My comtab does too." Quinn turned the card over, but it was unmarked. Then she remembered. "Lunesco!" Sebi Maarteen, Federation customs officer and revolutionary, had slipped this card to her as they left the *Solar Wind*'s shuttle on Lunesco. He'd been so casual about it, and she tried to match his demeanor. Then in the ensuing chaos, she'd forgotten about it. Strange he'd never mentioned it later.

"You want me to get my tablet?" Ellianne asked.

"No." Quinn shoved the card back into her pocket. "I'll look at it later. I don't want you running around the ship if we might launch soon."

"Cargo transferred," Maerk sang as he and Francine came into the lounge. "Money in the bank. Strap in and let's get out of here!" He clapped Quinn on the shoulder and continued to the cockpit.

Francine dropped into one of the armchairs and pulled out the hidden harness. "I was hoping to get some time on the dirt."

"I still don't understand why you're here." Quinn took the seat beside Ellianne. She flipped up the fabric flap and pulled the shoulder straps out of the hidden compartment.

When she tried to help her daughter buckle them, the little girl pushed her hands away. "I can do it. Time to fly, Sassy."

The caat stretched, then leapt off the girl's lap and strolled to her cubby under the bench built into the back wall.

Both women watched the animal curl up in her box. Francine's head shook slowly. "Too smart."

Quinn nodded. "It's kind of—"

"I know," Francine replied when Quinn broke off.

The caat's eyes closed to slits, and she purred.

SENDARINE HAD SEVEN MOONS, plus a scattering of smaller orbiting objects. Under Lou's direction, End piloted the *Millennium Peregrine* into orbit around one of the smaller bodies. When the *Swan* matched velocity, he extended the new inter-ship airlock. It connected with a muffled thump.

"Airlock secure," Stene called through the intercom. "They'll be coming over shortly."

"We'll keep the airlocks closed. No point in risking decompression." Lou glared at Lucas and End. "This is serious business, boys, so no screwing around."

End drew himself up. "I've lived on this ship my whole life. I think I know when to behave."

"Well, keep an eye on that one." Lou pointed at the younger boy. "And stop teaching him your stupid pranks."

Lucas muttered something under his breath. End put a hand on his shoulder, shaking his head an infinitesimal amount. When Lou stomped off the bridge, he squeezed Lucas' shoulder. "She knows you aren't stupid, but she likes to make sure everyone is on the same page. Think of it as re-running the checklist rather than nagging."

The younger boy shrugged. "At least she knows I'm smart. Better than Grandmother LaRaine. I'll take it."

End double-checked the settings on the autopilot, and the connections to his comtab. Any alerts would be transferred to him, so he didn't have to stay on the bridge. They followed Lou to the crew lounge.

A wall of chatter hit them when the lounge door opened. The entire Marconi family, plus extras, made a lot of noise. End threw his arms around his parents, while Lucas greeted his sister and mother. Dareen and Kert had laid out trays of snacks and beverages, and soon everyone relaxed—eating, drinking and talking.

"What have you been up to, Tony?" Maerk called out during a lull in the conversation.

Tony looked around at the faces surrounding him. "Fomenting discord and discontent," he said with a grin. "Amanda put me in touch with the leaders on a couple of different worlds. They're all this close to slipping the chain." He held up his fingers a few millimeters apart. "I thought Lunesco would be the catalyst, but everyone is still gun shy. They're each waiting for the next planet to act first." He sipped his drink.

"Is that what you're going to do now?" Lou asked sourly. "Fly around the galaxy trying to get frightened civilians to start a war?"

Tony shook his head. "We put plans in place. When the time is right, they'll act. We have to make sure we've got enough mayhem lined up to spread the Federation forces thin."

"What about the Russosken?" Francine asked. "Petrov was only one branch. I'm betting the *nachal'nik* is pissed. If she's identified us, they'll be coming our way. Soon."

"I know," Tony said. "That's why those kids spooked me. Until we've neutralized this situation, I think we need to stay off the ground —at least in large numbers. Meeting in orbit is much safer."

"How do you plan to 'neutralize the situation'?" Lou barked. "Unless you wipe out the entire Russosken, they'll keep after us until we're dead. And the Federation might be slow to respond, but they *will* come after you. We'd be safer to move to the other side of the galaxy."

"If you want to be safe, Gramma, by all means, do that," Tony replied sharply. "I had no intention of putting the family in jeopardy. That's why I left and joined the service. I'm sorry if my recent actions have made you a target."

Liz laughed. "Mom's been a target her whole life. She loves this stuff. If she didn't, she'd retire to Saen Petersberg and be done with it."

"What if..." Francine started, but Lou overrode her.

"If I'm a target, it's for my own actions." She chugged her drink. "The Marconis aren't afraid of the Russosken or the Federation, but we're smart enough not to kick the anthill."

"At least not more than usual," Stene said.

Lou growled. "Whatever. Let's eat dinner."

THE NEXT MORNING, Quinn set out schoolwork for Ellianne and Lucas in the *Swan's* lounge, then went in search of Tony. She cycled through the airlock and swung into the inter-ship airlock. The transparent material provided a stunning view of the stars and the barren moon they circled. She pushed off the *Swan*'s closed hatch, arrowing through the tube to the *Peregrine's* airlock. Pulling her legs in, she flipped around, meeting the opposite end feet first. She locked her elbow through a handle and hit the cycle button. When the hatch popped, she grabbed the upper edge of the opening and swung through. Artificial gravity kicked in and she flexed her knees to land.

With the lock closed behind her, Quinn made her way to the crew lounge. Tony sat at a small desk hanging from the outer wall, working on a tablet. He looked up when she walked in and smiled.

Quinn smiled back, but it faded. This was the first time they'd been alone since Lunesco—since Francine had asserted Tony was in love with her. Quinn still wasn't sure what to make of that claim. She and Tony had been friends for over a decade. She'd been married all that time. Now she was a free woman, and he was still here.

She shook her head. Francine was crazy. Besides, she had business. She cleared her throat. "You'll never guess what I found in my pocket."

Tony rose. "That's not how the joke goes."

She rolled her eyes and held up the data-card.

Tony took it. "This is the kind of throwaway card we use to pass messages in the business. Who gave it to you?"

"That's what's strange," she said. "Sebi Maarteen slipped it to me when we first arrived on Lunesco. When he helped me out of the shuttle. When you were busy being an ass."

He chuckled. "I play that role well." He turned it over again. "I don't remember him saying anything about it."

"He didn't. He slipped it to me and never mentioned it again. I stuck it in my pocket and forgot about it. Why wouldn't he have at least asked about it?"

"Delivering messages is part of his role." Tony returned the card. "He doesn't know what's on them or who they're from, and I'm sure he's encouraged not to ask. Who's it from?"

"You aren't going to believe it." She slid the card into her comtab. "Don't worry, it's a burner." With a swipe and a flick, a video started.

A sultry blonde with heavy makeup smiled out of the screen. "I'll bet I'm the last person you expected to get a message from."

"Tiffany!" Tony reached over and paused the video. "Maarteen brought you a message from Tiffany Andretti? This makes me question everything about him."

"I know." Quinn's lips twisted in distaste. "He said he carried a lot of messages. But how did she get it to him? She's not part of the underground, is she?"

"That is impossible to imagine." He laughed then motioned for her to start the message again.

"I hope we can put our differences behind us," the high-pitched voice warbled on. "I need your help, and I can offer you something valuable in return. And, no, I don't mean gold. I mean information. Assistance. I know you're in a bit of a jam, and I can help clear your name." One elegant, silk-clad shoulder shrugged. "If you care about that. All I care about is making *him* pay. I'm sure you want to, too. So, contact me."

"She's offering information," Tony repeated quietly. He took a turn around the room, drumming his fingers against his legs. "What information could she possibly have that we'd be willing to break cover to get?"

"She doesn't give any clues, does she?" Quinn crossed her arms. "I'm inclined to ignore her. How could the ex-trophy wife of a Space Force admiral help me clear my name? Except she managed to get this message to us, which worries me. How did she make contact with Maarteen? And how did she know he could find us?"

"How *did* he find us?" Tony asked. "He led us to believe he was looking for Doug—and meeting us was a happy accident. The fact that he came looking for and found us—" He broke off. "We need to talk to Maarteen."

"Are you supposed to meet up with him soon?" Quinn asked.

Tony shrugged. "I can get a message to Amanda, and she has access to Maarteen. We decided to be very careful with making contact. I'll send a drop message to her and see if she can set up a meeting." He picked up his tablet and started tapping.

"How is Amanda?" Quinn asked, looking anywhere but Tony. They had met Amanda McLasten and Myung Dae "Pete" Peterson on Lunesco. The two worked in the Federation's tax bureau but used their jobs as cover to meddle in local planets' affairs and push them toward revolution. Amanda had made no secret of her personal interest in Tony.

"She's up to all her usual tricks," Tony said. "I wish she'd keep her mind on her job. I get tired of fending off, you know?"

Quinn's lips quirked, but she bit back the grin. "I'm sure that gets tiresome."

"You have no idea." He grinned. "Tiresome as she is, she gets her job done." He flicked the device with a flourish. "There, message sent. She's supposed to check that box every three days, so we should hear back this week. Now, what do we do about Tiffany?"

"Do? We ignore her, of course," Quinn said.

"What if she has information we can use? I still think taking down Andretti is the key to this whole thing. Cut off the head... And no one hates him more than Tiffany. He left us to die, but we were collateral damage. He cheated on her, deserted her, then carpet bombed her home. That's gotta sting."

"True," Quinn agreed. "And have you ever been on the receiving end of one of her grudges? She might be small, but she has a huge ego, and an even bigger drive for vengeance. Remember Ambassador Richelea? His fall from grace was orchestrated by The Trophany."

Tony's eyes widened. "Wow, I had no idea." His forehead wrinkled. "That operation had all the hallmarks of a Commonwealth sting, but I never figured out who was behind it. Usually, I could tell. If it was really the Trophany, she could be more influential than any of us expect."

"If we can get to her without giving ourselves away." Quinn wrinkled her nose. "It could be a ruse to bring us in. Arresting us would make for big ratings on her show. Knowing The Trophany, that would trump her desire for revenge on her ex."

"Good point. Let's think about this. We probably want to talk to Maarteen first." He fiddled with the tablet. "Have you watched her show? Maybe we can gain some clues."

Quinn groaned. The Trophany in real life was bad enough. Listening to her on repeat, preening on that ridiculous stage and flirting with celebrities? "If we're going to watch her show, I need a drink."

He grinned, shaking his head in mock disapproval. "It's nine a.m.! But lucky for me, it's jump day. This afternoon, we can get sloshed and watch the Trophany Show."

CHAPTER 3

QUINN PLAYED the video for Francine, and a short clip of the Tiffany Andretti Show. Francine stared in fascination at the screen. "It's like a train wreck. Why do you call her the Trophany?"

"It's a concatenation of her name and the phrase trophy wife," Quinn said. "She was Andretti's fourth wife, and each one was younger than the one before. I think she was twenty-three when they got married. He was, like, sixty-eight."

Tony waved a bottle in their direction. "His newest one is nineteen."

"Why?" Francine demanded. "Why would either of them want—never mind. He's rich. She's hot. I guess that's a good deal for some people."

"I'm sure it's because they're deeply in love." Quinn kept her face almost completely straight.

"With some guys, I might believe that," Francine muttered. "But I've seen Andretti. He's creepy."

"In real life?" Quinn asked. "Have you met him?"

Francine wagged her head back and forth. "I've been in the same room with him. My parents were... I guess we could call them supporters?"

Tony burped. "'Scuse me. Francine's fam...fammy...family is one of Andretti's biggest fans. They pay him look...to look the other way. They got politicians in their pocketses, too. We gonna watch this train whack...wreck?" He waved at the frozen video on the big screen.

Quinn dropped onto the couch beside Tony and swiped the play button. On the screen, the Trophany came to life. She sat on a tall stool, her legs crossed and her ample cleavage on full display. She grinned, showing all thirty-two of her blindingly white teeth. Quinn's lips twitched. Tiffany Andretti always brought out the bitchiness in her.

Tiffany leaned forward, her blouse gaping further open. "Tell me, Luc-Pierre, when did you know it was true love?"

Francine hit the mute button. "Do you really think she's going to say anything significant to a b-list actor?"

"No." Quinn fast-forwarded a few more minutes. "This next bit is a power lifter, then she has a romance novelist."

"Maybe a different episode?" Francine suggested. "Find the one recorded close to when she made that video for you."

Quinn scrolled through the offerings and found the correct date. "If the metadata on that card is correct, this one was recorded the same day."

"Since the only metadata on that card was the date, that's prolly a clue." Tony lurched to his feet to dispose of his beer bottle and grab another. "You girls want some buffer?"

Quinn shook her head. "Much as I hate to watch the Trophany sober, I like jumping buzzed less."

"I'm good." Francine leaned closer to Quinn. "How much will he remember?"

Quinn glanced at Tony, who was struggling to open his twist-off bottle. "We'll probably want to give him a recap after the jump."

"Jump in five minutes." Dareen's voice echoed through the room and the nearby corridor. "Final check."

While Francine closed the door, Quinn reported in. "Francine and Tony are with me in the lounge."

"Is he drunk enough?" Dareen asked.

"I think so." Quinn eyed her friend. "He's staggering when he walks."

"Perfect. Dar out."

"Tony, come sit down and let's watch this video." Quinn patted the couch.

Tony staggered across the room and dropped into the seat. "Play!" He waved his arms wildly.

Quinn started the video.

"This week on the *Tiffany Andretti Show*," a deep voice intoned over inane music while a dance troupe performed. "Video star Lilienne Guandel, singer Jentry Korstence, and two-time Olympic juggler Randizi Chertanguali! Plus, the Tiffany Dancers, Melody Vilbrace, and the Funky-T band."

"Melody Vilbrace?" Quinn pulled out her own comtab to scroll through the show index. "What's she doing on the show? She despises the Trophany as much as I do."

"She's apparently the sidekick." Francine nodded at the screen. As the theme music played, a short, plump woman rose stiffly and moved over one seat to make room for the first guest.

Tony snored.

"Is that normal?" Francine pointed at Tony.

"Yeah." Quinn, still focused on the screen, barely spared him a glance. "I wonder why Melody would agree to help the Trophany. Hey, that's not Lilienne Guandel, is it?"

Francine looked at the screen. Her face went white. "No. That's my sister."

The intercom beeped. "Jump commencing, now."

The buzz of jump frizzed through Quinn's body. Francine's face went red then faded again. Quinn hit the pause button on the video. She glanced at Tony in time to see his eyes pop open.

He grinned and slapped his comtab. "Lounge is secure." He swiped the intercom off and looked at the women. "What did I miss?"

Mutely, Quinn gestured at the video screen and hit play.

"Before our scheduled guests arrive, we have a special request from Dusica Zielinsky." The Trophany put her hand on Dusica's arm. "There's nothing worse than a girl missing her sister."

"Really?" Quinn muttered. "*Nothing* worse than missing your sister?"

Dusica nodded, and a tear rolled down her perfectly made-up face. The resemblance to Francine was striking. Francine's face was a bit thinner, her features more pronounced, but anyone who saw them together would know they were family.

"Is that— Is she related to you?" Tony pointed, his eyes bulging.

"Shh!" Quinn and Francine hissed together.

"Tell my viewers what you told me," the Trophany said.

Dusica turned to the camera and blotted her eyes without smearing her mascara or dislodging the artistic tear on her cheek. "My dear little sister, Faina, is missing. She went to visit our sick grandmother a few months ago and never arrived at the *dascha*. We've been searching across the Federation, but to no avail. That's why we've turned to you, Tiffany, and your loyal viewers..." she smiled sadly at the camera. "...in our time of need."

"She's been missing for months, and you're finally looking for her?" Quinn muttered.

Francine's lips twisted. "I know why that is"

On screen, Dusica continued. "If you see this woman, please contact the number on the screen." A comm code scrolled across the lower part of the screen. "Do not approach her. We believe she may have been abducted by desperate villains and we don't want to tip them off." The camera zoomed out to include the stiff-looking Melody, then the scene faded to a formal portrait of Francine in an expensive business suit.

"You mean you don't want to tip *me* off," Francine said.

"Do they know you ran away?" Quinn asked as more still pictures of Francine streamed across the screen.

"More importantly, is this what Tiffany wanted us to see?" Tony asked.

"Yes, they know I ran." Francine jumped to her feet and prowled around the lounge. "How would Tiffany know I'm with you?"

"Maybe my mother-in-law leaked it somehow?" Quinn suggested. "It wouldn't surprise me to know Gretmar is connected to the Russosken. She runs Hadriana much like the Russosken run their planets."

"Except she doesn't have a private army," Tony said.

"What's up with Melody?" Quinn pointed at the screen.

"Are you still on that?" Francine asked. "We don't know why—"

"No, look at her," Quinn insisted.

"What am I supposed to see?" Tony asked.

"That's a duress signal." Quinn rewound and paused the video. "Look at her body posture." The woman's arms were tightly crossed, and the fingers of her right hand were positioned oddly. "Look at her hand. See how the ring finger is folded down, and the others are spread? And the coffee cup." A spoon balanced across the top of the cup.

"It's odd," Tony agreed. "But why do you think it's a duress signal?"

"It was a joke," Quinn said. "When Tiffany first got to Fort Sumpter, my friends and I made it up. If one of us got stuck talking to her, we'd use the duress signal to call for help. We had a pact. One of the others *had* to rescue you." She smiled, but it faded. "You started with one part—either the hand signal or the coffee cup and added the other if you were desperate. She's signaling me, asking to be rescued." Quinn made a face.

"When did you say this video was posted?" Francine asked.

Quinn froze the screen and tapped the metadata button. "About a week after we left Hadriana." She glanced at Tony. "We need to help her."

"Definitely someone on Hadriana tipped them off about Francine," he said. "Could have been the housekeeper. She was quite unhappy with us at the end."

Quinn sighed. "What about Melody? We can't leave her there."

"I'll see what I can learn about Melody," Tony said. "And it's useful to know the Russosken are looking for Francine."

"You won't tell Lou, will you?" Francine whispered. "She'll sell me out in a heartbeat."

"I don't think she will," Tony said slowly, but he didn't sound confident. "You've been helpful. You saved End from those *soldaty* on Lunesco. Not to mention the rest of the planet."

"Yeah, but Lou doesn't care about Lunesco." Francine's hands twisted in her lap.

"No, but she cares about End. Family first," Quinn reminded her. "As long as you keep the family safe..."

"I think it might be best if Francine moves back to the *Swan* as soon as possible," Tony said. "You might want to consider going back to N'Avon. You should be safe from the Russosken there."

Francine groaned. "So boring!"

Quinn raised her eyebrows. "You want safe? Safe and boring are usually a package deal. Or you could go back to Lunesco. Doug would be happy for the help."

"No thanks," Francine replied. "Lunesco is free from Russosken now, but if I know the *nachal'nik,* they'll be gearing up for another attack. She won't take that defeat lying down."

"That's what Amanda and I have been trying to prevent," Tony said. "Causing trouble in other Russosken-controlled planets, spreading their forces as thin as possible. We need to keep at it, until we break them completely."

"You'll never break the Russosken completely," Francine said. "You might force them to cut their losses, and damage their strength, but they've been around for centuries. They'll come back."

"Kind of like the Marconis," Tony said. "The family was a big deal when Lou was a little girl. That's why the name is so well known. But they were broken, and now we're all that's left. Give us a century or so, and we'll be back."

"So, the best we can hope for is a long period of hibernation, and hopefully a change in government that will keep them in check," Quinn said. "While we rescue Melody."

"We'll see." He swiped off the screen and cleared the browsing history. "First things first. Let's get Francine back to the *Swan*."

CHAPTER 4

FRANCINE WENT LOOKING FOR DAREEN. The *Swan* and the *Peregrine* had disconnected their inter-ship access tube before the jump. Theoretically, tandem jumping worked without problems, and larger ships like the *Peregrine* routinely carried shuttles attached to the outside, but most captains preferred to disconnect from other ships before jumping, and Lou and Liz were no exceptions. Returning to the *Swan* would require a shuttle.

Dareen and Francine boarded the *Fluffy Kitten*. The official name had been modified after Hadriana, but Francine couldn't remember the current designation. Sashelle strolled into the shuttle behind Francine.

"Is she supposed to be here?" Dareen leaned down to stroke the caat's soft fur. Sassy leaned against her hand, then stalked away without a backward glance. "Shouldn't she stay with Elli?"

Francine glanced at the animal as it leapt onto the copilot's seat, then onto the back of that chair. "She does what she wants. I suspect she'll ride back to the *Peregrine* with you." She sat down, and the caat stretched across the headrest, dropping a paw to bat at Francine's updo. Francine twisted in the seat to glare at the caat. "Stop that, or I will space you."

The caat's eyes closed to slits and she looked away, unconvinced.

Francine buckled her restraints. "Why didn't we connect the two ships again?"

"We want to arrive separately," Dareen replied. "We don't want too many people to know we're a team. Safer this way."

"Please don't use the potato adage again," Francine said. "I heard that more than enough on Hadriana."

Dareen grinned as she worked through her checklist in silence and fired up the engines. They pushed away from the *Peregrine* and crossed to the *Swan*. "*Swan of the Night*, this is the *Rubber Chicken* with a package for you. Request permission to dock."

"*Chicken*, you are cleared to dock," Maerk replied.

Dareen matched velocities with the *Swan* and hit the docking program icon. "The collar is mated. And we're locked...now." She swiped through the controls. "Pressure is good, and the board is green." She turned to Francine. "After you."

The two women stepped into the airlock with the caat on their heels. When the hatch popped open, Sassy launched herself through the free-fall of the flexible connector and landed gracefully in the *Swan's* airlock. She sat and lifted a paw to groom, ignoring the humans. When they entered the *Swan*, the caat streaked into the lounge and disappeared.

"What's her hurry?" Maerk stared after the caat.

"Who knows." Dareen threw her arms around her father. Francine waited while the pair exchanged hugs. She felt a twinge of jealousy—her own parents had never shown that much affection.

"Come on in." Maerk stepped aside to allow Francine to enter.

She hesitated inside the airlock. "I need to tell you something."

"Come in and tell us." Maerk took the bag from her hand. He led them to the lounge. "Obviously, you've reconsidered your decision to move to the *Peregrine*. Was it something Lou *did* or *said*?"

Francine paused a few steps inside the lounge.

Maerk chuckled as he set her bag on the bench then crossed to the couch. "Come on. Have a seat; give me the story. I'll decide how much to tell Liz."

"I heard that!" Liz's voice filtered through the open hatch to the cockpit. "If you want to keep secrets, you should close the door."

Maerk made an aborted movement toward the door, then settled back on his heels. "Close the door? Yes or no?" He raised a brow at Francine.

"You should both hear this," Francine started, but Liz's voice cut in again.

"Shut the door! I usually wish I *hadn't* heard statements that begin with 'you should hear this.' If it's important, I trust Maerk to tell me."

"Might be best, if it has anything to do with Lou," Maerk said as he closed the hatch. "Plausible deniability, if nothing else."

Francine glanced at Dareen.

The girl shrugged. "I can stay or go."

"She knows how to keep her mouth shut," Maerk said. "But the fewer people who know a secret, the better."

Francine threw up her hands. "Everyone will probably find out soon enough. It's easier if I show you." She pulled out her comtab and threw the saved video onto the lounge's big screen.

When Francine's face appeared on the screen, Maerk whistled. "I knew you were Russosken, but…"

"Yeah, you need to stay over here," Dareen said. "I love Gramma, but even I gotta admit she'd hand you over in a heartbeat if she thought you were a threat. Especially since it looks like your family has posted a reward for your safe return." She held up her own comtab to show them the page she'd found.

"Fantastic." Francine dropped into a chair, tired of pacing. Tired of running. "Maybe I *should* go back to N'Avon."

"It might be safer in the long run," Maerk said slowly. "But is that what you want?"

"I hated N'Avon," Francine said. "But I don't want to bring the Russosken down on you. No matter how careful we are, someone will spot me, or one of the kids, or Quinn, and then boom!" She grabbed her own throat and mimed choking.

"That ship has sailed," Dareen said. "After Lunesco, the Russosken are after us. I don't think you add that much threat."

"That's an interesting point of view," Maerk said. "But I think you may be right. For now, you may as well get comfortable. You don't want to leave the ship in Varitas."

"Definitely not!" Francine agreed. "I may as well hitch a ride back to Rossiya City. Why are we going to Varitas anyway?"

"Tony needs to talk to someone," Maerk said. "Which means this might soon be a very safe place for a Russosken refugee."

"Or a very dangerous one," Francine said. "All depends on who wins. And I don't want to be there in the interim."

"Go settle into your cabin," Maerk said. "We can make decisions later."

FRANCINE CARRIED her bag up to her cabin. The door stood partly open, but since everything she owned was in the bag in her hand, it didn't really matter. She pushed through and dropped it on the floor.

The cabin looked the same. Two bunks on one wall, access to the shared head at the far end, and a desk and chair on the other wall. Sufficient for sleeping, but not a place she'd want to spend long hours. Sassy lay on the top bunk, staring down at her through slitted eyes.

"You don't want to miss the shuttle back to the *Peregrine*." Francine scooped the caat off the bunk. "Elli would be heartbroken."

Not a problem, a deep, feminine voice said. The words felt like soft, thick fur.

Francine swung around, but the tiny cabin was empty.

The human kitten knows I have business here.

"What the—" Francine dropped the caat and stumbled back, banging her hip against the desk.

The caat landed gracefully, gave her a reproachful glare, then leapt onto the lower bunk. *I require scratching behind my ears.*

Francine rubbed the heels of her hands into her eyes. "I need a drink. Or more sleep. Or a nice long vacation on a beach somewhere."

I would find the last option agreeable, the voice said. *You will take me with you when you go.*

Francine crossed her arms over her chest, staring at the caat. "You can't be talking."

I'm not. The caat yawned and meowed loudly. *Talking, that is. However, I am communicating with you. With. My. Mind.* The last three words echoed in her head like a bad video voice-over.

"You're trying to tell me that you're sentient and have telepathy," Francine said. And a sense of humor—that seemed odd for a feline.

Ooh, big words, the caat replied.

"End!" Francine yelled. She barged out into the corridor. "Very funny."

Dareen's head popped up through the ladder access. "End isn't here. Remember, just the two of us came over. You feeling okay?"

"Uh, could you come up here, please?" Francine asked.

"Sure." Dareen bounded up the steps. "This ship would have been so cool when I was little. I would have loved to have lived here. I would have had a secret fort in that storage area. And your room is definitely bigger than my cabin on the *Peregrine*."

"Yeah, but I might have to share this." Francine stood back and allowed the younger girl to precede her into the cabin. "Right, Sassy?"

The caat blinked at the women.

"Oh, here you are." Dareen leaned down to scratch the caat's ears. Sassy purred loudly. "Are you staying with Francine, or coming back with me?"

"What did she say?"

Dareen stopped scratching the caat and turned to Francine with a puzzled expression. "What did who say? Ellianne? She won't mind if Sassy stays here." The caat batted her hand, so Dareen resumed petting.

"The caat didn't say anything?" Francine asked. "End was playing a joke on me—he transmitted a voice from the caat."

Dareen laughed. "That sounds like something End would do." She fiddled with Sassy's collar. "There's no speaker on here, though. He must have run it through the comm system." She glanced up at the corners of the room where comm speakers were usually hidden.

Francine looked, too, but didn't spot anything. "It was very realistic. I wonder how he got that beautiful voice. It was definitely female."

"His falsetto is terrible. Look, I gotta head back to the *Peregrine*. Is the caat staying with you?"

"I don't know." Francine turned to the caat. "Are you staying here, Sassy?"

I will stay with you.

"See?" Francine said. "Beautiful voice."

Dareen stared at her. "I didn't hear anything. You heard a voice? Do you have an integrated comm system? Maybe he hijacked it."

Francine rubbed the scarred skin behind her ear. "No, I don't. Not anymore."

"Maybe you need a nap." Dareen straightened. "Or a med check. I gotta run. I'll let you know if End is doing this." She gave Francine a swift hug and hurried out of the room.

I don't care for the name Sassy, the caat said.

"Ugh!" Francine glared at the caat. "Not funny, End!"

If by 'End,' you mean the Loud One, then I assure you he is not involved. Sassy jumped onto the pillow and kneaded it with her front paws. *His feet are too big, and he doesn't take care where he puts them. I have no use for him.*

Francine threw herself down on the bed, cracking her skull against the wall. "Ow!" She rubbed her head and stared at the caat. "Let's pretend you are really talking to me. Can you hear my thoughts, or only if I speak aloud?"

You don't usually think loud enough, Sassy said. *I can often read emotions, but human thoughts are unclear. Too weak. Too disorganized.* The animal arched her back, then sank, boneless, to the pillow. *It is better to speak. But I can feel disbelief rolling off you. What will it take to convince you this isn't a trick?*

"What did you do to my code on Lunesco?" She hadn't told anyone but Quinn that the caat had fixed the programming that froze the Russosken armor. And she hadn't told Quinn the details of how Sashelle had fixed it.

I deleted the extra character in the second function call. The caat closed her eyes and rolled over onto her back. *You spelled it wrong, but I fixed it. Scratch.*

Francine stared at the furry belly in shock. That was exactly what had happened. "So, not End," she said slowly. "I guess I'm going crazy. Hearing voices in my head."

The caat batted her hand. *Scratch! That's better. How can I convince you that I am really communicating with you?*

"Talk to someone else. If one of the others hears you too, then I know it's not in my head."

Not going to happen, Sashelle said. *You are my chosen one.*

"In the history of humans," Francine muttered, "no one has ever wanted to be the chosen one."

It is a difficult prowl, but a position of honor." Sashelle suddenly flipped to her feet. *Come, you must speak to the others.*

"My turn to say not going to happen." Francine crossed her arms again. "You tell people you hear voices in your head, you wind up in the looney bin."

But I have information to impart. The caat stared at her, unblinking.

"What information, Sassy?" Francine asked. "You tell me, and I'll find a way to tell whoever needs to know."

The caat sat. *First, we must get things straight. My name is Sashelle, Mighty Huntress and Eliminator of Vermin. You may call me Sashelle, but not Sassy.*

Francine narrowed her eyes. "So, you speak to Elli, then."

The caat flicked her tail. *What makes you say that?*

"If Sashelle is your real name, then you must have told her."

You are much brighter than the usual human, Sashelle said. *This is one of the reasons I chose you. Yes, I have spoken to the kitten. She didn't question my reality.*

"She's eight. She probably believes in unicorns, too."

Sashelle blinked and her ears twitched.

"Because unicorns are real?" Francine continued. "Is that what you're implying?"

I am implying nothing. What you infer is up to you.

Francine laughed. "You said my intelligence was one reason you chose me. What else?"

Sashelle stood and stalked to the far end of the bunk. *You are the most caat-like of the humans. Beautiful, aloof, superior.*

"Why, thank you. Most humans consider me snotty and condescending. Or so I've been informed by my loving sister."

Exactly, Sashelle said. *Caat-like. Any further questions will have to wait. My information must be shared before we land.*

"Fine. Let me have it."

The kitten has been in communication with the dirt people.

"The kit— Ellianne?" Francine asked. The caat stared unhelpfully. "Who are the dirt people?"

Those who stir up the dirt on my home planet. Sashelle's tail lashed back and forth. *The 'potato farmers,' I believe you call them.*

"Elli's been communicating with her grandmother?"

The caat declined to respond.

CHAPTER 5

QUINN SPUN and slammed her foot against the padded bag. It swung away and she kicked it again, stopping the swing. Punch, punch, kick. The sting of the bag against her wrapped fingers and bare feet made her feel strong and powerful. She unleashed a flurry of moves, then stepped back, breathing hard.

"Your form is getting really good," Tony said from the hatch.

She swung around in surprise. "Francine is a good teacher. Too bad she had to go back to the *Swan*," she gasped between breaths. "The gym here is much better."

"Maybe that's why she's on the comm," Tony lifted his comtab. "She wants to coach you."

Quinn laughed. "I'm sure that's it." She wiped her face on a towel and grabbed the device. "What's up, Francine? Missed me already?"

Francine's face was still and composed, as always. "I have some bad news."

Quinn dropped onto the bench near the hatch, her attention fully on the comtab. "What?"

"Ellianne has been talking to someone on Hadriana," the blonde said in a rush. "The signal is encrypted, and hidden, so I don't know who, or what has been discussed. I'd guess it was Reggie."

"That bastard." Quinn ground her teeth. "How'd you find it?"

Francine looked away. "I—I was bored. So, I ran a scan on the comms. I found the hidden signal and traced it back to its origin."

"How is she doing it?" Tony leaned over Quinn's shoulder to peer at the screen.

Quinn caught a whiff of Tony's subtle cologne. She'd always found it comforting, homey. Now, thanks to Francine's claim that Tony was in love with her, it was different. It still smelled the same, of course, but now she felt a twinge of adventure or even romance in response. She shook her head. Francine was ridiculous. At least in this.

"I'd guess someone slipped her a data-card that had a stealth program on it," Francine said. "Once she plugged it into a comtab, it probably walked her through setup procedures."

"She doesn't have a comtab," Quinn said sharply. "Where'd she get one?

"It's Dareen's."

"Then how do you know it isn't Dareen talking to someone on Hadriana?" Quinn asked, deflecting suspicion from her child by reflex.

Francine looked away from the screen again. When she turned back, she looked uncomfortable. "Good question. I can't tell you how I know. I'm running a decryptor on the latest message right now. I'll let you know when I break it." The screen went blank.

"That was odd." Tony slid down the wall to sit next to her.

"You think?" Quinn demanded. "Why would she jump to the conclusion that an encrypted message from Dareen's comtab came from Elli?"

He shook his head. "She must have a reason. Dareen doesn't know anyone on Hadriana, so there's that."

"Unless she was brainwashed by Ricardi while she was captive."

Tony laughed and nudged her with his shoulder. "Dareen was

captive for about twenty minutes. Maybe forty. Not much time to run a brainwashing program."

"What about that boy she met?" Quinn said. "The one who gave her the cloaking device?"

"I hadn't heard about him."

"She mentioned him the other day. Apparently, he was 'skinny but cute when he smiled,'" she said. "I didn't think she had his contact information, but maybe he gave her the data-card along with the device."

"That seems highly unlikely," Tony said. "I mean, unless he's a real ladies' man, why would he have had the data-card with him for a drop? And he would have no way of knowing who was going to pick it up. Plus, it would be extraordinarily bad craft. Dareen knows better. But either way, someone on this ship is communicating with someone on Hadriana. That's bad news. Let's go talk to Dareen and Elli."

Quinn pushed herself up from the bench, wishing she could shower first. But if someone on this ship was talking to Hadriana, they had to sort it out before they arrived at Varitas. She gulped water then followed Tony out of the tiny gym.

They found Ellianne in the mess hall, working on a math problem. The little girl pushed her tablet away the moment Tony walked into the room. "Tony! Mom! Can I be done, please?"

Quinn crossed the room and picked up the device. "You can take a break, but we need to talk to you." She scrolled through the files on the tablet and checked the settings. It was a standalone, blocked from even the ship's net except via parental controls. Of course, there was no guarantee Elli hadn't figured a way around those.

But Francine had said the person was using Dareen's comtab. She set the tablet down and sat in a chair next to her daughter. "Have you been talking to Daddy?"

Ellianne's eyes went wide, then she smiled. "He said you didn't know!"

Quinn's eyes narrowed. "Did he tell you to keep it secret from me? You know we don't keep secrets."

"That's what I told him." Ellianne nodded solemnly. "But we're planning a surprise, and surprises are okay to keep secret." She clapped her hands over her mouth. "Don't tell him I ruined the surprise!"

Quinn's face went hot, and a rush of anger filled her ears. Her teeth clenched. How could that bastard use her little girl—his own flesh and blood—like this?! Next time she saw him, she'd rip his head off and— A hand on her shoulder and a whiff of Tony's cologne cut through the anger.

"Why don't you let me talk to Elli, so we don't ruin the surprise." Tony squeezed her shoulder a little. "Go take your shower. It'll be fine."

Quinn glanced at Ellianne. Tears pooled in the girl's eyes, and her lips trembled. Quinn slid off the chair to kneel by her daughter. She pulled the girl close and kissed her cheek. "You didn't do anything wrong," she whispered. "You were right to tell me, and you didn't spoil any surprise. Talk to Tony, okay?" She pulled back to look at Ellianne's face.

"Okay." The girl sniffed. "You aren't mad, are you, Mommy?"

"Not at you, sweetheart."

"Don't be mad at Daddy, either."

"I'm not." It wasn't a lie—she wasn't mad, she was furious. "I'll be back in a few minutes."

Ellianne grinned and took Tony's hand. The two walked out of the mess hall to the more comfortable seating in the lounge across the corridor. Quinn gazed after them for a second, then headed for her cabin.

AFTER SPEAKING WITH ELLI, Tony gathered the family in the lounge. Ellianne and Lucas joined Kert on the bridge for "pilot practice" and to give the rest of the team time to talk.

"Dareen, we need your comtab." Tony struggled to keep his tone noncommittal. He didn't want to cast blame on Dareen.

"Sure." The girl handed over the device. "What for?"

Tony glanced at Quinn, but she clamped her lips tight. Probably still too worked up. He flicked the screen to life. "Elli has been using it to talk to her father." While the others exclaimed, he scrolled through the screens. "There's a hidden app." He threw the view onto the big screen. They all turned to watch. "See? If you hold this icon, then tap this one, it opens an encrypted message system."

Dareen gasped. "How did that get on my comtab?"

"Reggie," Quinn said, her tone clipped. "He got a data-card to Elli. We aren't sure how. She found a card on her desk. In the apartment in N'Avon. There was a note from her father. It told her to use this card next time she was in the Federation. I guess he thought the Commonwealth communications would have detection or blocking software. Once we got back to the *Peregrine,* she waited for a chance to grab someone's comtab. Reggie told her he was planning a surprise for me, and she shouldn't spoil it by telling anyone else."

Muttering around the room made it clear the others agreed with his and Quinn's assessment. He deleted the app, fighting a brief grin as he continued the tale. "She said the caat tried to talk her out of it. But eventually, she grabbed Dareen's comtab and loaded the software."

"How did she get your comtab?" Lou demanded. "And what does that software do?"

"She must have snuck into Dareen's cabin." Tony shrugged.

End jumped in. "When Tony discovered it, I—"

"Actually, Francine discovered it," Quinn interrupted. "She deserves the credit for that."

"How did *she* find it?" Lou asked, distracted by her distrust of the woman. "Was she mucking around in our comm systems where she doesn't belong?"

"I asked her to help me," End said firmly. "You told us we could do that, remember? She's a genius on computers. We've been taking turns installing encrypted stubs and then trying to find them. She must have found this one while scanning for my most recent. Which she hasn't found yet, by the way. I'm that good." He smirked.

Tony's lips quirked, but he was happy to see the boy standing up to Lou's prejudice. Maybe there was hope for him yet.

"Anyway," the youngster continued, "Tony told me to look for this file a few minutes ago, and I grabbed a copy. Comtab files are sent through the ship's comm system, you know. The program she uploaded doesn't attach any files to the message. And there doesn't appear to be any active pinging. Which is strange. It's stupid easy to include one of those, and then he'd know where we are."

"Yes," Quinn said, "but that would create a signal that could be found. Easier to insert location data into the message headers. Then he'd know where she was when she sent each message. Not as precise as real-time tracking, but less likely to get picked up in a scan like you and Francine do."

End nodded. "True enough."

"Give me the bottom line," Lou growled. "Does he know where we are?"

Tony, End, and Quinn all shook their heads. "He might know where we *were*," Tony said. "If the system has that location metadata. But Ellianne said she sent the last message before we jumped, and she didn't tell him where we were going. Now that we have the device, and Elli's password, we can look." He flicked the screen and the picture on the big screen changed to a message.

Dear Daddy,

I miss you so much. I hope you can come fly with us soon. We're having a good time on this ship. Mommy said I can never tell anyone the name of it, so I won't tell you. In case this message is intra-septid. But there are really nice people here. Maybe after you finish the surprise for Mommy, we can get our own ship and fly together.

Love, Ellianne

Tony glanced at Quinn, who had ducked her head. She swiped a hand across her eyes. "As you can see," he said, a little too loudly, to distract the others, "she didn't give him any clues. Quinn did a good job of training her."

End took the device and started swiping quickly through screens. He stopped on one that looked like gibberish to Tony.

Quinn sucked in a breath.

End growled.

"What?" Lou demanded.

"This is the metadata," End said. "It has a date-time stamp as well as location data pulled from the ship's navigation system."

"How'd he get that?" Tony asked in alarm.

"His software probably looked for a link from the comtab to any external systems," Quinn said. "Then it started mining data. You need to run a full scan to make sure he wasn't able to plant any bugs in the ship."

"He can do that?" Lou demanded.

"Reggie can't, but whoever he hired might be able to," Quinn said. "Reggie couldn't program his way out of a virtual paper bag, which means his coder could have done anything and be capturing data Reggie knows nothing about."

"No, it's fine," Dareen said. "I have an app that downloads the latest navigation data when I log into the ship's system. If I'd known Elli would 'borrow' my device, I would have disabled it. It replaces the standard location signals with the more accurate ship location data. I'll disable it now, but we still need to run full scans. Just in case."

"The upshot is, Reggie knows where we were yesterday afternoon." Tony took the comtab from End. "Make sure you run scans on every system on this ship. Dareen is probably right, but better safe than sorry. Get Francine to help you. We need to know if he's planted anything. Quinn." He handed her the comtab. "Take that apart and figure out how it works. Dareen, show Quinn how you've modified your device, but don't change anything—we need to understand how it's currently configured."

"Who put you in charge, young man?" Lou demanded. "This is my ship, and I'll decide who does what around here!"

"Sorry, Gramma." Tony gave the old woman a slight bow. "I'm used to taking charge when a breach is detected."

Lou scowled, but it faded quickly. "You do a fine job, but remember, this is my ship." She looked around at the assembled family. "For now, do as Tony recommends. We need to ensure the ship is clean before we do anything else. We're still twenty-six hours from Varitas. If that isn't going to be enough time to comb through everything, we'll fake an engine problem and slow down." She looked around the room.

"I can do that," Dareen said, her voice low. "It's the least I can do."

"This isn't your fault," Quinn said. "It's Reggie's. Don't take the blame for his nastiness."

"I shouldn't have left my comtab where Elli could get it, though," Dareen said. "I never thought she'd be able to override my security."

"We'll find out how she did." Quinn tapped the device against her palm. "I suspect the data-card installed a second user ID, so you never even realized she was using it. And I will talk to Elli about using other people's things."

CHAPTER 6

DAREEN LANDED the shuttle at Varitas Field, taxiing down the busy flight line toward the parking ramp. "We'll be at the loading dock in a few minutes," she said over her shoulder. "Where do you want to get out?"

Tony came forward, dressed in black. "Slow down as we pass behind that hangar." He pointed at her viewscreen. "I'm going to jump out there."

"What?" When she looked back, he was gone. Perfect. The inner hatch icon on her display flashed red, then green. The airlock cycled, and the outer hatch flashed red. She drove the shuttle along the strip, through bars of light and shadow, then slowed behind the hangar. The outer hatch light went green.

She flicked through the external camera views, spinning the video back ten seconds, but didn't see Tony leave the ship. Even the cam above the airlock missed him. The man was like a ghost.

Time to act innocent. She was good at that. She eased her ship into her assigned parking space and flicked through the automated payment screens. She shut down the system, walking through the checklists by the book, then she exited the ship and locked it behind her. Her cargo wasn't due for an hour, so she could visit the pilots' lounge.

A small, automated cart buzzed along its painted green line. As it approached, a message scrolled along the edge of the roof: Passenger Terminal, Flight Services. It slowed, sensing a potential rider. Dareen grabbed an upright and swung herself onto the wide seat.

Dim lights brightened overhead when she sat. The other seats were empty. Dareen leaned back and scanned the edges of the flight line, looking for threats. And for Tony. She didn't find either.

"Destination?" an androgynous voice asked.

"Is there a pilots' lounge?" Dareen asked.

"Maybe this will answer your question," the voice said. "Varitas Field has a state-of-the-art, twelve thousand square meter passenger terminal, servicing fifteen full-service commercial shuttle lines, three micro wineries, four microbreweries, and the newly renovated Space Burger that offers freshly—"

"Cancel inquiry." Dareen pulled out her comtab. "I'll figure it out for myself."

"If you'd like to rate this service—"

"Cancel," Dareen snapped.

"Arriving at the passenger terminal in fifteen seconds. Please wait for the vehicle to stop." Did the voice sound offended?

Dareen snickered and jumped off the cart before it stopped.

"Passenger safety is our number one—"

"Cancel!" Dareen yelled over her shoulder as she strode away. The cart ignored her and kept chattering.

Traffic at this time of day was light—only two people waited for the cart to return them to their shuttles. She nodded at them, noting their clothing. Passengers, not pilots. Or wealthy people with their own shuttles. Either way, they weren't going to know where the pilot lounge might be.

Inside the terminal, she wove through the badly-placed chairs to the closest gate clerk. The woman behind the desk didn't look up as Dareen arrived, but said, "Sorry, this flight is full."

"I don't need a flight." Dareen leaned across the counter. When the woman finally looked up, she gave a blinding smile. "I just landed my shuttle, and I'm looking for the pilots' lounge."

The woman nodded. "Take the cart to flight services. There's a bar behind the maintenance hangar." She looked Dareen up and down. "You'll have to show your credentials to get in. They don't allow passengers."

Dareen patted the pocket containing her comtab. "I'm all set. Thanks."

She started to turn, but the woman put a hand on her arm. "Be careful. There's a guy there who doesn't like female pilots much."

"What?" Dareen tried to make sense of this comment, but her brain stalled. "Why would he care what gender a pilot is?"

"You aren't from around here, are you?"

"Obviously." Dareen gestured to the ship's logo on her coverall. "I wouldn't have asked for directions if I was."

The woman looked around the room, then gestured for Dareen to lean in. "I get off in ten minutes. We can go somewhere safer than the pilots' lounge and talk if you want."

Dareen's eyes narrowed. "If this is a scam, I'm not buying what you're selling. And if this is a come-on, let's just be friends."

The woman flushed. "No, sorry. Look. You're young and pretty, and I don't want you to get hurt. Hanging out in that lounge with its current customer base is a bad idea. We can grab a drink—over there, if you want." She waved at a set of tables scattered in front of a sign reading, "World's Best Micro Wines."

"Okay," Dareen said slowly. "I only have an hour until my cargo gets delivered, though."

The woman shrugged. "We can have a quick drink. Or you can go back to your shuttle. Either one would be a safer idea."

Dareen glanced at the bar, then looked the woman up and down. Getting intel about the planets they landed on was one of her tasks. This might be better than the pilot's lounge. "Great, I'll wait for you there. Thank you."

The woman nodded and went back to her computer, so Dareen sauntered across the open space and sat at a table. Menus scrolled through the clear tabletop. She tapped it with a finger, and it stopped. With another tap, she ordered a non-alcoholic fizzy drink with a cherry and a lime on the side. It looked like a cocktail but allowed her to stay clearheaded. Gramma would ground her, literally, if she drank before flying.

She watched the passengers wander the terminal while she sipped her fruity drink, making mental notes. Very few solo women passed by. There were two groups of half a dozen, but most others were accompanied by a man. Interesting. She knew the Federation could be a bit backward on gender politics, but this was the first time she'd seen it in person. Women working in the terminal seemed to be the exception. Like her new friend, for example. Dareen waved as the woman strode away from her podium.

"I'm Hastri." The woman dropped her bag onto an empty seat. "What are you drinking?"

"I dunno." Dareen waved her hand over the menu. "I picked something at random. None of the drinks are familiar to me."

"You should have tried the wine," Hastri said. "We're famous for it."

Not anywhere I've been, Dareen thought. "I'm not much of a wine drinker, but I'll buy you a glass, if you'd like."

"No, I've got this." Hastri tapped the table and pressed her palm to the pay screen. "Employee discount. If you'd like another, I can…"

Dareen shook her head. "Don't have time. I have to load up and lift off in a bit."

The woman nodded. "What's it like?"

"Loading cargo?" Dareen purposely misunderstood her. "Boring. Mostly automated."

"No, I mean roaming around the galaxy." Hastri dropped her voice. "I would love to do that."

"There's a lot of sitting around," Dareen said. "It takes a couple days to get to and from the jump points, so that part can be boring.

Less time if you've got a more powerful ship, of course. Then you jump to the next system, and you wait a few more days until you're close to the planet. Depending on our cargo, we might unload at the station, or drop the shuttles dirtside. Captain tries to give us a little sunshine time every week, if possible."

"Sunshine time?" Hastri asked. A meter-high box, about twenty centimeters on a side, zipped up to their table. The door in the top slid open, and Hastri reached in to retrieve her drink. She tapped the top of the box, and gears whirred. A second door, lower down, popped open, revealing a steaming plate. Hastri put it on the table between them. "Nachos?" She tapped the top of the box again, and it zipped away.

"Thanks." Dareen pulled a loaded chip from the pile and stuck it in her mouth. "Oh! I don't know about your wines, but this is worth messaging home about!"

"They are good," Hastri agreed.

Dareen wiped her mouth and checked her comtab. "Sunshine time is what we call our planet leave. A chance to get some vitamin D from the natural sources." She shrugged. "Tell me about—" She waved her hands vaguely at the woman's uniform, the people in the terminal, and the planet in general. "Should I not have come alone? We didn't see any warnings on the net."

"You wouldn't," Hastri said, her voice low. She leaned forward to peer at the nachos, as if choosing the most heavily-loaded chip. "The government likes to pretend we're a modern society, but we aren't. Old habits die hard. Even though religion was outlawed when the Federation began, the attitudes of the people were heavily shaped by it. This area was originally colonized by a patriarchal religious sect."

Dareen contemplated the chips, then carefully selected another. "Don't take this the wrong way, but what are the odds that I'd run into an emancipated woman?"

"Higher than you'd think." Hastri grinned, but the smile didn't reach her eyes. "Any employed woman is likely to be a bit more independent than the population at large. The leaders don't like us working, but there aren't enough men to fill all the jobs, so..." She tipped her head toward the podiums at the gates. Most of the uniformed employees were women. "The shuttle services are from off-world, so they'll hire anyone. Women who work prefer less biased employers."

"Why aren't there enough men?" Dareen sipped her drink and looked around as if bored with the discussion. When Hastri didn't answer, she glanced across the table. The other woman had slid off her chair and moved to the next table.

"Has—"

Hastri coughed, her elbow jerking as she did. Dareen pulled another chip from the pile and casually looked in the direction Hastri indicated. Two men in black strode through the concourse, their heads on a swivel. They carried large, ugly weapons and riot shields clung across their backs. Each wore a small gold badge on their belt with ornate carving. At this distance, Dareen couldn't read the inscriptions, but she recognized the gear: Russosken *soldaty*.

CHAPTER 7

TONY CROUCHED behind a large ground vehicle, the huge wheel hiding him completely from the flight line. He reached into his bag and pulled out a bright orange vest. He slid it over his black shirt and strapped on a helmet with big ear covers, then he slung his bag over his shoulder and strode out into the light.

The key to going unnoticed, he'd learned back in the academy, was looking purposeful. He paused at the end of the vehicle, glanced at his comtab, then kicked the huge tire. With a nod, he tapped his device and headed to the next piece of equipment.

Three vehicles on, he darted into the shadows and ducked through a carefully-disguised hole in the fence. The electrical charge had been turned off for a ten-minute period—he'd made it with time to spare. Pausing to return his gear to the bag, he pulled out a mottled brown jacket. He jumped a ditch paralleling the fence, hid the orange vest under a bush because he didn't want to get caught with it, and hurried to the dark sidewalk beyond.

Vehicles whooshed by at high speed—travelers on their way to the shuttle port. Tony turned the opposite direction, darted across the road during a brief lull, and strode along the walkway as if he belonged there. Within ten minutes, a dark car pulled to a stop, and the passenger window slid down.

"Need a lift?" the woman asked.

"You shouldn't pick up strangers," Tony said. "Serial killers and circus mimes are only two of the potential dangers."

She smiled. "I can handle serial killers." She leaned across to push open the door.

Tony climbed in and shut the door. The window slid shut, and the car accelerated away. "I was beginning to think one of us had gotten the wrong day."

Amanda McLasten shook her head in mock dismay. "I would never get a date with you wrong."

"Not a date, Amanda," Tony said. "Can you turn the charm off now? There's no one to see."

"Sorry, sweetie." She gave him a slow look up and down. "This charm doesn't turn off when you're around."

Tony rolled his eyes. "If I weren't a Krimson agent, I'd file a sexual harassment report."

"Lucky for me." Amanda sighed. "If you really aren't interested, I'll back off."

Tony smiled. "I'm not, but I appreciate the admiration. What's the situation here?"

"A large portion of the male population has been conscripted," Amanda said. "Russosken are 'recruiting.' They don't take no for an answer."

"Putting unwilling conscripts into armor doesn't seem like a good plan."

"By the time they get armor, they've been fully threatened, blackmailed, and cowed. Fortunately for us, that takes time. It's slowing their deployment rate. And, of course, the hundred guys we took out of rotation on Lunesco helps."

Tony grimaced. "The Russosken have thousands of troops, though. It's only a matter of time before they launch another assault on Lunesco. Doug can keep them off the dirt for a while, but eventually, they'll get a ship through. If they're willing to take the kind of losses he'll inflict along the way."

"He doesn't have an unlimited supply of orbit busters," Amanda said. "We managed to 'find' a couple crates here and there, which have been diverted to him, but we need to distract the Russosken."

"What's my role here?" Tony asked. "You could have told me all this over encrypted comms."

"Isn't it enough that I wanted to see your pretty face?" She batted her eyelashes.

"Seriously, dial it down." Tony crossed his arms. "Why did you need me?"

"Believe it or not, the leaders of this community were unwilling to listen to me." She pressed her lips together in distaste. "I tried to bring in Sebi or Pete, but they're both busy. You were my next best option."

"Why were they unwilling? Because you work for the Federation? If that's the case, I'm a better choice than Sebi or Pete."

"No," she said in disgust. "Because I'm female. Can you believe it?"

"Sexists? I didn't know they even existed anymore. They certainly aren't tolerated by the Federation. Or at least not officially. Are you sure these are the guys we should be working with?" Tony asked. "If they don't treat women as equals, do we really want to help liberate them? I can't believe I'm saying this, but these people—or at least the female half—might be better off in the Federation."

"I know." Amanda turned the car down a brightly-lit highway. "It really chaffs my knickers."

"It what?" Tony thought he'd heard every colloquialism out there. "What the hell are knickers?"

"No idea," Amanda said. "But I like how it sounds."

She turned the car off the highway and drove along a wide street. At the corner, she turned into a parking lot near a tall building with three pointed towers. "Used to be a place of worship. I think it still is, but they're underground. The building is supposedly a cafe." She parked the car under the thick foliage in a corner of the lot.

Tony opened the door and climbed out. He turned to wait for Amanda, but she didn't open her side. "Aren't you coming in?"

Her head swung back and forth. "I told you, they don't want to talk to me. At all. Ever." She pulled something out of her low-cut cleavage and handed it to him. "That's your credentials. Good luck. I'll wait nearby and swing over when you come out. Or text "pizza" to this number." She swiped her comtab and used the nearfield link to send him a contact address.

"Pizza?"

"Someone's always ordering pizza. It's a universal constant. Safest code in the—well, in the universe."

"What if someone actually orders pizza?" he asked with a grin.

"If the order comes to me, they'll go hungry. Good luck." She raised her hand in a regal wave and stepped on the accelerator. The door swung shut as she drove away.

Tony watched the car for a moment, then trudged across the parking lot. She'd dropped him on the far side. Consistent with his training and experience, he walked close to the edge, near the heavy trees that bounded this side of the open space. He walked upright, his arms swinging slightly—a man out on a late-night walk. In a Russosken-controlled, misogynistic corner of the Federation. How had he gotten himself into this? He was supposed to be retired. Living on N'Avon, slowly wooing Quinn. Or sweeping her off her feet. Not traveling the galactic sector in a ship crowded with family, landing on dangerous missions. Someday. That was the dream.

A man hurried along the sidewalk by the building, looking around furtively as he jogged to the door. Tony sighed. Amateurs. He followed the guy up the side steps, carefully making as much noise as possible with his feet. The man started and swung around.

"Who are you?"

"My name's Tony." He held his hands slightly away from his body so this nervous Nellie would see he was unarmed. "This the meeting?"

"What's the password?"

Tony smirked. "If you don't know it, I'm not telling you."

The man's eyes narrowed. "Tricky. I know the password. Jackass."

"The password is jackass?" Tony asked. "That's not the one they gave me."

"Don't be a jackass."

"Look, I'm going to step over here, out of earshot." Tony pointed at the sidewalk. "You can use your password to get in, then I'll follow." Before the man could call him a jackass again, he ran down the steps and stepped onto the grass, into the shadow of a large tree. "Go ahead," he said in a stage whisper. He hoped this man's attitude and skills didn't reflect those of the rest of the organization.

The door opened and closed. Tony waited a few seconds, then approached. He knocked. A narrow panel at eye level slid open, light spilling out. "Password?" a hoarse voice asked.

Tony held out the data-card Amanda had given him. "You should probably turn off the inside lights." The eyes beyond the door narrowed at him, and the gap slid shut. He sighed again and waited, putting his back to the rough stonework beside the door.

Nothing moved in the empty parking lot—no animal sounds, which told him there were people out there alerting the local fauna. He tapped his comtab, and the device whispered the time through his earbud. He'd give them two more minutes, then he was calling for pizza.

The door opened. "Come in," a man whispered. "Hurry!" He slammed the door shut, nearly taking Tony's heel off in the process. "This way, honored guest."

"Hang on," Tony said. "If you're trying to keep this meeting secret, you're going about it the wrong way. At a minimum, either turn off the lights before you open the door slit or pretend this is a normal meeting. You couldn't look more suspicious if you tried."

The man rocked back in surprise, then nodded. "Yes, of course. Thank you for your counsel. Please, follow me."

Tony shook his head, sure Amanda must have told them the same thing. That was probably why the guy looked so surprised. They'd likely discounted everything she'd said. Idiots.

The man led him downstairs to a dim, dank hallway. They made their way between dusty crates, broken brooms, and stacks of old chairs. At the end, his guide opened a closet. He knocked on the inner wall, and a door opened. Light and noise spilled out. The man stepped out of the closet and gestured to Tony.

Why did everyone insist on building access to their secret room in the back of a closet? It was the first place he'd look. Especially since said closet had obviously been emptied recently. He shook his head and stepped into the warm, bright room.

Chairs were arranged in rows facing a single long table. Men sat or stood in groups, chatting, while the women stood silently near the walls, watching. The conversations petered out as the occupants of the room identified Tony as a stranger. Every head in the room turned in his direction. He sidestepped, surreptitiously putting his back to the wall.

The man who'd brought him hurried to the front of the room and engaged in whispered conversation with two men at the front table. They watched him as they spoke, a range of expressions crossing their faces: dismay, relief, curiosity.

Finally, the older of the two spoke. "Welcome, visitor. Please join us."

As Tony walked up the aisle, the others moved out of his way. Every eye in the room seemed to bore into him. Having spent his life as an agent, he was used to suspicion, but the underlying distrust felt personal somehow. Oh well, he'd experienced worse hostility. He reached the front and turned to face the assembly. "Hello, I'm Tony."

The man who'd led him to the room bowed to the older man and departed. The younger of the two apparent leaders narrowed his eyes. "Tony who?"

"Please, no last names," the older man said, holding up a hand. "We'll call you Tony. You may call me Bart. This is Edwin." He nodded to his companion. "We are the leaders of this community. We are working toward freedom from our oppressors. The woman said she would send us a liaison to help us. Please, have a seat." Bart and Edwin sat. The rest followed their example.

Tony picked a chair at the end of the long table and sat. "Tell me about your organization. How have you built it? How far does it extend? What are your goals?"

The two men looked at each other. "We thought the woman would brief you," Edwin finally said.

"We didn't have a lot of time on the handoff," Tony replied. "Plus, I like to get the story straight from the operatives."

Bart nodded. "Wise. I'll be honest, when your leadership sent *her*, I was concerned. Sending that woman to discuss political conflict? Ridiculous. We worried that your organization might not be a good fit for us. We prefer to work with people of action."

"Amanda is an excellent political analyst and operative." He looked around. "What's your problem with her? I thought you were sexist, but obviously..."

"We don't care that she's a woman," Edwin said. "There are people in some pockets of Varitas City that might, but most of us are more evolved. We're concerned that your leadership sent—" He broke off as if he couldn't stand to say the words.

"What?" Tony asked.

"A tax collector," Bart whispered.

Tony's brows furrowed. "What?"

"She's a tax collector!" Edwin said loudly. Everyone in the room shushed him.

"You're telling me you wouldn't work with Amanda because she's employed by the Federation Revenue Service?"

Heads nodded.

"Wow." Tony rubbed the back of his neck. "Not what I expected. I guess you'll have to make do with me. I've never collected a single tax. Tell me what you have."

Bart nodded. "These people are representatives from all over the planet."

Tony broke in. "All over the planet? That kind of travel must have alerted the planetary authorities! What precautions have you taken?"

"No, no. We're all local, but each of them represents an area of the planet. Kind of a local liaison, if you will." Bart threw a spreadsheet onto the large table display. "This is an accounting of our forces, spread around the globe. If you have questions about a specific entry, the local liaison can elaborate."

Tony stood to get a better view of the table. "You look to be well organized. What's this red column?"

"That's Federation peacekeepers," Edwin said. "After Lunesco, the Federation beefed up troops on this and other fringe worlds."

"What do you know about Lunesco?" Tony asked, alarm bells ringing in his head. How would these locals know about Federation strength? "Where did you get this data?"

"The Lunescans freed themselves of the Russosken," Edwin said. "They started the revolution!"

"*Semper Libero!*" The cheer went up around the room.

"Traders bring news," Bart said when the cheering had died. "And we have insiders in most of the Federation offices. Local people, loyal to our cause, who work for the oppressors so they can feed us intelligence."

"Lunesco was a unique situation," Tony said. "They had a small population, low economic importance to the Federation, no physical Federation presence, plus a wealthy man with military experience and connections that allowed him to acquire and install equipment you won't have access to."

"The woman said your organization would help us break free!" Edwin said. "Are you saying we should give up?"

Tony spread his hands. "I'm not saying anything of the kind. I am telling you that what worked on Lunesco isn't going to happen here. Different situations. However, with this information—" He gestured at the spreadsheet. "—we should be able to develop our own solution. Let's go through the numbers."

CHAPTER 8

QUINN TOSSED the comtab onto a towel-covered workbench. "Good thing we use burners." She stood and arched her back. "No one will ever use that device again. The good news is, it wasn't as bad as we thought."

End picked up the motherboard hanging from the case by a ribbon, then dropped it. "Did you get the original data-card? The one Elli used to hijack this thing?"

Quinn reached into her pocket and tossed it to him. "She gave it to me. She wasn't happy about keeping secrets from me. Good girl."

"We could put this into another burner and spoof the location data." End turned the card over in his fingers. "Then let Elli chat with Reggie. We have a filter to alert us if she used any of our names, ship names, etc. We don't want her accidentally spilling the beans."

Quinn's eyes sparkled. "That could be kind of fun. We can send him on a wild goose chase. Let's keep that as a later option, for now. Once we're sure he hasn't located us." She picked up the comtab's motherboard. "I'm kind of shocked that card didn't have more surveillance built into it. He could have recorded conversations."

"Maybe he thought Elli would have her own comtab," End suggested. "And he didn't want to listen to algebra tutoring."

Quinn grinned. "Reggie was never very good at exploiting all the opportunities. Lucky for us. He's also a tightwad. He probably picked up the cheapest software he could get. Minimal functionality. My real question is, what was he going to do with the information? Come grab the kids? And how did he get that card to Elli?"

End shrugged. "He probably paid someone to deliver it. There's a lot of shady commerce over the borders near Hadriana. We do that kind of work. Of course, we do it for the Commonwealth, not random jerk wads. And we're not shady." He grinned. "But, yeah, I'm sure he was going to scoop the kids up."

Quinn glanced at the hatch to make sure they were still alone. "But he doesn't really want them."

"No, but Gramma Moneybags does, right? And the Feds would love to have leverage over you. And us. Especially after Lunesco."

"Do you think they know that was us?"

"Always best to assume they know. That's what Gramma says." End handed her a comtab. "Here's one for Elli. I changed the location data, so we can input whatever we like here." He showed her an icon on the screen. "Right now, it says we're near Romara. If she sends a message, it will have that data in the header. Let's see how this plays out."

"Thanks, End." She took the device. "I'll hang onto it for later. When I'm ready to mess with Reggie. You're sure it's safe?"

"I burned the built-in locator chip. The only way it's getting location data is that app. It's not connected to the net. When you're ready to send or receive, you plug it in through our clean server here." He spun his stool and patted a box in the corner. "The signal will get bounced through our private net to a secret Commonwealth transmitter in the middle of nowhere. So even if he manages to track back, it will get him to a transmitter in a dead system. That's how we do all our comms."

"You sure this won't expose us to more danger?" Quinn asked.

"Nah, like I said, this is how we do all our comms. Commonwealth operatives have transmitters on rocks all across this edge of the

Federation. The server bounces through a couple of them and randomly assigns a location. It's as safe as you can get. And it's Commonwealth equipment, which means the Federation only has a poor copy. They try to steal all our stuff, but they mostly get bad fakes." He grinned.

"Could I use this system to send a message?" Quinn asked. "I was contacted by an—well, I won't call her a friend, but let's say acquaintance. She said she could help me. I want to know what she is up to." Although she didn't consider the Trophany particularly bright, *she* knew enough to hire the best. That made her more of a threat than Reggie.

"Sure," End said. "Record your message and let me know when you're ready to send. It won't be private—we run that filter I mentioned. It will alert me if there's anything that might pinpoint our location."

"I'm not worried about privacy," Quinn said. For one thing, there was none on a boat this small. "This can impact all of us. I need to talk to Lou before I send it. Probably Liz, too." And Francine, but she wasn't going to mention that to End.

"Good plan." End put away his equipment and threw the disassembled comtab into the recycler. "Let me know when you're ready."

FRANCINE'S FACE frowned from the screen of Quinn's comtab. "Are you sure this is a good idea?"

"I don't see how it can hurt," Quinn said. "And I need to know what the Trophany is up to. So do you."

"Can you stop using that stupid nickname?" Francine grumbled. "It always takes me a minute to figure out who you're talking about."

"I'll try, but it's kind of second nature. End says it's safe to send the message, and he set up a drop box for the Tro—Tiffany to send her answer. She knew we were in N'Avon, but your sister never came looking for us there, so that's a good sign they aren't working together. Or weren't at that point."

"Dusica in N'Avon," Francine laughed. "That's something I'd pay to see. She wouldn't have gone herself. But you're right, she didn't send any goons after me. Or if she did, they were incompetent."

"I suppose she might not have known you went there."

"I'm sure she has hooks into the public data in the Commonwealth," Francine replied. "We weren't exactly in the witness protection plan. Local records would have shown Francine Terrence rented an apartment there. And whoever ratted me out on Hadriana must have passed on my alias."

Quinn nodded. "I want to know how Tiffany's data-card got to Maarteen. Is his network compromised? We sent him a message, but it could be weeks before he responds."

Francine was silent.

"Well, I guess—"

"Quinn," Francine cut her off. "Should I go back?"

"Back?" Quinn echoed. "To Hadriana? Why?"

"No, to the Russosken," she said in a rush. "I could, I don't know, be a double agent. Pass info to Tony. Shorten the war by five years and save millions of lives."

"That last bit sounds like a quote."

"It was." Francine's lips twisted in a sad little grin. "I have no doubt I could help from there."

"Could you?" Quinn asked. "Wouldn't they watch you like a hawk?"

"I guess it depends on if they know I went to Lunesco," she said slowly, feeling her way through the idea. "There shouldn't be any record of me being there—I was on the shuttle or at Doug's most of the time. Unless there's a mole in Auntie B's network."

"We never did figure out who was sending info to the Russosken," Quinn said. "Not sure that's worth risking."

"I guess." Francine stared away from the camera for a few

seconds. "Okay. I won't make any decisions right now. But go ahead and send your message to Tiffany. I want to know what she and that snake Dusica are up to."

QUINN SAT in the cabin she shared with Ellianne and turned on her comtab. Making sure the wall behind her was blank, she flicked the video icon and hit record.

"Hi, Tiffany. I was surprised to hear from you. I see you're doing well. As you can imagine, I'm not eager to visit. Maybe if you give me more information, I can help you. Let me know." Nice and vague.

She took the comtab to End, and he sent the message out into the system. "The filter says it was clean—no hints in the text or video. Good job. We've got a one-time drop associated with that message. It will pass the response to your drop box through a series of random nodes with no pass-back, so Tiffany can't run a bounce tracker. When do you expect to hear back from her?"

"No idea," Quinn said. "Maybe never."

"Did you hear the *Peregrine* will be docking at Varitas Two?"

"The station? Do you know why?" Quinn asked. "Usually, Lou sends a shuttle to pick up cargo. Dareen should be back in a couple hours. Or you could go."

"It's big." End smiled at her wide-eyed reaction. "I mean, the cargo is physically big. Too large to fit into the shuttle, so she's docking the ship. We do that occasionally."

"But not often." Quinn gave him a sideways glance. He looked uncomfortable.

"No, not often." End scratched his head. "And almost never when we've got kids aboard. She must be sure it's safe. You gonna hit the station?"

Quinn laughed. "Visit a Federation station orbiting a planet controlled by the Russosken? I don't think so."

"I can't believe Gramma sent Dareen down there," End said. "She's usually careful about that kind of thing."

Quinn bit her lip.

"What?" End asked.

"I don't know Lou very well," she said slowly. "But does she seem a bit off her game lately? I mean, for the leader of a crime family, she seems to have made a lot of bad assumptions since I've been aboard." She garbled out the words in a rush.

"What do you mean?" End's face went tight. "There's nothing wrong with Gramma."

"I didn't mean there was anything wrong," Quinn said. "Like I said, I don't know her. It just seems like— First the cloaking device, then the poor cargo choice for Lunesco, now this..."

End's lips pressed together so tightly they turned white.

"Never mind. Forget I mentioned it." She should have spoken to Tony, not End.

CHAPTER 9

A MUFFLED clang vibrated through the *Peregrine* as they docked at Varitas Two. "Cargo lock sealed. Clamps secure. Board is green. We'll be dropping the gravity to zero-point-six-zero for cargo transfer...now." Lou's voice echoed through the ship. "Stene, you're cleared to open her up and load the cargo."

Quinn, Ellianne, and Lucas sat at the table in the mess hall, working on schoolwork. As she'd told End, Quinn had no interest in visiting Varitas Two. She'd help load cargo if they needed her, but she wasn't going outside the cargo docks for one second. Not worth the risk.

"Quinn, we need you down here," Kert called through the intercom.

Speak of the devil.

"You two finish your work," Quinn said.

"We want to come, too!" Lucas jumped to his feet.

"Yeah!" Ellianne backed him up.

"No. Stay here and finish your math. I'll be right back." She gave them her best mom-glare and headed out.

The cargo hold was a circus of activity. An enormous flatbed eased a giant shrink-wrapped package into the cargo hold, barely clearing the top. It wasn't particularly wide, but it had huge red arrows with the words "This side up" plastered on both the wrapping and the crate beneath.

"What the heck is that thing?" Quinn found Kert standing by the rear ramp controls.

"Portable medical lab." Kert checked his comtab. "Fully stocked, ready to drop into medical emergencies. We're pre-positioning a pair of 'em for—" He consulted the screen again. "MedCare Interstellar."

"Where?"

"Robinson's World in the Poinsettia System." Kert rubbed the back of his neck, not looking at Quinn. "You talk to her?"

"Talk to who?"

"The woman." He jerked his chin toward the station. "She said she needed to talk to you."

"And you told her I was on board?" Quinn demanded. "What the hell were you thinking! This is Federation territory! They're going to drag me off to prison!"

"Relax," Kert said. "She didn't ask for you. I'm not that stupid. She asked for Francine. I said she wasn't here, but she could talk to you."

Quinn shut her eyes for a moment. "I'm not sure that's any better." Her pulse pounded in her ears. "What name did you give her?"

"I didn't." Kert glared. "She asked for Francine. I said we didn't have no Francine. She said, are you sure, I heard she's on this ship. She described Francine. I said, no, we ain't got no blondes on the boat. You wanna talk to one of the gals? And she said yes."

"Tell her we're busy." Quinn rubbed her eyes. "Or get Lou to talk to her."

"Nah. Francine said you should talk to her."

"What? When did you talk to Francine?" Quinn resisted the urge to pull out her hair. Or what was left of Kert's.

Kert shrugged. "I called her. After I told the woman to wait over there." He pointed through the open rear of the ship, past the med lab now halfway into the ship. Near the office, Stene spoke to a man in station-branded coveralls. Beyond him, a blonde woman sat on a bench against the inner wall, ignoring everything around her while having an animated conversation with someone on her comtab.

Quinn gulped. "That's Dusica."

"Who?"

"Never mind." Quinn walked a few steps away, then turned back. "Francine said I should talk to her?" At his nod, she continued, "And you sent a picture? Of her? To Francine?"

Kert stared blankly at her. "Yeah, I sent a picture."

"I guess I'd better talk to her, then." Quinn looked wildly around then pointed at his head. "You got another one of those hats?"

"Sure." Kert waved at the inner wall of the cargo hold. A series of hooks held hats, coveralls, and other equipment.

"Thanks." After outfitting herself with the generic blue coverall and hat, she slid past the med lab and strode down the ramp to the blonde on the bench. "You looking for someone?"

Dusica Zielinsky's icey blue eyes flicked to her, then back to her comtab. She smiled brilliantly and tapped a button on the device. "You interrupted my filming." She slid huge sunglasses over her face.

"Sor—" Quinn started, but she broke off. She wasn't sorry. This woman was nosy. And dangerous. "What do you want?"

"I'm looking for my sister." She flicked the screen of her device. "I heard she might be on this ship." She held up her comtab. The screen showed a picture of Dusica and Francine together on a beach somewhere, bright-colored drinks in hand.

"Nope," Quinn said. "Guess you heard wrong."

The girl stared at Quinn, then rose. "I am worried about her. She is in a dangerous position, and I don't want her to get hurt." She pulled the sunglasses back off, her eyes pleading.

"I'm sorry to hear that. If I had a sister, I wouldn't want her to get hurt either."

"Look, I know she was on this ship." Dusica stepped closer. "Tiffany says I can trust you. I need to get a message to Faina."

"Tiffany?" Quinn took a step back. She wished she'd put a stunner in her pocket before coming out here. "Tiffany who?"

The woman stamped her foot. "Tiffany Andretti, of course. She sent you a message. You were supposed to watch the video. I need to get a message to Faina, and you're my best chance." As she spoke, her voice rose higher and louder.

Quinn made a hushing motion with her hands. "Please, calm down. If I could give your sister a message, I would."

Dusica looked away. "Faina is playing with fire. If the *nachal'nik* finds out what she's been up to, they'll kill her."

"What exactly do you think your sister has been 'up to'?"

"I know she was on Lunesco—or at least I think she was." Dusica looked around the cargo bay, but no one paid them any attention. She slid her huge sunglasses over her face again. They did nothing to disguise her appearance.

"Those glasses are going to get you noticed," Quinn said. "No one wears them on stations like this except celebrities trying to hide their identity."

"Do you know why we do that?" Dusica asked. At Quinn's headshake, she continued. "Because we all wear anti-paparazzi makeup. Which is illegal in the Federation. But if you add the sunglasses, it makes the make-up less noticeable to the cams."

"Thanks for the tip." Quinn had been afraid to wear the camera-scrambling foundation because she knew the lack of resolution would tip off the cameras. Why was this woman talking about it, though? Was she stalling? Or trying to build trust? "As I said, I'd really like to help you, but I can't."

"Quinn," Dusica whispered. "Please."

Quinn froze. "What did you call me?"

"Quinn. You're Quinn Templeton. I know my sister was nanny for your kids. And I know you left Hadriana with the children. I believe you took Faina with you. She was later spotted on Romara in the company of that man." She nodded across the loading bay at Stene. "Eventually, this ship went to the Lunesco System. Luckily for

Faina, it never landed on the planet, and no one is *positive* it was in the system. No one but me, that is." She pushed the sunglasses on top of her head where they still shadowed her face. "I know it's you. I haven't turned you in. I'm trying to help my sister."

Quinn glanced away from her earnest eyes. "Your sister isn't on this ship. But if I run into her somewhere, I'll tell her you're looking for her."

"Give her this." Dusica set a small item on the bench. Her chin dipped, and she adjusted the sunglasses onto her nose again. "I'll be in touch."

"Wait," Quinn said. "How did you find this ship?"

Dusica smiled. "That's a story for another time."

Quinn grabbed her arm. "I want assurance our ship isn't in danger."

The blonde froze, then turned back to Quinn. "Your ship isn't in danger. I haven't shared my information with anyone. Especially not the *nachal'nik*. Or the Federation. I have my own network."

"How can you be so sure the Russosken haven't infiltrated your network?"

"If they had, they'd be here, and I'd be dead," Dusica said flatly. "I have to go. My security team is loyal to me, but if anyone spots them in that bar, they'll know I'm here somewhere. And don't worry when that cargo handler follows me." She tipped down the glasses and over the top, her eyes jerked to the right. "He's mine."

She strode away, barely pausing long enough for the door to slide open. The cargo handler she'd indicated set down his inventory tablet and drifted after her.

Quinn sank onto the bench, leaning back and watching the crew load the second medical lab. After a few seconds, she leaned forward, swiping her hand casually along the seat. She scooped up the datacard that lay, almost invisible, on the bench. With a sigh, she got to her feet, adjusted her cap, and strode back to the ship.

CHAPTER 10

DAREEN SHIFTED her chair to put her back to Hastri, but close enough that they could still talk. She picked up her comtab and tapped her photos until she found one that looked like a call-in-progress. It wouldn't fool anyone who took a close look at the device, but it had kept annoyances at bay in the past. People were hesitant to interrupt if you were on a call. She leaned back in her chair and asked softly, "Is the Russosken 'recruiting' the reason there aren't enough men?"

Hastri hissed at the name. "They pull heavily from the local population. The rest of the planet aren't as accommodating, but the leadership here encourages young men to join the Russ—them. Which is kind of odd, since they don't want women working."

"No one ever said religious zealots made sense," Dareen muttered.

"Tell me about it. The rest of the planet is more progressive, but here, they stick to the old ways. I've thought about moving to New Darhil, out west. Have to get a job first, though, and those aren't easy to come by. Every woman in Varitas City wants out."

Dareen made a noncommittal noise. "Look, I gotta go load my cargo. Thanks for the nachos and the conversation."

"Oh, don't leave," Hastri said. "Have another drink."

Dareen pushed the half-eaten plate across the table to the seat Hastri had occupied. "Sorry, got a schedule to keep." She glanced at the other woman as she got to her feet.

Hastri grabbed Dareen's wrist. "Don't go."

Dareen pulled back, but the woman had a grip of steel. "What the hell?" She twisted her arm against the other woman's thumb.

With a soft yelp, Hastri dropped Dareen's arm. She cradled her hand against her chest. "I—"

Dareen's eyes narrowed. "Why are you trying to keep me here?" She turned, scanning the area. No one appeared to be paying them any attention. "What's your game?"

Hastri's eyes ranged over the concourse, but she didn't seem to find what she was looking for. "Fine, go. They aren't here anyway."

"Who aren't here?"

The warm friendliness was gone. "They said they'd pay for you, but—"

"What do you mean they'd pay for me?" Dareen's chest constricted. "For me, specifically? Or for any solo woman?"

But Hastri had already gathered her bag and stood. "If you want to find out, hang around. If you want to go back to your ship, you'd better go now." She strode away.

Futz. Dareen hurried to the flight line exit, her eyes wide, on the watch for the *soldaty*. She flashed her comtab, set to her pilot credentials, and the automated door slid open. She slipped out the door and ran for the cart pickup station.

Damn! There it went! She put her head down, arms pumping, running as fast as she could. The empty cart bumped on along the apron, following its painted line. Lungs burning, she put on a burst of speed and grabbed the upright bar. The cart brakes kicked in and she slammed into the back of the vehicle. With a gasp, she pulled herself onto the seat.

She slapped the emergency contact button on her comtab. "Local made an attempt on me. Don't know if I was targeted specifically or an easy opportunity. Headed back to the shuttle. Please advise." She hit send and hoped someone from the *Peregrine* would answer soon. In the meantime, she'd lock herself in the shuttle and wait for her cargo delivery with the engines hot.

She leaped off the cart before it stopped in the designated loading area. The voice reprimanded her, but she ignored it. Her comtab got her into the shuttle and she started the launch checklist.

The comtab vibrated. "Status?" Lou's voice barked.

"I'm in the shuttle," Dareen said. "Almost through the pre-launch. Do I wait for the cargo?"

"Leave it," Lou said. "It was a cover. We don't need it."

"What about Tony?" Dareen swiped and flicked through the sequence as quickly as possible.

"We'll send a full team to get him at the secondary location," Lou said. "Get off the ground ASAP, but don't skip the checklist."

"Going through it now, Gramma. Been flying long enough to know better."

"That's my girl. See you soon. *Peregrine* out."

Dareen finished the prep and set the comm to the local channel. Her hand hovered over the connect button, then she swiped and activated a voice modifier. "Tower, this is shuttle papa-november-seven-indigo-zero-three, the *Squeaky Toy* requesting permission to depart Varitas Field." Her voice transmitted in a lower, androgynous register.

"*Squeaky Toy*, Tower. You're cleared to taxi to runway eight-four."

As she pulled around the corner at the end of the runway, movement near her parking space caught her eye. Was it her cargo being delivered? Or something more nefarious? She zoomed the camera in. A truck loaded with crates and a sleek vehicle with Varitas Field Security emblems sat in the empty spot. Four men stood beside the vehicles, gesturing angrily at each other.

"*Squeaky Toy*, you are cleared to launch."

"Roger, Tower, have a nice day. *Squeaky Toy* out." She grinned as she pushed the throttle, and the shuttle rumbled over the tarmac, gathering speed. She flicked the attitude adjusters and kicked in the launch engines. Good-bye, Varitas Field.

QUINN RUBBED HER FOREHEAD, feeling a headache coming on. They'd been discussing the same lack of information for what felt like hours. Both ships had departed Varitas and were headed toward the jump point.

"Maybe that woman is part of a sex-trafficking ring?" End suggested. "She watches for solo women and delays them until the *soldaty* can pick them up?" He glanced around the table. Quinn, Dareen, Lou, and Stene sat there. Liz, Maerk, and Francine stared out of the big screen, transmitting from the *Swan*.

"I've never heard of *soldaty* doing that," Francine said.

Everyone stared at her.

"Don't get me wrong," she continued. "The Russosken definitely are involved in trafficking, but they don't use uniformed *soldaty* for pickups. Bad publicity. They use thugs and underlings."

"You think she was looking for me specifically?" Dareen gripped the edge of the table. "Or someone from this ship?"

"I don't know," Francine said. "Maybe Tony will have heard something. Where will we pick him up again?"

"Amanda said he'll meet us on Robinson's World." Lou poked her thumb toward the cargo hold. "That's where these medical labs are going. Where are you headed, Liz?"

"We've got a small shipment for a science station farther out in the Poinsettia System." Onscreen, Liz swiped through her comtab and threw a document at the camera.

"You contracted with Federation Research Service?" Lou exploded. "Are you crazy?"

"No." Liz stabbed a finger at her chest. "*We* have a clean record. They have no way to tie us to you. This ship is in Maerk's name. We have no reason to avoid lucrative government contracts. Plus, who knows what we might pick up along the way."

"She's right," Stene said. "Lots o' advantages."

"Fine." Lou got to her feet. "Anything else? I got a ship to fly."

After a chorus of negative answers, she stomped out of the ship's rec space. The rest of the group exchanged wary looks.

Quinn sighed. "I'm going to throw this out there." She carefully avoided End's gaze. "Does Lou seem different to anyone? Off her game?"

"Yes!" Liz cried amid a sea of muttering. She glared at Maerk, then stared at the camera. "She has been off since we picked up that stupid cloaking device."

"One could argue it was before that," Stene said. "She sent Dareen to pick it up."

"Hey, I've run pickups for her before," Dareen said. "Things went south when that stupid bird turned it on."

"Riiiight, a bird turned it on," End jeered.

"Can we stick to the topic at hand?" Maerk cut in through Dareen's angry howl. "We're talking about Lou, not Dareen."

"Thank you, Dad. And I agree, Gramma has not been herself."

"But no one knows what's going on?" Quinn pressed. "I don't want to start a mutiny, but should she be in charge?"

Stene sucked in an angry breath but before he could respond, Maerk cut in again. "This is probably not a topic of discussion for the crew at large. Maybe Liz, Stene, and Kert should talk in private. We will back you up on whatever you decide." He gestured at the people gathered around the two tables.

Francine muttered something, but the mics didn't pick it up. Probably a good thing if she wanted to stay aboard the *Swan*, Quinn thought. "Francine?"

The woman looked up.

Quinn glanced at the others to make sure they weren't paying attention and pointed at her comtab. Time to discuss her sister's visit.

"GO AHEAD and look at the data-card," Francine said from the screen above the desk in Quinn's cabin. "I don't have any secrets."

"Are you sure about that?" Quinn's lips twisted. "We didn't know you had a sister until a few days ago."

"Fair point." Francine tapped the desk. "There's no way for you to get over here, though. Not until after we jump. You'll have to look at it. Better you than one of the others."

Quinn nodded and loaded the card into another burner comtab. At the rate they were going through these things... An icon popped up and she flicked it.

Dusica's face appeared on the screen. "Faina," she said, followed by a garble of a language Quinn didn't understand. Her auto-translator offered no assistance. No wonder Francine hadn't been worried about her hearing the message. She waited for it to end. "What did she say?"

Francine's lips pressed together tightly. "Pretty much what she said to you. That she has my best interests at heart, and she wants to keep me safe. She wants me to come stay with her."

"Do you believe her? That she cares about your safety? And can she really keep you safe?"

Francine looked away for a few seconds, thinking. "Neither of us was happy with the way the *nachal'nik* runs things. I ran. Dusi was smarter than me. She's built her own network over the years. Wouldn't surprise me if she takes over the whole thing at some point. Which is a problem. If the *nachal'nik* realizes what she's doing, she'll be viewed as a threat and removed."

"Is this *nachal'nik* related to you?" Quinn asked.

"She's my father's brother's mother."

"Father's broth— Doesn't that make her your grandmother?"

"No. My dad has several half-siblings. He's not related to the *nachal'nik* by blood." Francine drummed her fingers on the desk again. "I think I'm better off here, if the Marconis will let me stay. I hope. If Dusi was able to find me, then so could others."

"Your sister said she's the only one who knows you were on Lunesco." Quinn shrugged. "And soon, if Tony is successful, your *nachal'nik* will be too busy to bother with you." The comtab in her hand vibrated. "Hey, there's a second message on here." She hit play.

The *Tiffany Andretti Show* appeared on the screen. "There's no audio on this file." Quinn turned her back to the camera on her comm panel so that she and Francine could watch together. Sitting on her ridiculous set, Tiffany spoke to a sequin- and glitter-bedecked celebrity Quinn had never seen before. "This isn't the broadcast footage, though. Look, you can see backstage." In the wings, Melody stood by a tall table. She carefully balanced a spoon across a coffee mug. Then she stared straight at the camera and crossed her arms, right ring finger folded down.

"I guess Dusi wants us to help Melody," Francine said. "That's odd. She doesn't usually do 'help'."

"How can I help Melody? I can't go to Romara," Quinn said. "Too big a price on my head."

"You aren't going to believe this," Francine said, "but Tiffany doesn't film on Romara. She's located on Robinson's World."

CHAPTER 11

ROBINSON'S WORLD, located in the Poinsettia System, was home to many low-budget video producers. Quinn's hasty research revealed the planet had an excellent communications net, and although it was on the edge of "civilized space," it was well connected to the rest of the Federation. It also, apparently, required a couple medical labs. Quinn's eyes narrowed, and she stared up at Francine's image on the screen. "Do you believe in coincidences?"

"Not usually," Francine replied. "But this seems too subtle for Dusi. Plus, Liz and Maerk aren't going to Robinson's—we're headed for the FRS station circling the gas giant. If this is a setup, it's for you, not me."

"Great. I wish I knew what to believe. I guess I could go visit Tiffany's set. And wear some of that camera-scrambling makeup your sister mentioned." Was this why Dusica had brought up the subject? She knew Quinn would need it?

"Do you need some?" Francine asked. "Maybe I can borrow the skiff once we get to Poinsettia and bring it to you?"

"No worries. Lou gave me some before Lunesco." Quinn dug through the drawer in her desk and pulled out the little jar. "For my trip through the Romara Prime station. But I didn't use it—I was afraid it bring more attention to me." She turned the small cylinder over in her fingers. She was seeing conspiracies everywhere.

"Jump in thirty minutes," Lou's voice echoed through Quinn's cabin. Her comm system pinged, and a green banner appeared below Francine.

"Got a message." She reached toward the controls.

"We're going to jump soon," Francine replied. "I need to help run a check. Gotta earn my keep. Let me know what you think we should do. Before you do it." She winked at the camera and signed off.

Quinn brought up the message. It was a text from Lou: come see me after jump. That didn't look ominous at all.

QUINN STRODE onto the bridge of the *Peregrine*. "You wanted to see me, Captain?"

Lou heaved herself out of the command chair. "You got the conn, kid," she said to Lucas, who sat at navigation.

Quinn stared at her son, then back at Lou, eyes wide.

"Yes, sir!" Lucas smiled widely, his eyes sparkling.

Lou grinned and stomped to the door. After it shut behind them, she turned to face Quinn. "End's watching from the comm station. Not leaving a teen in charge of the ship."

Quinn started to point out that End was barely twenty himself but changed her mind. "What did you need?"

"My office." Lou swung around and led the younger woman the length of the ship to the crew lounge. She carefully closed the door behind them and dropped into one of the armchairs. "Have a seat."

Quinn perched on the edge of the couch.

"I have a mission for you," Lou said. "Need you to pass a message for me."

"Pass a message? You mean make a drop, like Dareen did on Hadriana?"

"That was a pickup, but same-same," Lou said. "I have a data-card that needs to get to someone, and I don't have any trusted assets in place. You owe me, so it's time to pay up."

"If you're spending your favor on this, it must be a big deal."

"Hardly," Lou said, her face blank. "This is an easy pass-off. It doesn't begin to clear the slate—just a little payment toward what you owe me."

"Who's keeping the tally on this favor-owing thing?" Quinn folded her arms. "I'd like to know what the conversion rate is, so I know when I'm paid up."

"That's not how these things work. You do what I need you to do. In addition to the favor you owe me, you basically work for me here on the *Peregrine*. I'm letting you stay aboard. Maybe we should consider it rent."

"If I do this, it's a *favor*," Quinn said. "I'm already paying my rent by working as a member of the crew."

"Yeah, but you're working for three,."

"Lucas is apprenticing to you, so he doesn't count against me," Quinn countered.

Lou grinned. "Fair enough. Will you do me a favor?"

"Who am I delivering to?"

"Tiffany Andretti," Lou said.

Quinn froze. "What do you need to deliver to her?"

"None of your business," Lou snapped.

"If I'm delivering, it's my business."

"That's not how this works," Lou said again. "If you're working for the family, you have to trust. And sometimes trusting means not knowing the details."

"I saw how well that worked for Dareen on Hadriana." Quinn crossed her arms and leaned back against the couch's stiff arm. "I'm not agreeing to anything blind." Especially not anything involving Tiffany Andretti.

"Your friend Tiffany—" Lou began.

"*Not* my friend." Quinn snapped a hand up in protest.

"Whatever. Tiffany has requested my assistance in a matter, and this is my response to her request." Lou fingered the data-card she'd pulled out of a pocket.

"I've seen way too many of those lately." Quinn cleared her throat. "What matter?"

Pink washed over Lou's wrinkled face, then receded. She heaved a sigh. "She asked us to do a job for her. She obviously has no idea what kind of work the Marconis really do. I am telling her we can't help her with her request."

Quinn waited, but Lou did not elaborate. "You aren't going to tell me what the request was?"

"Something we don't do." Lou's voice went colder. "Does it matter? Maybe she wanted us to build a bookshelf or cater her latest book signing. It doesn't matter what it was, because we don't do that."

"Fine," Quinn said. "Did you *agree* to do anything?"

"I agreed to send her a response via a trusted agent." Lou's tone practically dripped icicles. "That's you. For now. Any more questions?"

"Growl all you want, Lou. I told you a long time ago there's no more crap to be scared out of me." Quinn leaned forward. "If I'm playing messenger girl, then I need to know the details. Otherwise, it's no deal. Take it or leave it."

"That's all there is," Lou said. "She asked for something we don't do. I said no. Nothing more to tell. We'll dock at RW Prime to deliver the labs to MedCare Interstellar. You will take the 'vator down to Crusoe City and deliver the data-card at the studio where Andretti is recording. She's there every morning from eight to three, more or less. Catch the afternoon 'vator back up and get on the ship. Done."

"The *Peregrine* will be docked all day?" Quinn asked. "Isn't that risky?"

"MedCare isn't known for their timely delivery or retrieval. Plus, it will take most of the day to find the paperwork involved in this transfer. How they lose so many electronic files is beyond me."

"And what if I don't make it back to the ship before you have to leave the MedCare berth?" Quinn asked. "Or if the Federation sends inspection teams aboard and finds my kids?"

"Lucas and Elli are assigned to shuttle practice." Lou leaned her elbows on her knees. "Dareen will take them on a little field trip through the moons of Xury. It's a gas giant. The jump insertion point is near Xury's orbit, and the moons there offer some interesting opportunities for low-g landings. We've used them before, when End and Dareen were younger."

"You have everything planned." The level of detail made her more nervous instead of less. "What if the *Peregrine* gets delayed or impounded?"

"Liz and Maerk will be at the research station near Xury." Lou's eyes, under her half-closed lids, bored into Quinn, as if challenging her to ask more questions.

"Fine." Quinn held out her hand. "I'll do your delivery run."

"I'll give this to you when we get to RW Prime." Lou tucked the card back into her pocket and patted the outside. "I'd hate for it to get lost. Right now, Stene could use your help setting up the next trade. That'll be all."

Quinn pinched her lips together and rose. "I'll go help him, then." She barely resisted the urge to throw a rude gesture at the old woman as she left.

CHAPTER 12

FRANCINE LAY ON THE BUNK, staring up at the ceiling. Should she try to contact her sister or Tiffany? Or Quinn's friend Melody, perhaps? How would she do that without giving away her location? Of course Dusi hadn't had any trouble finding her.

Francine's eyes widened and she sat bolt upright. What if Dusi was tracking her? People tracked their kids. Could Dusica have— She yanked off her top and ran her hands over her arms and upper body. Twisting around in front of the mirror, she tried to inspect her back. What if Dusica had added an extra circuit to her birth control implant? She clapped her hand over her left shoulder, feeling the tiny bump. Dusi had taken her to the med pod as a teen to have it inserted. What if—

Sashelle sauntered into the cabin. She glanced at Francine, twisting and turning in front of the mirror, then leapt onto the desk. *Is this a new dance?* The caat yawned and curled up on top of Francine's comtab.

"No," Francine said. "I'm trying to see if my implant looks normal."

It looks the same as always, Sashelle said. *At least, it hasn't changed since the last time you wore a sleeveless blouse on Hadriana.*

"Not helpful, housecat," Francine muttered.

I suggest you modify both your tone and your phrasing, Sashelle said loftily.

"Or what?" Francine stopped twisting and yanked her shirt back on. "You might hock up a hairball on me?"

I might choose not to grace you with my wisdom, Sashelle said. *Besides, you're tedious when you're frantic. We have a mission, and I don't want to put up with that.* The caat's tail snapped through a couple of horizontal arcs.

"Mission? What mission?"

We need to go to Robinson's World. The Purveyor of Tuna may require our assistance.

"The Purvey—you mean Quinn?"

Yes. The Purveyor of Tuna. The caat sank into a puddle of fur and closed her eyes. *After, I wish to return to the kitten.*

"You don't like it here?" Francine didn't care if the caat preferred the other ship, but she was curious. That's all, just curious.

The kitten is more affectionate.

"Like you care about that."

The caat ignored her.

"How are we going to get to Robinson's World, oh great huntress?"

Mighty Huntress, Sashelle replied without opening her eyes.

"Fine, Mighty Huntress and Eliminator of Vermin, how, pray tell, will we get to Robinson's World?" Francine curtseyed to the caat.

That's your job, Sashelle said. *I can't think of everything.*

LIZ INPUT the coordinates of the Xury research station and swiped the engage button. The *Swan* pulsed her attitude adjusters to rotate into the correct direction, then fired the thrusters. Acceleration pressed Liz back into her seat until the artificial gravity caught up. Then she snapped open her harness and walked into the lounge. "We should be there in twenty-nine hours. Those new engines really give us some speed."

"I told you they were worth the extra credits." Maerk looked up from the mess of parts scattered across the table and smiled.

"I didn't say they were worth the extra cost," Liz corrected him. "I said they're fast. We'll see if they pay for themselves."

Maerk went back to soldering something. "I'm not worried. They will."

Francine climbed down the ladder and jumped the last couple steps to the deck. "What's our ETA?"

"Twenty-nine hours," Liz said. "You got a hot date?"

Francine glanced up from her comtab. "Kind of. I need to hit Robinson's World, and there's a system circulator scheduled to stop in thirty-three hours. Good timing."

"Those things are slow," Liz said over her shoulder as she dug through the fridge, looking for lunch. "If you really need to get to the planet, we could probably arrange something."

Francine shook her head. "I don't want to draw any attention. The circulator is safest."

"What are you going to do on Robinson's?" Maerk asked.

"I'm meeting my sister."

"What?" Liz's head jerked up in surprise. Pain chopped into her skull when it met the bottom edge of an open door. "Ow!" *Damn cupboard doors!* She slapped the overhead shut and rubbed the back of her head. "I thought you fixed the auto-closers on these things!" she snapped at Maerk.

"Sister?" Maerk didn't even acknowledging Liz's howl. "Wasn't she on Varitas Two? How many sisters do you have?"

"Only the one." Francine paced across the room, chewing on her lower lip. "I'm not sure she's here, but…"

"Suppose you tell us what this is all about." Liz pulled a chair away from the table and sat, still rubbing her head. "I need to know if my ship or my family is in danger. Spill."

"I thought you wanted plausible deniability." Francine looked from Liz to Maerk and back.

"That was before I knew who you were. Now that I know that much—" Liz shot a glare at Maerk. "I need to be informed."

Francine told Liz and Maerk about Dusica's message, and Quinn's analysis of Melody's signals. "I think Quinn needs backup, but I also want to talk to Dusi. I can do both those things if I get to Robinson's."

"If Dusica is even there." Liz jumped up from her seat. "But I'm more concerned about Quinn. You can't help her if you're three days late! By the time that circulator gets you to Robinson's, she'll be back on the *Peregrine*. If everything goes right." She headed to the bridge.

"What are you doing?" Maerk called after her.

"We're going to make a slight detour."

The others followed her, squeezing onto the bridge. Liz paused the autopilot, letting the ship continue on course without accelerating. Then she pulled up the system's public transport schedule. "Poinsettia is a well-connected system. They have circulators and connectors everywhere. Here it is." She pointed at the screen. "The in-bound circulator stops at Kreutznaer Station halfway between Robinson's and Xury. We can be there in a few hours."

"Thank you," Francine said slowly.

Liz shrugged. "We're probably all safer with you off the ship."

Francine smirked. "Thanks anyway."

⸻

THE *SWAN'S* AIRLOCK CIRCULATED, and the lights turned green. Francine hit the release, and the hatch swung inward. She stepped onto the gangplank leading to Kreutznaer Station's airlock.

"I don't think they allow animals on the circulator," she told Sashelle. "And you're too big to fit in my bag. Plus, I'm sure they'll run it through the security system, and you'd get busted."

The caat swished her tail a few times. *Don't worry about me. I'll meet you on board.*

The *Swan's* hatch closed behind them, and they hurried through the access tube to the station. The transparent tube provided a panoramic view of stars, station, and the docked ship.

"The *Swan's* bigger than I realized." Francine tapped her comtab and entered the station's public access code. The hatch hummed, then dinged and swung open.

Enough chit-chat, Sashelle said. *They'll think you're crazy if you talk to yourself.*

"I'm talking to you. That might be a little crazy, but there are plenty of crazy cat-ladies in the universe."

They won't see me.

Francine closed the outer hatch behind them and waited for the cyclers to run. "Why not? You're pretty big—hard to miss."

They won't, Sashelle insisted. *I'll meet you on the ship.*

The inner hatch popped, and noise assaulted her ears. A crowd filled the open concourse—talking, whispering, arguing. Children ran and yelled. Laughter bounced off the huge windows behind her. Francine stared. She hadn't seen this many people in this small of a space since she left N'Avon. She glanced down, but Sashelle had vanished. With a shrug, she pushed through the crowd to a podium bearing the Poinsettia Circulator logo.

"Good afternoon. The circulator is fully booked, but I can put you on the waitlist." The man behind the podium wore a name tag that read, "Bob, Customer Service."

"I have a seat." Francine flashed her comtab at the kiosk reader. The screen beeped green. "I wanted to ask what's going on. Why's it so crazy here?"

Bob looked around the room and frowned. "Crazy? This is pretty normal for a Friday. Everyone's headed dirtside for the weekend."

"Thanks." She'd lost track of the date. She turned just in time to see the *Swan* fall away from the station, the maneuvering thrusters nudging it over. She hitched her bag higher on her shoulder and strolled to the window to watch.

When the *Swan*'s main engines ignited, it blasted away in a blaze of light. Why did it feel as if she was being abandoned? She'd left a lot of places and a lot of acquaintances over the years; this was nothing new. Besides, she'd be back with them soon. Fighting the sinking feeling in her stomach, she turned to look for Sashelle.

She knew the caat was here, somewhere, but she didn't see her. She tried thinking the animal's name, but shouting inside her head was harder than books made it sound. Still, she focused on calling the caat.

What? Sashelle's long-suffering tone was comical, and Francine's lips quirked.

"Where are you?" She tried thinking but ended up whispering.

A heavy sigh echoed through her mind. *I'm up here. Don't look! I'm not invisible, just good at hiding.*

"Sorry," Francine replied aloud.

You think much more clearly when you speak aloud. But try not to draw too much attention to yourself. I'll find you on board.

While they were "talking," Francine had surreptitiously scanned the open ceiling. Large beams and pipes crisscrossed above the concourse. A few heavy bulkheads cut through at regular intervals. Those would surely slam shut in the event of a decompression. Finally, she spotted the large caat lying stretched across a beam near the airlock. How had she gotten up there with no one noticing?

CHAPTER 13

TONY SAT on a bench in front of a half-constructed building. Behind him, beyond a transparent dust barrier, robots installed windows and wiring. Across the transit trench, people came and went under his observant stare.

He'd been watching this building on Robinson's World all day. Early this morning, Tiffany had arrived in a private transport. Those were extremely rare on Robinson's. Two hours later, a stylishly-dressed man emerged from another private vehicle, accompanied by an entourage including three well-trained security personnel. One of Tiffany's guests, perhaps.

He hadn't seen Melody at all. She might have entered at the rear, or perhaps she'd arrived before he had. Or maybe she lived in this building. The upper stories might hold apartments. It was hard to tell on Robinson's. All the buildings were built to strict design themes. In this region, it was Late-Earth with slick-sided glass monstrosities.

Tony adjusted his hat to protect his nose from the sun and strolled down the street. He'd loop over the intersections and return on the other side of the transit trench, then take up a new observation post. After he got a sandwich. The drone he'd left on top of a nearby trashcan would keep watch while he took a break.

A LITTLE AFTER three in the afternoon, the streams of people entering the building had reversed, with more leaving than arriving. Tony checked his comtab, and the drones watching the rear doors gave him clear picture and sound. Before long, the glittering male celebrity and his massive entourage exited through the front. One of the security team scanned the area, his eyes catching on Tony.

Tony dropped his chin a fraction, knowing the trained professional would see the small movement. Hopefully, he'd think Tony was part of Tiffany's security crew. For a few tense seconds, the other man stared, motionless. Then he gave his own infinitesimal nod and climbed into the private transport.

"Act like you belong." That was his motto for operations. Ninety percent of the time, it worked. The rest? Well, he could run. Time to move.

He crossed the pedestrian bridge and strolled to the building's wide entrance. From earlier reconnaissance, he knew security guards sat behind a tall desk at the rear of the huge lobby. According to his sources, they changed at precisely 3:30. He loitered by a food cart, dithering over the selections for a few minutes and annoying the people lining up behind him. Before they could get irate enough to start paying attention to details, he selected a bag of something and a bottle of something else. It didn't really matter what, since he wasn't going to consume them.

He took his purchases and strolled to the building's entrance. A man scooted in front of him just as he reached the revolving door and dove into the rotating entrance. Tony paused, waiting for the next wedge to open. That was when he recognized the woman exiting the building through that exact wedge.

"*Futz.*" He yanked his hat a little lower over his forehead and stepped away from the entrance. With a savage twist, he yanked the bottle cap off his beverage and raised the bottle to cover the lower part of his face. A few more steps back, turn a bit, and he was leaning against the glass wall, checking his comtab for the time, waiting impatiently for someone.

Tiffany Andretti breezed out of the building with three flunkies at her back. One raced ahead to open the door of the private transport that had whooshed to a halt at the transit stop. Another hurried behind, taking notes on her comtab. The third's head flicked left and right like a bird, clearly watching for fans to fend off. There weren't any.

Tony's lips twitched, and he took a sip of his drink. Agonizingly sweet liquid washed over his tongue, making his teeth throb. What the hell was this stuff? He glanced at the brightly-colored label, but it was as painful to look at as it was to drink.

Tiffany got into her vehicle, followed by the three assistants. The second it pulled away, Tony tossed the bottle into the trash and pushed into the building. He'd barely make the shift change.

He strode across the wide lobby as if he owned it, watching the security guards from the corner of his eye. The four black-clad individuals chattered together while two of them collected items scattered around the desk and the other two waited to stow their own belongings. None of them watched the lobby.

Tony stepped behind a large plant near the elevator hall. A few seconds later, a group exited one of the elevators and pushed past the security desk, chattering and laughing. Tony slunk behind them and into the car before the doors slid shut. Easy.

On the thirty-eighth floor, he fought his way through another crowd of departing workers to exit the elevator car. Except for low walls dividing the desks and evenly-spaced support beams, the entire floor was open from the elevator to the floor-to-ceiling window. He hadn't realized the Late-Earth theme extended to the interiors. Too much open space could be a problem.

He strode around the elevator shaft, watching for late workers, but the floor appeared to be deserted. Apparently, everyone got off at three-thirty. He found the stairwell and used an app on his comtab to unlock the door. Robinson's World building codes required these to be locked at all times. What would happen if the building needed to be evacuated?

He climbed two flights to the fortieth floor and exited. This time, the door opened to a small lobby with a half-dozen closed doors. Each had a green light above indicating it was safe to enter. He pushed open Studio B.

The room was dim. Tall tiers on either side of the entrance held utilitarian seats, each row lower than the one behind it. He walked between the bleachers and stepped onto a low stage. A padded chair, slightly higher than normal, sat next to a long, low couch. Overhead a huge sign, currently unlit, read "the Tiffany Andretti Show!"

Tony tried out the couch and it was as hard as it looked. Maybe uncomfortable guests gave better interviews? He moved the tall chair and settled back to wait.

He didn't wait long.

"Comfy?" Marielle LeBlanc strolled in.

THE NEWLY RENAMED *Dark Avenger* fell away from the *Millennium Peregrine*, maneuvering thrusters pushing and rotating it. The straps cut into Dareen's shoulders as her body fought with the ship's movement. "If you set the antigravity at one-quarter before you release from the ship, it's more comfortable for your passengers," she said.

Lucas glanced at the screen in front of him, his finger hovering over a slider. "This one?"

"Yup. Slide it—slowly!—up to twenty-five percent. Normally, you'd want to make an announcement, but since it's only the three of us..."

Lucas grinned and flicked the intercom icon. "This is your pilot. We're going to one-quarter gravity in five, four, three, two, mark." He slid the controller, and they settled into their seats.

"Talking on the intercom is the best part," Ellianne said.

"No, it's not," Lucas retorted. "Flying is better. Can I fire the engines?"

"Is your course set?" Dareen asked. "Always double-check. You don't want to end up in the far reaches of the system without enough fuel."

"Aye-aye, ma'am!" Lucas nodded sharply and pulled up the navigation screen. "We have a course laid in for Xury Five. Why do these moons have numbers instead of names?"

"You're cleared to Xury Five," Dareen replied. "I dunno. Maybe there are too many of them. There are, like, fifty."

"Fifty-seven, plus assorted asteroids," Ellianne said. "Two of them are big, and they have names: Defoe and Daniel."

"I know," Lucas moaned. "I learned about the system, too. Firing engines now." Their location on the screen changed, but the low acceleration was dampened by the artificial gravity.

"Well done," Dareen said. "Increase speed and set an alert to notify us when we are near Xury."

"How close?" Lucas asked.

Dareen smiled. "That's up to you. You're the pilot."

"When do I get to fly?" Ellianne asked.

"Lucas will do a bit of velocity matching near the smaller moons, and then you'll have a chance to fly us to the larger one. Don't worry, there's plenty of time for everyone to fly. And no one out here to bother us."

CHAPTER 14

A FLASH of light drew Francine's gaze to the window. A small ship—smaller than the *Swan*—drifted toward the station, rotating in several directions until the airlock matched the gantry. With impressive economy, it gently kissed the station and clamps locked on.

"The Poinsettia Circulator bound for Robinson's World has arrived," a voice announced. "Please clear the corridor so new arrivals can exit the ship."

The crowd surged toward the airlock, ignoring the announcer's command. Francine stayed by the window. They all had assigned seats, so why were these people so anxious to get aboard? She'd rather stay here where she could stretch her legs.

She glanced at the overhead beam, but Sashelle was no longer visible. Maybe the caat had her own cloaking device?

The man from the podium—Bob—pushed through the crowd. "Please, step back! Make a hole! We have passengers who need to exit the ship before you can get on." He pressed through the crowd, physically pushing people aside. "Over there. Wait over there! We do this every week, people! It's not that hard!"

"No one ever gets off," someone grumbled nearby.

The airlock hatch popped, and the crowd leaned forward, then ebbed. A pair of young women and a man stepped into the concourse, and the crowd parted like magic to let them through. As soon as they passed, the space filled behind them. Finally, Bob allowed them to board, a dozen at a time, each passenger flashing their comtab at the reader as they did.

Francine trailed behind the last few people. "Why are they in such a hurry?" She flashed her comtab again.

"You ever lived on a small station?" Bob followed her into the airlock, checking the telltales as the hatch sealed. "It gets old, really fast. They want to have a nice weekend on the dirt."

"I get that. I live on a ship—even smaller. You're coming too?"

"Hell yeah. This is the last trip to Robinson's for a while."

"Why is that?"

He looked around and leaned in close. "Because of the unrest."

"What do you mean?" Francine feigned surprise and confusion.

Bob eyed her. "Nothing. There are rumors— Never mind. I hope you have a seat."

Rumors of unrest? Was this evidence of Tony and Amanda's work? She'd have to wait for a more private setting to ask questions. "I have an assigned seat. " Francine waved her comtab at him.

"Don't count on it." He pushed her ahead of him through the access tube. "That's why they're in such a hurry. They don't pay much attention to assigned seats."

"I don't care where I sit," Francine said. "But I paid for a seat. I need to get to Robinson's."

"Oh, you'll get there. But it might not be as comfortable as you'd hoped."

The circulator's hatch popped open, and they followed the last few passengers into the airlock. When the inner hatch popped, the wall of noise crashed over them again.

"These are the loudest people I've ever encountered," Francine said.

"What?" Bob yelled.

She gave up.

When everyone had finally stowed their bags and taken a seat, Francine still stood by the hatch. Bob—whose nametag now read "Steve, Flight Services"—grinned at her. "Told you."

"Where's my seat?" Francine gave Bob/Steve her best frosty glare.

"You get the jump seat." He pushed past her and folded down a hard shelf by the hatch. A compartment above the hatch opened to reveal shoulder straps. "Enjoy. You do know how to open the airlock manually, right?"

Francine glanced at the unpadded perch, then at the hatch. "If I can't, will you assign me a new seat?" A small plaque about halfway up displayed a picture of a spoked wheel and an arrow showing which way to turn it. "I think I can handle it." She tucked her bag into the netting hanging below the seat and strapped herself in.

Across the aisle, Steve unfolded another seat and tucked away his own bag. "You wanna make the announcement?" he asked with a grin as he latched his harness.

"Please, proceed."

Steve pulled a wired handset from the wall. "Welcome to the Poinsettia Circulator." His voice echoed through the ship. "Next stop, Robinson's World Prime."

A cheer deafened Francine. She closed her eyes and rotated her shoulders. Thank all the gods, this trip was only a couple hours.

"Strap in, if you haven't yet," Steve said. "We'll be leaving the station in—whoops, we've already left."

Francine peered through the tiny window in the hatch. The station fell away, rotating out of sight.

"Get your stuff stowed and—" Steve continued.

"This is the captain," another voice cut in over Steve's. "Thrusting in three, two, one, mark."

Acceleration pushed Francine against her harness, then the artificial gravity dampened the force.

"We'll arrive at RW Prime in three hours," Steve said after a pause. "The captain is cutting gravity to one-quarter, as usual, for the duration of the trip. Stay strapped in unless you need to use the loo. Try not to drink too much. Y'all know the drill. Have a safe flight."

Francine glanced at Steve. "Not much of a safety briefing."

"Everyone on this ship has done this before. Many, many times." He looked her up and down. "I know 'em all. And you just arrived—on an interstellar-trader—so I wasn't worried about you. What's your story?"

Francine shrugged. "Seeing the galaxy, one small ship at a time."

"Rich kid on tour or working your way?"

"You don't beat around the bush, do you?" Her stomach complained briefly as the gravity lightened.

He grinned. "Usually, I can guess. You look like the rich kid type, but you don't have enough luggage."

She smiled back. "I'm working. When I need to. I have a friend on Robinson's, so this leg will be fun." Something brushed against her ankle and she swallowed a yelp.

"You okay?" Steve asked. "You're looking kind of nervous."

"I'm fine. Thought I left something on the ship, but it's in my pocket." She tapped her jacket pocket. At the same time, she pushed her foot against the bag in the netting under the seat. She didn't want to draw Steve's attention to it, because she was pretty sure Sashelle had climbed in next to the bag.

AS SOON AS Kert lowered the cargo ramp, Quinn slipped out of the ship and across the MedCare loading bay. She'd never been to RW Prime, but like every other Federation station, it had a downloadable map and plenty of signs. She followed the blinking arrow on her comtab, exiting through the personnel airlock. Three other people stepped into the lock with her. She kept her eyes on her comtab, watching the others out of the corner of her eye. They ignored her and each other.

Following Dusica's suggestion, she had applied the camera-confounding makeup before leaving the ship and wore a pair of thick-framed glasses. She hoped the wig and glasses would prevent anyone from recognizing her as the convicted Federation traitor.

The others turned left when they exited the airlock, but Quinn's comtab directed her to the right. She kept her head down, watching her feet and device, as she followed the red line painted on the wall. They really didn't want anyone to get lost on this station. She glanced up as she reached an intersection, but there weren't a lot of people roaming the corridors. Three junctions later, she turned left and went through an open hatch set in a thick bulkhead.

Another turn brought her to transparent doors that slid open at her approach. Voices assaulted her ears—many people talking too loudly in a confined area. She spotted the red sign leading to the Robinson elevator and stepped into the line.

"I was wondering when you'd get here," Francine said.

"You scared the crap out of me!" Quinn swung around, her heart pounding in her chest. She took a couple deep breaths. "How'd you get here so fast?"

"Liz dropped me off at Kreutznaer." Francine looked up at the overhead supports.

"What are you looking for?" Quinn asked.

"Sashelle."

"You brought the caat? They won't let us take her to the surface. Robinson's has a strict quarantine for pets."

"I didn't bring her. She brought me." Francine continued scrutinizing the upper reaches of the space. The line shuffled forward a couple of steps.

"She brought you?" Quinn started to scoff, then remembered how Sashelle had led them to Dareen's shuttle on N'Avon.

Francine looked around, but no one paid them any attention. "The caat can talk," she whispered.

Quinn leveled a look at her. She could believe the caat was smart, but talk?

"I mean it." Francine rubbed her eyes. "It sounds crazy, but the caat is sentient. Or is it sapient? Maybe both. She talked to me."

Quinn raised her eyebrows. "The caat talks."

"Not out loud." Francine grimaced. "I knew I shouldn't have told you."

"You're serious."

"Completely."

"Dareen said Sashelle was a native Hadriana caat. I suppose they could be sentient. But talking?" Quinn's brows drew down. "She speaks Standard? How's that happen?"

Francine shrugged. "She's lived with humans. She picked it up. Plus, she's telepathic, so that probably helps."

The line moved again, people purchasing tickets and moving into the loading area beyond the double-doors.

"A telepathic caat." Quinn picked up her bag and scooted forward a few steps. "Sure, why not? There's got to be other intelligent life out here somewhere. Why not Hadriana caats?"

"You believe me?" Francine gaped at her.

"Not really, but I'll humor you." Quinn snickered.

They reached the kiosk at the head of the line. Quinn punched the "round trip" button and swiped the number-of-tickets box to two. She flashed her comtab at the screen to register payment, and the door ahead opened. "Let's go."

Inside, a hallway curved away from them on both sides, with doors located every ten meters on the inner curve. A green arrow flashed on the floor, leading them to the right. They followed the lit pathway, joining a small group of passengers who had been in line ahead of them.

The doors opened, and they stepped inside. The car was wedge-shaped, with rows of seats facing outward. Quinn and Francine took seats near the middle and strapped in.

"Where is Sashelle now?" Quinn asked. "Can you hear her?"

Francine's lips pressed together. "I don't know where she is. She said she'd meet me on the surface. She managed to get from Kreutznaer Station to RW Prime by herself. I'm not worried."

"You look a little worried," Quinn said.

"Whatever," Francine huffed. "I don't want to lose her. Elli would be devastated."

"Yes, she would." Quinn nodded. "That's why I was upset to hear you'd brought her. Why risk it?"

"I told you, she brought me." Francine pulled her comtab out of her pocket and stared at the blank screen. "She thought you might need help. I don't know how she knew that."

"That's sweet." Quinn patted Francine's arm. "I hope she's okay."

"She'll be fine." A smile lit Francine's face. "She just crawled under my seat."

"What?!" Quinn snapped her mouth shut as heads turned her way. She smiled apologetically at the people staring at her. "Sorry," she mouthed. When they turned away, she leaned forward to check her own bag. Sure enough, the caat blinked at her from under Francine's seat. "How the hell did she—"

"Don't know." Francine swiped at her device, unconcerned. "I told you she can take care of herself."

THE DROP to Robinson's World took six hours. A shuttle or drop ship would have been faster, but Robinson's severely limited the number of ships entering the atmosphere. The elevator was more economical and less intrusive on their environment—or so the bright graphics on the large screens above the doors claimed.

"I wish they'd turn off the ads and put on a video," Francine grumbled. "We get it, you're green here."

"I have crayons in my bag, if you need a distraction," Quinn said with a sly grin.

"We're almost there, dear." A woman in front of them turned to address Quinn. She glanced at Francine and her eyes widened. "I thought you were talking to a child."

Quinn bit back a grin.

Francine glowered.

The woman gave a disapproving look and faced forward.

"We're on final approach to Robinson's World," a soothing voice announced through the cabin. "Please return to your seats and fasten your safety harnesses. The restroom and snack machines are now closed. Prepare for arrival."

The lighted vending machine went dark, and the seatbelt icon appeared on the advertising screens. The large panels on either side of the door faded to transparent, giving the occupants a view of clouds stretching to a curved horizon. As they dropped closer to the planet, the clouds dispersed, and a slice of city came into view at the bottom of the window.

"Is Robinson's one big city?" Quinn asked. "I don't see anything except buildings."

"It's heavily populated," Francine said. "I think there are agricultural areas farther out, but the elevator is tethered in the middle of Crusoe City. Luckily for us, that's where *she* is."

"Which *she* are you looking for?"

"I'm not looking for anyone. I told you I'm here to help you. Who are you looking for?"

"I feel like we should have discussed this before we left the ships," Quinn grimaced. "I'm here to deliver something to the Tro—"

Francine held up a hand. "Got it. I'd like to ask her about my sister." She glanced around, nervously, but no one paid them any attention.

Quinn nodded. "I want to talk to Melody, too, and make sure she's okay. I have the address of the studio."

Francine gave her a thumbs-up and closed her eyes. "I don't like the landing part of these things."

"You've been on one before?" Quinn focused on the windows. "I haven't."

"The last bit is a little disorienting." The younger woman leaned her head against the seat back.

As the elevator dropped, it seemed to increase speed. The city grew closer at an alarming rate until it felt like they'd crash into it. Then they braked hard, the seats pressing up against their legs and rears. Suddenly, they were within a forest of buildings, and the car stopped, bouncing a little as the last of their downward speed was absorbed.

"Welcome to Crusoe City," the soothing voice said. "Please check under your seat for your belongings. This car will return to RW Prime in twenty minutes. All passengers are required to exit for cleaning. If you are returning immediately, find the quick-return line at the left side of the lobby as you exit. Thank you for riding with us."

The doors slid open, and people around them surged to their feet, banging bags and packages into their neighbors in their haste to depart. Quinn and Francine waited for the rush to slow before standing.

"Is Sashelle—" Quinn asked.

Francine shrugged. "She's gone. I'm sure she'll find us out there."

As they exited, a pair of white-clad elevator employees waited outside the doors, cleaning implements in hand. They nodded as the women left the car. "Hope no one got sick this trip," one of them muttered as they passed.

In the lobby, beyond a clear barrier, a line of people snaked toward the entry doors. On this side, planetary security ran new arrivals through a screening process. Francine and Quinn flashed their comtab IDs and walked through the weapons and biohazard detectors. "No, I didn't bring any fruit," Quinn said when asked.

"I have Gummy Froots." Francine held up a bag of candy. "Do you want some?"

The security agent rolled his eyes and passed them through.

Outside on the sidewalk, Francine grinned. "It always throws 'em when you offer them candy. He didn't notice the knife in my shoe."

"You have a knife in your shoe?" Quinn's brows shot up.

"You don't?" Francine looked around. "Now, where's that caat?"

They turned slowly in place, forcing an eddy in the stream of pedestrians flowing along the sidewalks. Tall buildings blocked the late afternoon sun. Commuter pods zipped down wide trenches between the buildings. Low pedestrian bridges crossed the trenches at each intersection, angling at forty-five degrees to form an X high over the crossing lanes. In the middle of each block, a covered transit stop protected passengers.

"We can catch a ride there." Francine pointed to the transit stop. She slid her duffle straps onto her shoulders and strode down the sidewalk.

"What about Sashelle?" Quinn hurried after her.

"The caat will take care of herself."

CHAPTER 15

QUINN FLASHED her comtab at the kiosk and entered the location of Tiffany's studio. The kiosk screen turned green and displayed a message, "Your ride will arrive in twenty seconds." As the countdown reached zero, a pod eased to a halt in front of them. Two people climbed out, and the door shut.

"SwifKlens is being run for your protection. Please wait ten seconds before entering the pod."

The door of the pod popped open again, and Francine and Quinn stepped inside. As they settled in, the door lowered. Just before it snapped shut, Sashelle squeezed through the gap.

"There you are," Francine said. "I was almost worried."

The caat stared at them.

"She says she doesn't like the smell of the cleaner." Francine dropped into a seat.

"That's what she says?" Quinn asked. "She's been MIA for hours, and that's all she has to say?"

"The smell is pretty nasty." Francine's nostrils flared. She considered the animal for a few seconds, then nodded. "She said she has her ways, and we shouldn't worry about her."

"Sure," Quinn said. "Have you considered you might be having hallucinations?"

Francine held up both hands. "I'm only reporting what I'm hearing. Maybe it's Sashelle, maybe it's my subconscious. She's usually right."

The cat meowed loudly.

"No, you aren't *always* right," Francine muttered. "Fine, I can't name a time you were wrong, but we've only been conversant for a few days. I'm sure— Never mind." She shot a look at Quinn. "I'm not crazy. Or if I am, I'm really creative."

"I'll give you that." Quinn looked through the translucent pod at the buildings towering overhead. "I haven't been in a city this big since Romara." She shivered.

"This place is a lot looser than Romara. Less Federation death-grip."

"Does that mean there's more of your *family* influence here?"

Francine glared. "I— Look, Elvis."

Quinn nodded, acknowledging the diversion. Francine was right —public transport was not a good place to talk about the Russosken.

The pod slowed and drifted to a halt beside another transit stop. The two women and the caat stepped out. As the door snapped shut to run the SwifKlens cycle, Francine and Quinn peered up and down the street.

Sashelle sauntered across the sidewalk, slinking between the pedestrians hurrying out of nearby buildings. None of them seemed to notice the large caat weaving between their legs. Francine hurried after the animal. With a shrug, Quinn followed. The caat walked to the door and waited for the humans to catch up.

They pushed through the revolving door. Inside, their footsteps echoed through the large, empty lobby. A tall desk at the back stood empty. Sashelle strolled across the polished floor, tail swaying over her back. With a shrug at Francine, Quinn followed.

A half-full cup of something hot steamed on the desk beside a partially-eaten sandwich. "I guess the guard had something important to do," Quinn said as they passed.

"Sashelle says an alarm was triggered in the basement. How do you know that?" Francine looked at the caat. "She's not telling."

"Tiffany's studio is on the fortieth floor." Quinn waved her hand at the call sensor.

"I doubt she's still here. It's kind of late for entertainment types."

"Really?" Quinn eyed her companion in surprise. "How do you know that?"

Francine gave her a haughty look. "My family is basically D-list celebrities. I've been on these shows before."

The elevator whooshed up and stopped on forty. The doors opened, and Sashelle led them out. They walked down the hall and found the correct studio.

"Do you think anyone is here?" Quinn asked.

"Only one way to find out." Francine pushed the door open and strode inside.

The studio was dim, except for a lighted stage, which held the set of Tiffany's show. Two people sat on the couch. As Quinn and Francine entered, they looked up, squinting into the darkness between the tiers of seats.

"Quinn!" Tony said in surprise. "Francine? What are you doing here? And what's with the caat?"

"Long story," Francine muttered. "What're you doing here?"

"I told Lou I'd meet the ship here." He stood as they reached the stage and gave each of them a one-armed hug. "Didn't she tell you?"

"No," Quinn dropped her small duffle onto the coffee table and turned to Tony's companion. "Marielle. How are you?"

"Fantastic," Marielle said.

"Where's Melody?" Quinn asked.

Marielle glanced into the shadowed wings. "She's at home, I guess."

"What are you looking at?" Quinn demanded.

Marielle glanced at her. "Melody usually hangs out there when she isn't here." She pointed at the tall table off stage, then the couch. "But if she isn't either of those places, she's probably at home."

"Why are you here? I thought you were going back to the Secret Service." Tony sat at the end of the couch so Quinn could sit between him and Marielle. Francine perched on the tall chair. Sashelle prowled into the wings.

"It seems Tiffany has a bit of a hold on our Marielle," Tony said.

"Should we be discussing this here?" Francine gestured to the sign over their heads. "If Tiffany is blackmailing Marielle, this doesn't seem to be the safest location."

Tony picked up his comtab and waved it at Francine. "State-of-the-art jammer. This place should be empty until tomorrow, so it's as safe as anywhere."

"Why is Tiffany blackmailing you?" Quinn asked.

Marielle's eyes hardened. "She wants me to kill Andretti."

Quinn's jaw dropped. After a second, she found her voice. "I guess that's not too surprising. She always was the vengeful type. Are you going to do it?"

"No," Marielle answered flatly.

"No offense," Francine said, "but you killed people for a living. And he left you to die, too. Why not do it?"

"I didn't kill people for a living." Marielle spat. "The FSS *protects* people. Sure, we're trained to take out threats, but we don't go around *executing* people. I won't lie—I want to see Andretti rot in hell for what he did—but I won't lower myself to that level. I'm not a hired gun. Now, if he happened to wander in..." She left the words hanging.

"Is that why you're here?" Quinn's wave encompassed the studio. "Tiffany's hoping he'll wander in someday and you'll be here to take him out?"

"That's her daft plan," Marielle replied. "She's been trying to lure him in for weeks. I keep telling her the harder she tries the more he'll be on guard, but you know Tiffany when she gets an idea in her head."

"How did she convince you to come here?" Quinn asked. "And what's she holding over you?"

Marielle gave Quinn the stink-eye. "So you can hold it over me, too? I don't think so. She invited me. We used to be friends—before Sumpter. I was here, so I thought I'd see if I could forgive and forget. Turns out, I'm not very good at either."

Tony had been listening quietly to the discussion, but now he leaned forward. "Now we're all caught up, why are you two here?" He glanced from Quinn to Francine.

"I'm here to find out what my sister is up to," Francine said.

"Lou asked me to bring a message to Tiffany." Quinn patted her pocket. "Since I wanted to check on Melody, I agreed."

Marielle eyed Quinn. "You have a message for Tiffany? I think she's lost it. I mean, a serious mental break. She told me she wanted me to track Andretti down and kill him, and I said no. I told her I wasn't prepared to die in a Federation prison over him, because you know that's where I'd end up." She nodded at Quinn. "Sorry that happened to you, by the way."

Quinn grimaced. "Me, too."

"I'm the one who suggested she invite him to be on her show. He never could resist talking about himself." Marielle wrinkled her nose. "She must have botched the invite, because he declined. Then I told her maybe she should let it go for now, and she freaked out. The next day, she had that stooge from FIS here. You saw that episode?"

Quinn nodded.

"Ejaz Xavier," Tony said. "Federation Investigative Services."

"You remember his name?" Quinn asked in surprise.

Tony shrugged. "I try to remember the names of people setting me up."

"Yeah, Ejaz," Marielle laughed. "All looks, no brain. He spewed out the party line like a seasoned actor, though. After the show, Tiffany offered me a deal I could not refuse. So here I am."

"Why are you here so late in the day?" Francine asked. "Are you living here?"

"She set up a little apartment in the dressing rooms." Marielle pointed her thumb over her shoulder. "The staff think it's for her. I didn't have anywhere else to go."

"Don't they notice you're here when they come in to clean?" Quinn asked.

Marielle shook her head. "It's all automated."

"And why is Melody here?" Quinn asked.

"She's here because her husband, Ted, is under Andretti's thumb, just like everyone else. He sent Melody to find out what Tiffany was up to," Marielle said.

"Andretti made Melody spy for him?" Quinn said. "Melody would make the worst spy in history! She's completely transparent."

"I didn't say it was a good plan," Marielle said. "I think he's running out of stooges and their spouses."

"Ted never struck me as being one of Andretti's yes-men," Tony said. Quinn nodded in agreement.

"He isn't," Marielle said. "But he works for Andretti, and they have kids. Threats were made, and Melody came here. Tiffany was clueless, of course. She thinks Melody loves her."

Quinn snorted and rolled her eyes. "Of course she does. Is she okay? Melody, not Tiffany. Are her kids safe?"

Marielle shrugged. "She's as safe as anyone is these days. Probably safer if you don't contact her, to be honest." She raised her eyebrows at Quinn. "I'm sure Andretti is watching, and he'd love to get his hands on you."

"She's not wrong," Francine told Quinn. "So now what? You came here to check on Melody. If you believe her—" She nodded at Marielle. "—Melody is safe, for now. Until we can figure out how to get her husband and kids away from Andretti, she's safer left alone."

Marielle and Tony nodded.

Quinn ground her teeth. "I can't leave her here."

"You can and should." A blonde woman sauntered into the studio, with Sashelle trailing behind.

"Dusica?" Francine gulped. Then she glared at the caat. "You couldn't warn me?"

CHAPTER 16

FRANCINE JUMPED off the tall stool, her eyes darting around the sound stage. The caat stretched out under the table. *I tried, but you weren't listening.*

"You didn't try very hard," Francine muttered. If Dusica was here, there would be security as well. How many had she brought? "What are you doing here, Dusica?" she asked, louder. "How many do you have with you?"

"Just one," Dusica said.

Tony rose, but Francine couldn't tell if he was being polite or preparing for an attack. Probably both, knowing Tony.

A blonde man followed Dusica out of the dim backstage area. "I suggested we come."

"They love their dramatic entrances, don't they?" Marielle muttered.

"Fyo?" Francine threw herself off the dais and into his arms. She hugged him tightly, then let go. Her eyes stung, and her chest tightened. "How are you alive?" She swung around to glare at her sister. "How could you bring him here?"

"He's perfectly safe. Let's get the introductions out of the way, shall we?" She turned to the women sitting on the couch. "I'm

Dusica, Faina's sister. This is our brother Fyotor. You must be Tony. Quinn, nice to see you again. Marielle."

"Dusica," Quinn and Marielle said at the same time, their voices equally cold.

"We should leave," Dusica swung back to her sister. "I don't expect to be interrupted here—I set this up so that we could safely meet—but I don't like to tempt fate. I've been to this studio three times, which is twice too many. Let's go."

Tony stiffened. "*You* set this up?"

"We're supposed to just follow you out of here?" Quinn asked at the same time. "We don't know anything about you—except that you're Russosken. Based on our recent history, I don't think going anywhere with you is a great idea."

"I agree." Tony held a mini blaster, although it was pointed at the floor. "I want to know a little more before we go anywhere. You said you set this up. What's your plan?"

Dusica blew out an exasperated breath. "I want Faina to come home. I have a safehouse—a very comfortable estate. Fyotor has been there for ages. Tell them, Fyo."

"It's comfortable," he agreed. "It's not so fun being stuck there, but it's big enough that I don't go crazy. The people in the village have no idea who I am. And no one is trying to kill me, so that's a plus."

"Why would they try to kill you?" Quinn asked.

"Fyo was involved in a coup attempt," Francine said. "A couple years ago, our father tried to take over, but the *nachal'nik* crushed them. Fyo was only seventeen, but the *nachal'nik* took out everyone involved. I never knew—until today—that he'd escaped."

Marielle stood behind the couch now. Francine wasn't sure when she'd moved, but she looked ready for anything. "What happened to your father?"

The Zielinsky siblings glared at her.

"Okay, then. Sorry for your loss. I say we go with them."

"What about Tiffany's blackmail?" Quinn asked.

Marielle rolled her eyes. "Please. I took care of that the day I arrived. I've been waiting here for this."

"This? What do you mean?" Tony grabbed Quinn's arm and urged her away from Marielle.

"Don't you see? This was all a setup." Marielle heaved a dramatic sigh. "Tiffany invited me here because she wants me to kill Andretti. I didn't have anything better to do, so I humored her—hung around. Then Dusica arrived, and she and I made a deal. I get you all here. Ideally, Francine would come with, but if not, we could use one of you as hostages and make a trade for her." She nodded to Francine as if thanking her for being so considerate.

"We're leaving. I don't really care if the rest of you come. I want Faina." Dusica fluttered her fingers at the others. "The rest of you can do wherever."

Francine crossed her arms and glared at her older sister. "What if I don't want to come? I ran away, remember?"

"You left the Russosken," Dusica agreed. "But they're closing in on you. If I could find you, it's only a matter of time before the *nachal'nik* does. And after that fiasco on Lunesco, she won't be happy with you. If you come with me, you'll be safe."

"I don't want to hide on your estate for the rest of my life," Francine said. "If I wanted to be safe, I could have stayed on N'Avon."

"What do you suggest, then?" Dusica demanded. "Hide with the Marconis? That won't last much longer. The only other option is to overthrow the *nachal'nik* yourself. We all saw how that ended last time."

Tony and Quinn exchanged a look.

Francine glared at them. "You aren't seriously suggesting..."

Tony caught Dusica's eye. "Could we speak with your sister, alone, for a few minutes?"

"So you can plot against me?" Dusica asked.

"I think we're on the same side," Tony said. "You aren't happy with the status quo, and neither are we. I can't expose certain details to you at this point... You understand, I'm sure."

Dusica glanced at her comtab. "I'll give you ten minutes. We'll wait in Marielle's *cozy* apartment." She gave Marielle a smirk. "Then we're leaving." She nodded at Fyo, and the two of them disappeared into the shadows.

"You, too, Marielle," Quinn jerked her head at the exit.

Marielle rolled her eyes but followed Fyo.

Tony opened his mouth, but Francine held up a hand. "Sashelle?"

Very well, Sashelle said inside her head. *This one time, I will run security for you.* She followed Francine's siblings out of the room.

Tony watched the caat leave, then gave Francine a worried look. "What was that all about?"

"Don't ask," Quinn said, her lips twitching.

They're in the apartment, Sashelle said. *I'm going to look for a snack.*

Francine tried to ignore the mental picture of Sashelle catching a mouse. "We're clear."

Tony nodded in an exaggerated fashion, as if to a crazy person.

"I'm not crazy," Francine muttered.

Tony waved the comment away. "Is Dusica planning a coup? And if she did, how would that impact the planets we're already engaged with? If we're going to work with her, I want to make sure they aren't worse than what we've already got."

"I'm not sure Dusi wants to be *nachal'nik*," Francine said. "If she did? I think she'd be better than the status quo. She really does care about me and Fyo. She's fair to her employees. As far as Fyo... The family would never accept Fyo. He's much more distantly connected to the current *nachal'nik* than we are." The faces around her registered confusion. "He's our half-brother. Same mother, different father—even though he worked with our—my—father on the coup. Russosken families are confusing."

"It would be good to know who might take over," Tony said. "But not necessary. A coup would create chaos we could use to our advantage. I'd like to go with Dusica and work out a plan."

"What if she isn't going to do anything?" Quinn asked. "She seemed pretty set on getting Francine somewhere safe. That doesn't sound like someone ready to cause chaos."

"Then we get a free trip to wherever she's got her secret lair," he replied. "And maybe we can sow a little chaos of our own. If she doesn't want to work with us, we go back to plan A."

"What if she won't let us leave? I don't want to live with Fyo, Marielle, and Francine for the rest of my life." She wrinkled her nose at Francine. "No offense."

"None taken," Francine said. "I'm not ready to settle down in her utopia either. The fact that she's kept Fyo hidden from the *nachal'nik* for years makes me think we can trust her. And I'm pretty sure we can get away if we need to escape."

"We escaped Sumpter," Tony said with an easy grin. "I think we can escape Dusica. We need to talk to Marielle, though." He hurried out of the room and returned a few minutes later with Marielle in tow.

"I'm ready to get away from the crazy lady," Marielle was saying as they returned to the stage. "I *need* to get away from her. She's driving me insane."

"What about your husband?" Quinn asked. "He was Andretti's exec. Is he still on active duty? Hasn't he been curious about your new situation?"

"He's dead," Marielle said flatly.

"I'm sorry," Quinn said. "I hadn't heard."

"It's fairly recent. And don't be. I'm not." Her lips pressed together.

Francine considered pressing for more information, but decided she'd prefer to keep all her limbs. "What's your plan, then?"

"We might be able to use your help," Tony added.

"Who's 'we'?"

Tony started to answer, but Quinn cut him off. "Before we give you any more information, I want to know where your loyalty lies. You helped Dusica get us here. Who's pulling the strings, you or Dusica? And what about Melody?"

"And how did Tiffany get that first message to Quinn?" Tony added.

"Tiffany's an idiot," Marielle dropped to the couch with a tired sigh. "Not to mention crazy. I told you about her plan to kill her ex. I came because I had nowhere else to go after Reno died. The FSS didn't want me back—too old, they said. I'm only twenty-eight!"

She glowered. "After Tiffany tried to get me to off Andretti, Dusica showed up. She convinced Tiffany that Quinn could help her —being a desperate escaped traitor and all. I helped make that video, and Dusica passed it to you. I don't know how she did that." She turned to Quinn. "I don't suppose you want to kill Andretti?"

Quinn shrugged. "I'm not the killing type, but if he happened to wander in..." She grinned as she repeated Marielle's earlier suggestion.

"If he happened to wander in, you'd give him a stern talking to," Francine said with a chuckle. "You're not a killer."

"Hey, I— No, you're right." Quinn shrugged. "Revenge isn't one of my strengths. Besides, if you don't forgive your enemies, they control you."

Marielle gave Quinn a quick up-and-down and raised an eyebrow. "Sure."

"Did Melody tell you about the duress signal?" Quinn asked.

Confusion flashed over Marielle's face and disappeared. "Of course she did."

Quinn's eyes narrowed. "Right. Where is Melody?"

"I told you she's safe." Marielle said. "Look, if she was actually in danger, I'd tell you. I like that little fireball. She's fine. Bored? Maybe. Worried about her family? Of course. But as long as Andretti doesn't realize there's a connection between her and you, she's safe. If he finds out you two were BFFs, all bets are off. He'll use her in a heartbeat to get to you. He wants you dead."

Quinn snapped her mouth shut.

"So, with the exception of Melody, this whole thing was a plan to get Francine back to Dusica," Tony slid the blaster back into his pocket. "I say we go along and see what kind of lemonade we can make. Or at least, Francine and I can go. Quinn, you can go back to Lou."

"I'm not leaving you alone in the grip of the Russosken. We should get a message to Liz and— That reminds me. I was supposed to give this to Tiffany." Quinn pulled a data-card out of her pocket.

"Who gave you that?" Tony asked.

"Your gra— Lou."

"She asked you to deliver it to Tiffany?" His brows lowered. "Have you looked at it?"

"I was told in no uncertain terms that was 'not how it works.'" Quinn's mimic of Lous was spot-on. "But yeah, of course I did. It's a text message saying, 'We cannot accept your contract. Sincerely, L. Marconi.' She told me Tiffany asked her to do something and she said no. I don't know why it had to be delivered in person. Lou said she'd agreed to deliver the message by trusted courier."

"Dusica put her—Tiffany—up to it. To get you here," Marielle said. "She hoped Francine would come too."

"Sounds like Dusi," Francine agreed. "She certainly has pulled all the strings so far. She'd probably make a great *nachal'nik*."

"You mean a terrifying one," Tony said. "But you're right. Let's go."

About time, Sashelle said inside Francine's head. *The mice here taste like SwifKlens.*

CHAPTER 17

TONY LEFT an encrypted message in Liz's drop box, telling her the three of them were on a mission, leaving the system via a private ship, and they'd meet at Taniz Alpha in a few days. Quinn sent the same message to Lou, with an additional message for the kids and a video of Sashelle.

"Elli will be very impressed that Sashelle is helping us," she told Francine as they took seats in Dusica's private ground vehicle.

"You know the caat talks to her, too," Francine whispered.

"Why wouldn't she?" Quinn gave the caat sitting on Francine's lap a sour look. "But she won't talk to the person who fills her tuna bowl. Not that I believe she talks," she added when the others glanced at her.

"The caat is talking?" Dusica asked. "To whom?"

"It was a joke," Quinn said.

Dusica's eyes flicked from face to face. "That's a shame. I've heard Hadriana caats might be sentient. It would be exciting to make first contact."

"Sentient caats?" Fyo scoffed. "Sure, why not."

"We're almost at the shuttle port," Marielle called from the front of the transport pod.

"How'd you get clearance to land a shuttle on Robinson's?" Quinn asked.

Francine and Dusica both gave her disbelieving stares. "Russosken, remember?" Francine waved a hand between herself and her sister. "We kinda own the place."

"Robinson's is a *bit* more difficult than most planets." Dusica rubbed her fingers together in the ancient sign for credit. "But like anywhere, local officials respond to enticements."

"Bribes," Quinn said.

"Exactly," Fyo agreed cheerfully. "What's the point of having piles of credit if you don't use it to improve your situation?"

"Said like a true Russosken." Francine gave her sister a sour look "Well done, Dusi. To the manor born."

The massive pod slowed in front of a tall wall. A gate slid open before they came to a complete stop and they accelerated through, turning into a transit trench that paralleled the fence. After passing several large hangars, they eased to a stop in front of one plastered with a huge SwifKlens logo. Bright lights made the logo glow in the dark like a beacon.

"We're taking a SwifKlens shuttle?" Marielle asked.

"We own them," Dusica said. "Or rather, they're a subsidiary of a corporation that is owned by a shell company…You know how it is."

"We don't," Quinn said dryly. "I assume your *nachal'nik* can't trace this to you?"

Tony made eye contact and gave a light nod. A warm swirl of approval curled through Quinn's chest.

The pod door popped open. "Of course not. I'm not stupid. Let's go." Dusica stepped out, pulling her massive sunglasses over her face, even though it was dark.

Francine chuckled.

"What?" Quinn patted down her pockets looking for her own specs. If Dusica thought they were necessary in the dark in front of a hangar belonging to a company that was a subsidiary of— whatever. She pulled out the glasses and slid them on.

Francine's eyes flicked to the caat, and her lips twitched. "She doesn't like SwifKlens, remember?"

Tony slid a hat low over his eyes, and Fyo wrapped a scarf over his head and the bottom of his face.

"Very stylish, little bro." Francine donned her own shades and slid her hand through the crook of his arm.

"Thanks. There's not much to do on Fortenta, so I've become quite the fashion icon." He flipped the end of the scarf over his shoulder.

Quinn ducked to avoid the beaded fringe that flew past her face and followed them out of the pod. The caat bounded ahead of her.

"*She* might be a liability," Marielle said as she followed Tony and Quinn. "Unmistakable and huge. Anyone looking for us just has to scan the videos for the caat."

"That's harder than it sounds," Tony said. "We've tried on the ship."

Quinn frowned. "Why bother?"

He chuckled. "Gotta keep End busy or he causes trouble. I told him to keep track of where Sashelle goes. He can't find her."

"What do you mean?" Marielle gestured to the feline waiting by the closed hanger door. Seated on her haunches, her nose nearly reached the doorknob. "She's huge. How could you miss her?"

Tony shook his head. "I have no explanation. If you look at the video, she's there. But if you try to search video for her, she doesn't show up."

"Facial recognition software probably doesn't work on animal faces," Quinn said. "Too different from humans."

"It's not that," Tony replied. "I had End modify the code. He used a program he pulled from the Commonwealth archives—software that tracks endangered species. It doesn't register Sashelle. It's the weirdest thing."

"I need to see that," Quinn said. "Why didn't you have me or Francine look at it?"

"End thinks he's a computer genius," Tony said. "I don't like to crush his ego completely. Plus, it was a busy work thing. We might want to look into it when we get back, though. Maybe she has some natural distortion we can mimic."

"That would be worth a fortune," Marielle said.

"It could also be useful to those of us who are wanted by the Federation," Quinn said dryly.

They followed the rest of the group into the hangar. Enormous, automated doors were already rolling open on the flight line side of the building. The Zielinskys climbed the portable steps to the open shuttle door.

The caat stopped on the top step, nose and tail switching in agitation. Dusica and Fyo ignored her and went inside. Francine stooped down and said something. With the low whine of the shuttle's startup sequence, Quinn couldn't hear what the woman said. The caat narrowed her eyes, then rose and stalked onto the shuttle.

"She really doesn't like the smell," Francine said as Marielle, Tony, and Quinn reached the top step.

Tony took a deep breath. "I'm not particularly fond of SwifKlens, but I don't smell it here."

The airlock—both ends open to allow easy access—led to a short hallway. A small galley took up the opposite side of the shuttle, and an open hatch on the left led to the cockpit where two uniformed pilots worked their way through a checklist. To the right was the main compartment. This was furnished with wide, plush chairs, fold-down desks and tables, and a thick, gold carpet. A door at the rear read "cargo" and another held lavatory signs. Fortunately, the whole thing smelled of eucalyptus and vanilla instead of SwifKlens.

"This shuttle is for company execs," Fyo told them. "We'll dock with their long-distance cruiser in orbit for the journey to Fortenta. The shuttle could do it, but it's too primitive for that long a trip."

"Too primitive?" Quinn mouthed at Francine.

A tinge of pink washed over Francine's face.

Dusica settled into one of the chairs near the back. She pulled a folding desk down across her lap and placed her comtab on it. "Tell them we're ready, Fyo." She pulled a pink satin mask over her face and reclined the chair to horizontal.

"Yes, ma'am." Fyo made a face at Dusica then knocked on the cockpit door. Francine grinned.

Quinn settled into a chair near the middle of the craft, pulling the restraints out of their hidden compartment. Sashelle curled up in a chair across the table.

Tony sat next to Quinn. "You flown on one of these before? You found those straps pretty easily."

"Most of these high-end birds are built by the same company. Reggie and I flew with his father once, before he died. Same equipment, different-colored upholstery."

Marielle sat across the aisle, promptly leaning her seat back. Fyo and Francine took seats close to the front.

"I can't believe she thought her brother was dead all this time," Quinn watched the two younger siblings. They sat with their heads close together, whispering and giggling. "She always seems so cool and emotionless."

"Maybe that's how she copes with loss. I'm sure they were trained to present a professional image at all times. Probably from birth." Tony flicked his comtab and activated his jamming program.

"Won't that interfere with the navigation or something?"

He shook his head. "That's a myth. Besides, this particular program has a very small radius. Can't even detect it more than two meters away."

With a tiny lurch, the shuttle pulled out of the hangar and turned toward the runway.

"This is a lot nicer than our last few trips," Quinn said. "I mean, the *Peregrine* is fine, but the drone flight from Romara? No thanks. And that freighter we took to Lunesco." She gave a dramatic shudder.

"That wasn't so bad," Tony said. "Nobody was out to get us, and we had the sergeant to keep us company."

"Please don't ever buy Sergeant Sinister's again." Quinn managed a more realistic shiver. "I can't believe I used to drink that stuff. Hey. How are you going to manage jump?"

"I sincerely doubt the Russosken are dry." Tony mimed tossing back a shot. "Speaking of them, what do you think about Dusica?"

"Are you sure that thing works?" She nodded at the comtab laying on their table.

He nodded. The shuttle rolled into place at the end of the runway.

"This is the pilot," a deep voice said. "Prepare for launch in five...four...three...two...launch."

The ship surged forward, rumbling over the runway, gaining speed. Tony's comtab rattled on the table. He grabbed it and stuck it into his chest pocket. From across the table, Sashelle opened one eye a fraction of a centimeter, then closed it again, ears twitching. Acceleration pressed them back into the seats as they lifted off.

"I don't think we should trust her." Quinn leaned close to keep her volume low. "Clearly, she's used to getting what she wants—whatever she wants. I don't know why she suddenly wants Francine back."

"From what she says, she's been looking for Francine since before we met her on Hadriana. And she's managed to keep her brother safe."

"True. But I wouldn't put it past her to turn us over to the *nachal'nik* if she thinks it will give her an advantage. We aren't family."

"You'll get no argument from me," Tony agreed.

"I'm kind of surprised you wanted to go," Quinn said. "Don't you have a revolution to start?"

"I've put most of my pieces in place." He grinned. "It's not like a shuttle—you can't just press the start button. And I think Dusica might be able to give us some insider information at least."

In the state-of-the-art shuttle, the trip to the long-range ship in orbit took very little time. Once they'd docked, the pilot opened the airlock and came to the back to inform Dusica. "We've arrived, ma'am. We'll return to the surface as soon as you depart."

Dusica ignored them as she strolled past.

Tony smiled at the pilot. "Thanks for the flight."

"My pleasure, sir."

CHAPTER 18

THE SHUTTLE FIRED reverse thrusters and slowed to orbit Xury Eighteen, a small moon in the outer reaches of Xury's influence.

"Well done, Elli," Dareen said. "Now, what would we have to do to land on this rock?"

"I could plot a descent and landing using the auto-nav," the girl replied.

"What are you going to use for beacons?" Lucas asked derisively. "There aren't any landing beacons, so how are you going to set your destination?"

Ellianne's hands fisted and she glared at her brother. Dareen tried not to roll her eyes. Surely, she and End hadn't been this annoying when their mother taught them to fly? "Lucas," she said over her shoulder.

The boy subsided but didn't bother hiding his own eyeroll. She saw it reflected off the screen. Then he lifted his comtab and started tapping. She knew he was probably playing a game, but since his flying skills were well beyond Ellianne's, she couldn't blame him.

"Here's how I'd do it," Dareen leaned forward to show Ellianne how to program in the parameters. "You'd need to be careful—landing on a moon this small with no runway is dangerous. That's why we aren't going to try it. Someday, maybe, but not today. For now, plot a course past this asteroid. I want to go close enough to get good video, but well within the safety parameters. Don't engage until I check it."

"Yes, ma'am!" Ellianne did her customized salute and leaned against the straps to work on the problem. Her tongue stuck out of the corner of her mouth, and she hummed as she worked.

Dareen loosened her restraints so she could twist around to look at Lucas. "What ya playing?"

He started guiltily, then swiped his screen. "Nothing. Just looking at stupid stuff."

Dareen's eyes narrowed. "That might fool your mom, but I'm not buying it. What were you doing?"

"Nothing bad," Lucas said. "Messaging a friend."

"What?!" Dareen lunged against the straps, flinging her hand out to Lucas. "Give me that! You know we can't message people off the ship!"

He held the device out of reach. "It's a gaming friend. I didn't tell him where we are. He doesn't even know my real name."

"Give it to me. Now." When he hesitated, she doubled down. "If I have to come take it from you, you won't have a comtab until you're eighteen. Gramma will back me on this."

Lucas heaved a dramatic sigh. "Whatever. Here." He spun the device at her.

They had the artificial gravity off so the kids would feel the real thrust from the engines as they flew. The comtab sailed across the space, spinning, and she snapped a hand up to grab it.

"How long have you been in contact with this person?" She swiped the screens and icons. Settings showed it connected to a server at Kreutznaer through an interface she didn't recognize. "What program is this?"

"It's the GameServe connector," Lucas said sullenly. "Mighty-Kihn is a guy I've played against. I told you, he doesn't know anything about me."

"But you're still using the same gamer handle you had back on Romara!" Dareen cried. "T-Rexplode! End told you not to use that anymore!"

"That was on a different platform." Lucas rolled his eyes again.

"You think people aren't smart enough to know you're the same person?" Dareen demanded. "Do you think End doesn't know what he's talking about? He's been gaming since he was younger than Elli, and he's been living on the *Peregrine* his whole life. He knows how to keep us safe, and using this handle isn't safe!"

"Fine," Lucas muttered. "I'll change my handle. Can I have my game back now?"

"Not on your life," Dareen retorted. "I need to figure out how badly we're compromised. But first, Elli, let me check your work."

She looked over the nav screen, then flicked it back to the girl. "Engage, Number One."

"I'm number one!" Ellianne sang as she hit the icon. "Engaging!"

The mild thrust settled them into their seats while Dareen worked on the comtab. "I wish End were here. He's much better at this."

"Look, there's another spaceship!" Ellianne pointed at the contact screen. "Is that Lou coming to get us?"

"What?" Dareen shoved the comtab into her pocket and swiped up the screens. "No, that's not Lou." Her eyes narrowed. "I don't know who it is—their transponder is off. This is not good. Elli, I'm taking the stick." She slapped the nav screen to disengage the current flight path and angled the craft away from the newcomer.

"Are they bogeys?" Ellianne asked.

"We don't know," Dareen said. "But probably. Good guys don't usually turn off their transponders." They bought fake ones. In fact, only stupid people would turn off their transponder. It was an obvious giveaway that you were up to something.

"Elli, bring up the secure comm." Dareen sent the shuttle toward the nearest moon. "We need to let Gramma know what's going on."

"This green one with the waves, right?" The girl flicked the icon.

"You got it," Dareen replied. "Now hit the red button."

Ellianne giggled. "You're never supposed to push the red button!" She stabbed it gleefully.

"Only in emergencies," Lucas grumbled from the back seat. "Maybe Elli and I should switch places. I can help better than she can."

"No, you can't!" Ellianne cried.

"Quiet!" Dareen roared. "No one is moving out of their seat until we're safely hidden. And make sure your straps are tight. Great, that all went on the message. Oh well. This is Dareen. We're being followed by at least one ship with its transponder turned off. Taking evasive action now. In addition, there's been a comms breach with possibly-identifying information exposed." She shook her head. "Lucas used the same gamer handle on a new site. What was it called?"

"GameServe," Lucas mumbled.

"GameServe," Dareen repeated. "He's been in contact with a player using the handle..." She glanced over her shoulder.

"MightyKihn," Lucas said, spelling the name. "But he's fine. He's just another kid, playing games."

"You don't know that," Dareen snapped. "I'll update as soon as possible. Dar out. Hit the stop button, Elli." She slid the artificial gravity up to an eighth.

"Hey, you're supposed to announce—"

"Lucas, shut up." Dareen swung the ship around an asteroid and changed direction as soon as the rock blocked the other craft. "Elli, hit send."

"Message sent," Ellianne said.

An alert bleeped. "Damn it," Dareen said.

"What?" Ellianne asked.

"They're definitely following us. And that asteroid wasn't big enough to hide us for long. I'm heading back to Eighteen. It's big enough to give us better cover." If they could get behind it before the other ship caught up. If whoever was following them didn't have a faster ship.

"See where Eighteen is on the screen?" Dareen pointed. Didn't pay to waste a teachable moment, her mom always said. "We aren't headed directly toward the moon—we're aiming for a tangent off the far side. Just outside of orbit. That's the shortest distance."

"Ooh, trigonometry," Ellianne said. "I love that."

"You're crazy," Lucas muttered.

Dareen ignored him. "Exactly, trig. Once we're 'behind' the moon, relative to the other ship, we'll angle this way. They'll probably be expecting that, because that vector keeps us hidden for the longest time, based on their current location and speed. But there's nothing we can do about that. They can do math, too. And we'll punch the engines up to full throttle as soon as we're hidden. No need to show them our capabilities before we have to. We have enough lead to make this work."

They flew in silence while Dareen went through options, and Ellianne ran calculations on her tablet. The little girl held it out. "I think if we take this vector, we can stay hidden longer."

"Good work," Dareen replied. The change would only buy them a second or two, but she didn't want to discourage the girl.

As they neared Eighteen, another craft swooped out from behind the moon.

"*Futz.*" Dareen yanked the stick over, changing their direction. The turn pressed them down in the seats, easily overcoming the weak artificial gravity. "Hold on!"

FRANCINE PEERED out the porthole as they approached a huge intersystem passenger ship. The shuttle matched orbits and locked on to the *Savoy One*. Francine trailed her siblings out of the airlock, followed by Sashelle, Tony, Marielle, and Quinn. In the lobby, a huge blue and green logo proclaimed the ship belonged to Savoy-Interstellar, Incorporated.

They gathered around Dusica. "Where is the purser?" Her foot tapped impatiently. "It's not like they didn't know we were coming."

"Who's they?" Tony asked.

"This ship belongs to a friend," Dusica said. "They're making a slight detour to drop us at our destination."

"You're friends with an interstellar conglomerate?" Marielle leaned against a bulkhead.

Dusica's lips pressed together. "Obviously not. My friend is on Savoy's board. And one of his shell companies owns a majority of the stock in Savoy's parent company."

Marielle's eyes sparkled. She clearly enjoyed tweaking Dusica.

This ship smells better, Sashelle told Francine. *I detect meat. And fish.*

"I only smell lemongrass." Francine nodded at a diffuser running in the corner.

My senses are superior. The caat leapt onto a chair and stretched out across the back.

The internal door slid open, and a woman in a white uniform with blue and green trim hurried in. "I'm so sorry to have kept you waiting, madam. I am Elena Cantrel, the purser of *Savoy One*. Please come with me. I have staterooms for all of you." She bowed to Dusica, then turned and strode out.

The ship looked like a cruise liner, all white walls and tasteful art. Francine had ridden on many vessels like this in her life. They all looked the same. Posh staterooms. Elegant meeting spaces with full communications suites. They passed through a large dining room with linen-covered tables and a lounge with deep leather chairs. At the rear of this compartment, a door slid open revealing a long hallway.

"The rooms with green access screens are available. Choose one and register your comtab or handprint to access it later." Elena mimed the actions. "Meals are served when you wish, although we close the kitchen from one to six a.m. The meeting rooms and gym are on the next level down. The captain will join you for dinner tonight at seven. Is there anything else I can do for you?"

"When do we arrive at Fortenta?" Fyo asked.

"We'll reach the jump point in thirty-four hours." Elena looked expectantly at each of them. When no one asked further questions, she bowed and gestured to the hallway. "Please, enjoy your stay."

As they filed through the door, Francine stopped by Elena. "Do you have tuna? Or something else my caat might enjoy? She's hungry."

To her credit, the woman didn't even blink. "I'm sure we have fish in the kitchen. Shall I have a bowl delivered to your stateroom?"

"Yes, thanks."

Sashelle ignored the woman as she preceded Francine into the hallway. *I approve of this ship.*

"I'm sure you do." Francine followed the caat to the nearest available room. After sending the access code to her comtab, she went inside. Typical corporate transport room with a large bed, desk, communications gear, extra chairs, small couch, large wall screen, and spacious head.

Sashelle jumped onto a deep, barrel-shaped chair. *This will be mine.* She curled up in the seat. *Additional blankets, if you please.*

"Of course, ma'am." With a grin, she pulled a throw-blanket off the foot of the bed and tossed it over Sashelle and the chair.

Very funny, human. The caat did not sound amused.

Quinn arrived in the open doorway. "Nice boat your sister borrowed. I can see why you wouldn't want to live this way."

"It's nice for a while." Francine waved her inside. "This is definitely better than the bunk I have on the *Swan*. But there are too many strings attached."

"Gilded cage?"

"Exactly." Francine dumped her bag onto the bench at the foot of the bed. "Did you get a cabin?"

"Yeah, I'm one door that way." Quinn pointed to her left. "Didn't have much to unpack, though. I hope we don't have to dress for dinner."

"I'm not sure there's anyone on board except us," Francine said. "In fact, I very much doubt Dusica would risk the trip if there were. You can wear whatever you want. I'm going to work out. You want to join me?"

"No. But I'll do it anyway."

CHAPTER 19

IGNORING THE INCOMING COMMUNICATIONS ALERT, Dareen pressed the engines as far into the red as she dared. Her parents were docked at Xury Station, but she didn't know if she could make it that far. She set in a direct course and engaged the autopilot. The second ship stayed on their tail, drawing closer as they ran.

"Maybe they just want to talk to us." Ellianne pointed at the blinking indicator. "Do you want me to answer?"

"Play the incoming message," Dareen said, "but don't respond."

"Aye-aye!" Elli swiped the screen and tapped the icon.

"Attention, shuttle," a gravelly voice said. "This is the *Intrepid*. We are conducting operations in the name of the Federation. Cease acceleration immediately and prepare to be boarded."

"Federation operations?" Lucas's voice cracked.

Dareen sneered. "That's not a Federation ship. They don't turn off their transponders. It's probably Russosken or some other hired thug."

"Hired thugs?" Lucas repeated. "That means pirate, right?"

"Are we going to let them board?" Ellianne asked.

"Not technically pirates," Dareen said. "And no, we aren't going to let them board. Give me the comm board. You watch the navigation. Let me know if anything changes."

Ellianne nodded solemnly.

"Attention, *Intrepid*," Dareen said. "This is shuttle hotel-lima-seven-eight-five-golf. We will not submit to boarding by an unidentified ship."

"Listen, hotel-lima," the deep voice responded immediately. "I just identified us. We're the *Intrepid*."

"Your transponder is off," Dareen said. "To me, that says pirate."

"We aren't pirates," the Intrepid said.

"If you aren't pirates, then give us video," Dareen said. "Hiding behind a graphic and voice modulator says 'pirate' as loudly as no transponder."

The screen went blank, then a man appeared, an eyepatch covering one eye.

"Pirate!" Ellianne screamed.

"What?" The man jumped, then tapped his eyepatch. "You mean this? I can't believe you discriminate against the mono-ocular." He grinned as if daring them to respond.

"Last I heard, the Federation provided their employees with prosthetics." Dareen said coldly. "When do you get yours?"

"Ya got me. We aren't Federation agents, and this isn't the *Intrepid*." The man leaned toward the screen; his eyes focused below the camera. "There, our transponder is back on."

Dareen swiped her own screen and pulled up the contact screen. The unknown ship now showed a registration out of Hadriana.

Blood pounded in Dareen's ears. A ship out of Hadriana, demanding to board them. Lucas communicating with an unknown "friend." This did not look good at all. "What do you want, pirate?"

"I told you, we're not pirates. My name is Dean, and my friend Reggie and I were cruising—"

"Reggie?!" All three occupants of the shuttle demanded at once.

"Daddy?" Ellianne asked. "Is my daddy there?"

"Are you Ellianne?" Dean asked. "Can you turn on your video?"

"No!" Dareen hollered.

At the same instant, Ellianne said, "Sure!" and she poked the button.

Dareen slapped the control. "No." She muted the communications channel. "You know we can't let anyone know where we are!"

"But it's Daddy!" the girl said. "I missed him so much, and now here he is! Can I visit him on his ship?"

Dareen stared at the child. "Elli, if you go over there, they'll never let you come back. Your daddy doesn't want you to live with your mommy and the rest of us."

"He wouldn't do that!" Ellianne said. "I'll go visit, and then I'll come back."

"He won't let you come back," Lucas chimed in. "Remember? He'll take us to Hadriana, and we'll have to live with Grandmother LaRaine. Again."

"Ugh," Ellianne said. Before Dareen could stop her, she slapped the comm controls again. "I want to visit Daddy, but then go back and live with Mommy. Can I do that?"

Dean smiled. Dareen didn't think it was a nice smile. "Of course you can, sweetie. Let's dock these ships and you can come visit." The screen went blank.

"I don't think Dad's over there," Lucas whispered. "And even if he is, he won't let you come back."

Ellianne unfastened her safety restraints and pushed herself out of the chair. With the gravity dialed down, she flew upward. Dareen grabbed her ankle to pull her back into her seat.

"We aren't docking with them," Dareen said. "They've given us zero reason to believe your father is aboard, and even if he was, I couldn't let you go without your mom's approval."

Ellianne's face fell. "Oh. Mommy is mad at Daddy, so I don't think she'd let me go."

"Duh, yeah, she's mad at him," Lucas said. "He's a—"

Dareen hurriedly cut him off. "Doesn't matter. He's not on that ship. Which means 'Dean' is a pirate. Or at least lying to us." She swiped the comm controls. "If Reggie LaRaine is on that ship, I want to talk to him."

"Sorry, girlie, he doesn't want to talk to you," Dean said. "He wants his kids."

"Fine, then get him in front of a camera, and start him talking."

"He's, uh, he's asleep."

"Dude. Did you even think about this before you called? Obviously, he isn't there. And we aren't waiting." She cut the comms and opened the weapons panel. "Spinning up the em-cannon."

"Don't shoot Daddy's ship!" Ellianne cried.

"I'm not going to shoot his ship," Dareen said, trying to calm the girl. "Okay, I am, but I'm not going to hurt anyone. I'm just going to mess up their sensors and stuff. Life support will be fine." At least she thought it would. The em-cannon wasn't strong enough to take down a ship that large, and anyone with a brain in their head would shield their life-support system from this type of attack. Em-cannons weren't exactly new technology. On the other hand, Dean didn't impress her as a forward-thinking guy. "Keep an eye on that other ship, okay, Elli? The one behind us."

She eased off the engines, cutting their acceleration to zero. The other ship pulled up beside them. Dareen hit the maneuvering thrusters and spun the ship, pointing the bow directly at the Intrepid's side. Then she fired the em-cannon. The little puck flew across space and snapped onto the hull.

Dareen hit the activation button as she spun the ship and slammed the thrusters to full. The shuttle zipped away. She changed course by forty degrees. If her plan had worked, the other ship shouldn't be able to maneuver. "Watch the screen!" She shoved the contact screen up so Lucas could see it. "Tell me if they turn."

She pushed the shuttle to full throttle, heading toward Xury Station. "Status!"

"Still headed the other way," Lucas replied. "They haven't turned at all."

Dareen grinned. "What about the other one?"

"It's still behind Eighteen," Ellianne said. "Are you sure my daddy wasn't on that ship?"

"Yes, I am." He might be on the other one, but she wasn't going to mention that. "We need to get to safety. Flying lessons are over for today." She set in the course, turned off her own transponder, and shut down the thrusters. On their current trajectory, they should reach Xury in a couple of hours. Long before the other ships could get a fix on their dark shuttle.

CHAPTER 20

TONY TOOK a seat at the white-draped table in the executive dining room. He ordered a drink from the attentive waiter and sat back in his seat. The others hadn't arrived for dinner yet, but he had a date.

"Mr. Marconi." Dusica sailed into the room like a queen. "Thank you for meeting with me."

"My pleasure." He rose to pull out her chair. "But you called me Tony before."

"We weren't talking business before." Dusica sat. The waiter scurried over to take her drink order. "White wine, Sinclair. Chateau Frinsell. Turn of the century."

"Very good, madam." He hurried away.

"Sounds fancy," Tony said.

Dusica eyed him. "Don't use that hick act on me. I know you're a highly-trained Commonwealth agent. Don't you all drink martinis, jiggered, not blended?"

"I used to, before I retired." Tony raised his glass of beer. "In reality, I'm a simple man. What business did you want to discuss, Ms. Zielinsky?"

She held up a hand, pausing the conversation as the waiter arrived with her wine. The two of them went through the whole ritual: sniffing the cork, admiring the color, tasting the vintage. In the meantime, Tony drank half his beer.

"Thank you," Dusica finally told Sinclair. "Leave the bottle." When he returned to the kitchen, she raised her glass to Tony. "To a mutually profitable endeavor."

"How about a mutually successful endeavor? Profitable sounds so fiscal, and my current mission is more than just credits."

"I'll drink to that." Dusica sipped. "My current mission is the safety of my family. What's yours?"

"Cutting straight to the core, are we?" Tony leaned forward, eyes locked on hers. "Excellent. My mission is freedom in the Federation. I'm working with a number of planets who would like to even the playing field, business-wise. Currently, the Federation—and the Russosken—have a chokehold on those planets. I would like to loosen the noose. Greater financial freedom includes the potential for much higher returns. Surely that's a good thing? For the Federation and for the Russosken."

"You clearly haven't spoken with the *nachal'nik*." Dusica set her wine down. "She believes control is more important than freedom."

"What do *you* believe?"

"It doesn't matter what I believe. I told you, my mission is to keep my family safe."

"How far are you willing to go to do that?" Tony asked. "So far, no one knows Fyo survived the extermination, but they know Francine is alive and free."

"Faina," Dusica snapped. "Her name is Faina."

Tony held up his hands. "She introduced herself as Francine. And that's how she's known out in the 'verse. Too many people know she's out there. It's only a matter of time before someone realizes who she is."

"That's why I'm taking her to Fortenta," Dusica said. "We can stage a fake death for Francine, if we need to."

"I'm not sure that's what she wants."

"I don't care what she wants." Dusica's hand clenched around the stem of her glass. "She's my little sister, and it's my duty to keep her safe, not happy."

"What if we can do both? If we work together, we can—" He paused for a moment, searching for the right word. "We can loosen the *nachal'nik's* grip on both businesses and your family."

"You've been reading too many fairy tales, Mr. Marconi." She downed the rest of her wine and set the glass down with a loud clink. Sinclair appeared as if by magic to refill it.

Tony watched the man return to the kitchen. "Can he hear what we're saying?"

Dusica waved that away. "He's watching from the kitchen cams. They are muted. And pixelated to prevent lipreading. Too many high-powered deals are made in this room for anything else. Furthermore, he's been vetted and is loyal to the company. Which means he'll keep any secrets. But I know you have a jammer. I assume it's active?"

Tony smiled. "Of course. This ain't my first interstellar rodeo."

"Can you give me a detailed plan, Mr. Marconi?" Dusica asked. "Exactly how you would accomplish this 'loosening?' Then we can talk about whether I think it's possible."

"I can't lay all my cards on the table. That would make me too vulnerable. Not to mention my allies. The *nachal'nik* would love to get her hands on such a plan."

"I'm already vulnerable," Dusica said through gritted teeth. "My whole family—everything I care about—is here, on this ship. You're coming with us to my private safehouse. That's as vulnerable as it gets. If you won't trust me after all this, then I can't trust you. I'm sure you know what the Russosken do with people they can't trust." She stood and emptied her glass again. "I suggest you think about that. If your story hasn't changed by breakfast, we have nothing more to say to each other."

"That went well," Tony muttered to himself as she stormed out.

Francine slipped in through the other door. "What went well?"

"My discussion with your sister." He gave her a rundown. "We might need to sneak away in the night."

"Good luck with that," Francine said. "You don't have a ship nearby, do you?"

"I could contact End," Tony mused. "But I doubt Dusica's captain would allow him to dock."

Francine took Dusica's deserted seat and poured some wine into one of the remaining glasses. Before she finished, the waiter had materialized with a new one. "That's a red wine glass, madam." His fingers twitched, as if he itched to yank it out of her hand.

"I'm quite aware what kind of glass it is," Francine snapped. "I prefer this shape. Is that a problem?"

"No, madam." He backed away. "Not at all."

Tony widened his eyes at Francine. "Remind me not to get on your bad side."

"Just channeling my inner *nachal'nik*."

"Did you learn that in Russosken school?"

"Of course." She sipped the wine and nodded. "Dusi always could pick wine. Look, I know you're hesitant—" She smiled at the mild word. "—to trust her, but Dusi has kept Fyo safe from the *nachal'nik* all these years. She might not want to help you, but she's not going to get in your way as long as Fyo and I are safe."

"Is that what you want? To be safe? Last time we had this discussion, I didn't think that was the case. She's going to pack you in bubble-wrap and lock you away."

"No, I don't want that." Francine's hand tightened on the stem of the glass, much as Dusica's had earlier.

Tony reached across the table and took it from her. "Don't want to upset the waiter by breaking that." He set it down. "If we can loosen the *nachal'nik's* grip, you wouldn't have to live that way."

"That waiter would probably be thrilled if I broke it because then he could force me to use the right glass." She laughed sourly. "You aren't fooling me. 'Loosening the *nachal'nik's* grip' means eliminating her. She's not going to give up power, and that's exactly what you're proposing."

"Do you have a problem with eliminating her?" Tony asked. "After she 'eliminated' your father?"

Francine shook her head in one short, sharp movement. "No. I don't want to do it, but I have no problem with it being done. My father is not the only one she has eliminated. The problem is anyone who might take her place is going to have the same political philosophy. 'Squeeze 'em dry and shoot the dissenters' is practically the family motto."

"Then we'll have to make sure whoever takes over doesn't feel that way." His gaze bored into her.

She made a comical face. "Surely you don't mean me. They would never accept me."

The door opened, breaking the tension. Quinn walked in. "Sorry, am I interrupting something?"

Tony shook his head. Now that the seed was planted, it was time to change the subject. "Not at all. Come join us." He pointed to the third chair.

The waiter hurried out, the glass still clutched in his hand. "Would you care for a glass of wine, madam?"

"Yes, please," Quinn said. "Whatever you have is fine."

A pained look crossed his face.

Francine snorted daintily. "You know how to make a sommelier extremely unhappy, Quinn."

"What?" Quinn retorted. "It's not like I asked for a box of the pink stuff. I do like the pink, though."

The waiter choked back a sobbing sound, poured the wine, and left.

Tony turned to Francine again. "Tell me about the caat."

"The caat talks," Quinn said with a laugh. "Or so she claims."

Francine glared daggers at Quinn. "She does talk."

"I haven't heard anything," Tony said.

"She only talks to me." Francine lowered her voice. "Inside my head."

"Why does she speak only to you?"

Quinn jerked in surprise. "You believe her?"

He shrugged. "Have you done any research on Hadriana caats? I've tried. There isn't much information out there."

"That's not what Dareen said," Quinn muttered. "She wrote a whole paper on them."

"When she was seven," Tony said. "Not very stringent research required at that age."

"I'll give you that," Quinn said. "She implied it was more recent. Okay, I'll go with it. Sassy's certainly done some things that the average house cat can't."

Something hissed. Their heads snapped around to stare at the caat who sat on a chair at the next table.

"How long have you been sitting there?" Francine asked.

The caat curled her tail tightly around her legs and looked away.

"What did she say?" Tony watched the caat.

"She didn't. She frequently doesn't reply." Francine shrugged.

"Why does she only speak to you?" Quinn repeated Tony's question.

"She told me I am the most caat-like of the humans." Francine flushed. "Beautiful and aloof."

"From her point of view, I'm sure that's a compliment," Tony said.

"I dunno." Quinn glared at the caat. "*You* say thanks when someone feeds you."

Tony chuckled. "I can see Francine as a caat. What does she want?"

"What?" Francine asked blankly.

"What does Sashelle want?" he repeated. "Why, after nearly a century of sharing the same planet with humans, has she revealed her species' sentience? What's their end goal?"

"I—I hadn't thought to ask." Francine turned to look at Sashelle.

The caat stretched out across two chairs, eyes half-closed. "She insisted we come to Robinson's to help Quinn."

"Me?" Quinn choked on her wine. "Really? Why would she want to help me?"

After a pause, Francine answered. "Ellianne. She wants to keep you safe for the kitten. That's what she calls Elli."

"What does she call me?" Quinn leaned forward to look at the caat.

Francine bit her lip. "Uh. The Purveyor of Tuna."

Tony burst out laughing.

"I knew it!" Quinn pointed an accusing finger. "She expects me to wait on her but offers no appreciation. Not nice, Sassy."

"She hates that name. If I call her that, she ignores me. More than usual." Francine shifted her chair, so it faced the other table. "Oh, Mighty Eliminator of Vermin, Great Huntress—what?" She paused. "Fine. Oh, *Mighty* Huntress and Eliminator of Vermin, pray tell us, why are you here?"

A deep, feminine voice answered, *I believe the traditional answer is forty-two.*

CHAPTER 21

QUINN AND TONY stared at Sashelle, eyes wide.

Francine choked down a laugh at their expressions. "I think that was a joke."

They nodded, still speechless.

"Very funny, Sashelle," Francine said. "Seriously, what do you want? Why are you helping us?"

The caat jumped off the chair and stalked around the tables, tail swishing back and forth. After a tour of the room, during which the humans remained silent, she returned. She leapt onto the empty chair at their table and sat tall, like a statue, her tail wrapped around her feet. *I want to get rid of the dirt people.*

"Dirt people?" Quinn whispered.

Why did that sound familiar? "Oh, yeah, that's what she called your in-laws, Quinn." Francine laughed. "The potato farmers."

Tony finally found his voice. "Seems appropriate." He gulped down the rest of his beer and raised the glass toward the kitchen door.

After Sinclair brought another beer and retired, they all turned to face the caat again. "How does coming with us help you eliminate the dirt people?" Tony asked.

The caat yawned, showing off her sharp white teeth. *It doesn't,* she said. *Not directly. But I have time. I have grown fond of the kitten and have prioritized the Purveyor of Tuna's life on her behalf. Perhaps, out of gratitude, you will assist me in my mission.* Her eyes closed to slits.

"You have time?" Tony repeated. "What does that mean? How much time?"

My species lives many years. I have time. Sashelle stretched then curled into a tight ball, barely overhanging the generously sized seat. She closed her eyes.

"When you say you want to get rid of the dirt people, are you talking about everyone on Hadriana or only the potato farmers?" Quinn asked.

The caat said nothing.

"I think that's all you're getting." Francine shrugged. "I'm not sure how we're going to help her get rid of the dirt people."

"Removing the LaRaines from Hadriana would be like—" Quinn scrunched up her face. "Harder than getting the Russosken out of the Federation. Gretmar thinks the family has a divine right to that land."

Tony rubbed the back of his neck. "We'll try to help you, Sashelle. We owe you. But we need to focus on the Russosken and the Federation in general. Once that's done, we can look at Hadriana."

Sashelle opened her eyes a slit and nodded regally.

"Our to-do list is getting long," Quinn said. "Maybe we'll be ready to start after dinner."

AS THE SHUTTLE approached Xury Research Station, Dareen contacted station comm. "This is shuttle hotel-lima-seven-eight-five-golf, the *Magic Unicorn*, requesting permission to lurk in your shadow."

"This is Xury. You're who? Requesting what?" a voice replied.

"The *Magic Unicorn*," Dareen repeated.

"Aren't all unicorns magic?" Lucas scoffed.

"Hush, I'm on the comms. We are being tracked by a pair of unidentified ships, and they tried to board us. I want to hide."

"Shuttle hotel-lima-seven-eight-five-golf, I need to check with station command," the voice said. "I don't have a standard protocol for requests to lurk."

"You don't?" Dareen asked. "You're a Federation station. Hasn't anyone in the history of the Federation asked for protection from pirates?"

"I suppose, but it's not in the manual, *Unicorn*," Xury replied, the tone huffy. "Hold one."

"What if they won't help us?" Lucas asked.

"They have to," Dareen said. She hoped.

"In the vids, good guys always help people attacked by pirates," Ellianne said. "But I don't think they were pirates. That man is a friend of Daddy's."

"He *says* he's a friend of Dad's," Lucas retorted.

"Enough," Dareen said. "We've had this argument forty-seven times in the last two hours. It doesn't matter who he was. Their transponder was turned off, and they didn't ask permission to dock. As far as I'm concerned, that means 'pirate.' And I'm still in charge here." She glared at Lucas, who now sat in the co-pilot's chair, then turned to cast the evil eye on Ellianne in the jump seat. "If the station won't help us, Mom and Dad are supposed to be here. Somewhere."

"*Magic Unicorn*." Xury Station came back online. "The commander would like to speak with you. Please dock at berth three."

"Wait— You mean talk in person?" Dareen asked. "Can't we just chat on screen?"

"He would prefer to speak in person," Xury replied. "Apparently, we've had reports of unregistered ships in the recent past. We're collecting data." His voice shifted to a mutter. "Would have been nice to know."

Something about his tone gave Dareen the heebie-jeebies. "Um, I don't have authorization to pay docking fees." She muted the comms.

"Lucas, use my comtab—see if you can get Mom or Dad. I don't see the *Swan* here."

Xury Station was small, and two other ships were locked onto the docking arm. If the *Swan* was there, it should be with the others. Dareen flipped through pages on her device and pulled up the schedule Liz had sent. According to this, they should be here now.

"Docking fees are waived if you cooperate with our data collection," Xury replied.

"Uh, I didn't want to tell you this..." Dareen had never heard of a station waiving docking fees. Ever. "I'm not very good at docking. My captain doesn't let me visit stations I've never been to before. She doesn't want me damaging anything." She made a face at Lucas as she told the whopper.

The boy gave her a thumbs-up. Then he pointed at the comtab and shook his head. No response.

"Look, I'll send a report and head back to my ship," Dareen said.

"We can bring you in, *Unicorn*," Xury Station said. "Once you're within two hundred meters, we'll send out the drone tugs."

"No, that's okay." Why were they so anxious to get her ship locked down? "I'll, um, figure things out. I'll shoot a report when I get a chance. Bye!" She snapped her hand down on the icon, deactivating the comms. "I guess it's time to run again. Keep trying Mom and Dad."

Lucas nodded, his face pale. "When will we meet Lou?"

Dareen glanced over her shoulder at Ellianne. The little girl looked unconcerned. "Not soon enough. We need to find the *Swan*. They were supposed to be here. I can't— Where could they be?"

"Maybe they met the pirates, too," Ellianne said.

"When would they have done that?" Lucas demanded. "We just left the pirates. They didn't have time to track down Liz and Maerk, too."

"Could you two stop?" Dareen yelled. Their mouths snapped shut.

Dareen plotted a course to their rendezvous point. "We'll take the long way to meet Gramma. If we detour this direction, maybe the pirates won't find us." She pointed out the course.

"We only took out one of them." Lucas indicated the dot that said Xury Eighteen. "The one we fried should still be here. But that other guy followed us. If we can find him, then we can set our course to avoid him."

"Good idea," Dareen said. "Scan for the transponder, as well as their engine signature. If they turn their transponder on and off, it's likely they have multiple IDs. But engine signatures don't lie. I'm going to try Mom and Dad again."

After what felt like forever, they received a return message from Liz, routed through their drop box system. "That explains why it took so long." Dareen flicked the file onscreen and hit play.

"We've had a comms malfunction," Liz said, her voice clipped.

"Mom is mad," Dareen said.

"Your father assures me he can get it running again shortly, but it means we couldn't dock at Xury as scheduled." Liz glared off screen, then turned back. "We're in orbit near the station, but since we can't talk to anyone, we went dark. Probably should have followed standard shipping protocol, but family training dies hard." Liz's lips pressed together. "By the time you get this, you'll probably be out of range, but we've turned the transponder back on. You can dock with us. If you're already too far away and can't get back to Lou, try Tony. He said they're headed out of the system. He didn't say who they're flying with, but he has connections. Love you. Be careful. Mom out."

CHAPTER 22

QUINN WOKE in her executive stateroom aboard the *Savoy One*. The huge bed with zillion-thread-count sheets filled only a small part of the massive compartment. Between the bed and the desk, there was enough room to hold a party, and the bathroom—or head, as they insisted on calling it—was a lesson in luxury.

The room was cool, but the blankets were thick. She listened, blinking in the darkness, wondering what had awakened her. Nothing. Must have been her brain spinning out options and scenarios of how their current situation could resolve. Or get worse. Those were always fun.

There it was again. Singing.

Climbing out of bed, she wrapped a blanket over her sweatpants and tank top. She laid her ear against the door, but the singing was indistinct. Only their party was aboard, so unless a random employee had decided to risk their job by bothering the passengers, the singer had to be one of her friends. She unlatched the lock, then pulled the door open a few centimeters and blinked to clear her sight.

Fyo and Francine sat on the floor, singing. And they were drunk. Very drunk, if she was any kind of judge. She hitched up the blanked so she wouldn't trip and padded over.

After a few moments and another verse, Fyo looked up. "Hiya, Quinn-pin!"

Francine's gaze bounced up to the ceiling, then her chin slowly dropped until her eyes fell on Quinn. "There she is!"

"Why are you out here in the hall?" Quinn asked. "People are trying to sleep."

"Not a hall," Fyo said. "Def-def-an def-nit-ly a passageway. We're in space."

"Didjya see the stars?" Francine waved an expensive-looking wine bottle. "All around."

"Yes, I saw the stars. Why are you in the passageway?" Quinn pointed at the hatch leading to the dining room. "There's a bar a few meters that way. And another one in your suite, if it's anything like mine."

"Y'get great acoo-stix in the hall," Fyo said. "Perfic for singing!" He launched into another song.

Tony's head popped out of the next doorway. "What the hell?"

"Apparently, it's good for singing," Quinn said.

"It might be good for singing, but singing isn't good for sleeping," Tony strode over to the pair and reached down. "Could you move somewhere less right outside my door?"

Fyo yanked Tony's hand.

The older man had anticipated the move, though, and stayed on his feet. "Cute, but I've dealt with drunks before." He leaned back and pulled.

Fyo flew to his feet and the two of them crashed into the bulkhead across the passage.

Marielle opened her door. She wore lacy panties and a tight camisole. The ruffles, pink lingerie did nothing to soften the appearance of the stunner in her hand. "Party's over. Now."

Fyo stared so hard his eyes went crossed. Marielle's nostrils flared and a low growl issued from her. Fyo jumped back, hands in the air. "Ah'm goin'!" Then he staggered into the wall.

"Quinn, open Fyo's door, will you?" Tony grabbed drunk man

around the waist and pulled the other man's arm over his shoulders. "Then we'll come back and get Francine."

"I've got her." Marielle's stunner had disappeared. She crossed the hall and pulled Francine to her feet.

"Pretty pink PJs," Francine said popping each word. "Pretty pink PJs!"

"Let's get you into bed." Marielle slid Francine's hand away from the lacy fabric. The two stumbled to the next door, and Marielle pushed Francine's hand against the access panel. As the door slid shut, behind the two women, Sashelle streaked out.

That was unpleasant, she said inside Quinn's head. *I will be in the lounge.* She turned and sauntered away.

"How's she going to get the door open?" Quinn lifted Fyo's hand and pressed it against the access panel. Or tried to. Each time it got close, he yanked it away with a high-pitched giggle.

The door at the end of the passageway slid open, and Sashelle wandered through.

"Like that." Tony shrugged and grinned.

"Fyotor Zielinsky, stop that at once!" Quinn commanded.

"Yes, ma'am." Fyo meekly pressed his hand against the panel, and it flashed green.

"You forgot his middle name," Tony whispered as the door slid open.

"If I knew it, I'da used it." Quinn grabbed Fyo's other arm and slung it over her shoulders.

They stumbled across the room and dropped the younger man onto the bed. He flopped back, staring at the ceiling. "The room is spinning."

"Pull off his shoes," Quinn said. "I'll get him under the covers."

"She's gonna get me under the covers," Fyo said to Tony. "She's kinda old, but still hot, so's 'kay."

Tony glared. "She's not old, and her hotness is none of your business, little boy."

"He's drunk, Tony." Quinn laughed as she tucked the blankets under him then rolled him onto the open side of the bed. "Besides, I'm kinda flattered. He's, what, twenty-two? I'll take it."

Fyo snored. She reached across him to pull the blankets, and Tony's hand closed on her wrist. She looked up. Tony's eyes locked onto hers.

Everything stopped. She couldn't breathe. The only reality was Tony. His hand on her wrist, his eyes on hers.

And that annoying beep. What the heck?

Tony growled and let go of her hand. He pulled out his comtab. "What, Dareen?"

"Dareen?" Quinn whispered.

Tony held up a finger. "We're scheduled to jump in three hours. Can you get here by then, or do I need to— Okay. I'll talk to the captain. We'll be ready." He put the device in his pocket and pivoted for the door. "Come on. Dareen and the kids are inbound. They need to dock before we jump." He ran.

Quinn flipped the blanket over Fyo and raced after him.

"SHOULDN'T YOU BE DRINKING?" Quinn asked as they paced in front of the airlock hatch. "We're scheduled to jump in an hour."

Tony grunted. "They're almost here." He held his comtab so she could see the tiny screen. A blue dot designated *Savoy One's* position in the center of the screen. A couple of tiny red and green arrows moved around them, with one heading directly toward the blue. "About ten minutes. I can drink once we know they're safe."

"I can't believe Reggie was tracking them!" Quinn said. "How did he— Dusica must have a way to scan the shuttle and their comm equipment. She wouldn't allow—"

"Wouldn't allow what?" Dusica stood in the doorway to the airlock lobby, resplendent in a white silk robe and fur-trimmed, high-heeled slippers. Her hair looked perfect, even though she'd retired to her stateroom several hours before. "The captain says we've got visitors coming?" Her voice was cold and sarcastic.

"My kids are on their way here," Quinn said. "With Tony's cousin. My ex-husband found them, and I want to get rid of whatever he was using to track them. I figure you must have something."

Dusica's expression hardened. "You're bringing a shuttle that's been compromised to my ship?"

"My kids are on that shuttle," Quinn repeated. "I'm not going to leave it floating around the system where that *crepic* can get them."

"Maybe you two should climb aboard and head out with them," Dusica said. "Family comes first. In this case, that means *my* family."

"Lou is in-system," Tony said. "And Liz and Maerk, too. We could find them and follow you later."

Dusica went completely still. "Follow me later? How would you do that?"

Tony smiled. "I can't reveal all my secrets. But believe me, I can do it. Unless you have some way to stop me find my tracker, in which case you can scan the shuttle."

Dusica threw up her hands. "Yes, we have a way to scan the ship. Fine. Bring your children aboard." She pivoted sharply, then stopped and turned back around. "Does this mean you've reconsidered your stance on my proposal, Mr. Marconi? If you want sanctuary, you must agree to my terms."

Tony nodded. "I'll tell you what you want to know, in exchange for allowing the *Magic Unicorn* to dock and the opportunity to discuss cooperation between our factions." He held out his hand.

Dusica crossed her arms. "And?"

"And...we'll bake cookies?" Tony said. "I'm not sure what else you want."

"You'll help me keep *my* family safe," Dusica said.

"Of course," Tony replied. "That's what I said—cooperation between our factions."

"No," Dusica replied. "Business is separate. I'm saying I'll protect your family if you'll protect mine. All other cooperation is TBD."

"Agreed," Tony said at once.

Dusica stepped forward and shook his hand. "I am going back to bed. The captain said this arrival will delay our jump by an hour, and I prefer to sleep through that. I'll see you in the morning."

"We'll try to keep the noise down," Tony said.

"Don't worry about that." Dusica waved her hand as she headed for the door. "My cabin is soundproofed."

"I guess that's why she didn't hear Francine and Fyo earlier." Quinn peered through the porthole in the hatch. "How much longer?"

"You should see them approaching," Tony said. "I'm surprised the captain agreed to this before he checked with Dusica."

"Maybe he doesn't really work for her," Quinn said. "I mean, not directly. Savoy is a big company. He probably doesn't know exactly who she is. There they are!"

The internal door swished open, and Elena Cantrel, the purser, stepped into the compartment, holding a comtab. "The docking program is pulling them in. They'll be locked on in three…two…one…now."

A muffled thud echoed through the room. Quinn peeked through the porthole again, waiting for the *Unicorn's* hatch to pop. After what felt like hours, it swung wide, and Lucas and Ellianne bounded into the connector.

"*Unicorn*, this is Savoy One," Cantrel said, speaking into her comtab. "We'll lock the clamps for jump. Your shuttle must be completely shut down. Pass control to us."

"Understood," Dareen's voice came through the device. "Setting control now."

The airlock opened, and the kids hurtled into the lobby. Ellianne squealed as she threw herself at Quinn. "Mom! Daddy's a pirate!"

CHAPTER 23

DAREEN AND ELLIANNE bunked with Quinn, since the ship only had six staterooms. Lucas slept on Tony's couch. She got everyone settled just in time to jump to Fortenta. After sleeping in late the next morning, they gathered for brunch.

"I've never heard of Fortenta before," Quinn said as she set her loaded plate on the table. The chef had provided a full buffet with foods she'd only seen on video: caviar, Saurian eggs, Deviled Tomicon.

Francine sipped her hot tea, leaning her head against her hand. She looked terrible.

"Are you okay?" Quinn asked.

The blonde spread jam on a piece of toast. "I took hangover-meds, but I feel like crap. I should know better than to drink before a jump. It intensifies the hangover."

"You've never heard of Fortenta because it's not real," Fyo said, ignoring his sister. He looked like he'd just woken from a long, deep sleep and had a massage.

"We're going to a place that isn't real?" Ellianne's eyes sparkled.

"It's a real place," Francine said wearily. "But the name isn't really Fortenta."

"Exactly." Fyo jabbed his knife in her direction. "We never use the real, legal designation when we're out of the system because we don't want anyone to know where it is. If too many people know a secret, it's not secret anymore."

"That's why I had to keep the surprise secret from Mommy." Ellianne nodded wisely. "Then she figured it out, and the surprise was ruined."

"Parents do that sometimes," Fyo whispered.

"Was the pirate ship a surprise?" Quinn asked. "Did Daddy tell you they'd be coming?"

"No," Ellianne answered. "That was a surprise for me, too. But Dareen wouldn't let me visit Daddy."

"Smart lady." Francine fist bumped Dareen.

The door slid open, and Tony strolled in. "Lucas is still asleep."

"He's thirteen," Quinn said. "I'd be amazed if he was up before one."

"Kid sleeps like a rock once he finally stops talking." Tony grabbed a plate and worked his way through the buffet.

Francine sipped her tea. "What system is it?"

Fyo smiled and shook his head. "Nope, not out here."

"But we're in the system." Francine pulled her comtab out. "I can look it up."

"You could, but we aren't at Fortenta," Fyo replied. "Dusica's ship will meet us here, and then we'll jump to Fortenta."

"Clever," Tony said. "I was wondering about Dusica trusting the crew of this ship."

"When will we meet Dusica's ship?" Quinn asked.

Fyo glanced at Francine's comtab, lying on the table. "About twenty minutes."

"What?" Quinn asked.

"I need to pack," Dareen said at the same time.

"Marielle isn't even awake yet!" Francine said.

"Where's Sashelle?" Ellianne demanded.

"What packing can you possibly have?" Francine asked Dareen. "You just got here."

"Come on." Fyo pushed his chair back. "I'll help you find Sashelle."

The little girl jumped out of her chair and pelted across the room. Fyo shoved a piece of bacon into his mouth, waved cheerfully to the group, and followed her out the door.

"How do you know Marielle isn't awake?" Quinn asked Francine.

Francine blushed. "Uh, because she's not here."

"Dusica isn't here either." Quinn said with a sly grin. "Nor Lucas. Interesting that you focused on Marielle."

"She was the last one I saw last night." Francine rose. "Or this morning. Whenever it was. She took care of me, so I'm going to take care of her." She swallowed the last of her tea and stalked out.

"Who's Marielle?" Dareen asked.

"I'll explain later," Quinn said. "You'd better go pack."

"I don't have anything to pack. That was a joke. But I do need to get the *Unicorn* ready for departure." She dropped her napkin on the table and stood. "Are y'all going to fly with Dusica or with me?"

"Doesn't really matter," Tony said. "I suspect you'll have to dock the *Unicorn* to Dusica's ship before we jump anyway. She's not going to give you the coordinates to her secret planet."

"I'll know where it is when we get there," Dareen said.

"You heard what Fyo said," Quinn replied. "The more people who know a secret, the less secret it is. She's going to try to keep us all in the dark as long as possible."

"Don't talk to me about keeping secrets," Dareen said. "Marconi, remember? I know about keeping secrets. That's practically a family motto. I guess I'll see you when I get docked on Dusica's ship."

"Do you need anything from the stateroom?" Quinn asked.

"Nope, I got it all here." Dareen picked up her bag and slung it over her shoulder. She waved and strolled away.

Tony pulled the comtab out of his pocket, flicked something, and set it on the table with a sheepish grin. "Not really necessary, but I hate eavesdropping. I mean other people eavesdropping. I'm okay with doing it myself."

Quinn laughed. "We're going to discuss super-secret stuff?"

"I'm sure we will at some point," Tony said. "But mostly this is about privacy. Just because Dusica is trusting us and vice versa doesn't mean she should be privy to everything we say."

"Fair enough." Quinn picked up a piece of bacon. "I guess you got enough alcohol before the jump?"

"It was close, but I managed," Tony said. "I use the hard stuff for emergencies."

"It doesn't have to be beer?" She put the bacon down. For some reason, this inane conversation was making her nervous. She and Tony had been friends for years; why would she be uncomfortable? Sure, there'd been that moment in Fyo's room...

Tony smiled at her, and her insides turned to goo. There it was. After all these years, now that Reggie was out of the picture, maybe it was time for something more than friendship. She smiled back.

"All passengers, please report to the lobby for debarkation," the purser's voice announced over the loudspeaker.

With a wry grin, Quinn picked up her bacon and stood. "I guess that's us."

"See you down there," Tony said. "We can share secrets later."

FRANCINE STARED through the porthole as the ship-to-ship access extended to connect them. Dusica's ship looked like an ore freighter. Big, boxy, grungy—nothing like the sleek *Savoy One*. "That's your ship? Clever camouflage."

"It's not really a disguise." Dusica lifted her chin. "It actually carries ore. But it's a little nicer than it looks."

"And faster," Fyo agreed with a grin. "But nobody would expect it to have a scion of the Russosken *nachal'nik* aboard."

"Technically, it doesn't," Francine said. "And won't. None of us are related by blood."

"Good thing, too," Dusica said. "We'd be locked up like fairytale princesses if we were."

"You mean like me?" Fyo patted his hair. "I'm a superb fairytale princess,"

"No, you're not," Ellianne exclaimed. "You're not a girl."

Fyo gasped. "You're right! I'm not! Oh, the horror." They both dissolved in giggles.

"How long has he been on your estate?" Quinn asked in a low voice. "He's enjoying eight-year-old humor, so I'm guessing it's been a while."

"Fyo's always liked kids," Dusica said. "It's one of his few endearing qualities."

"Don't forget my stunning good looks." Fyo winked at Ellianne. "And my stellar video gaming skills."

"What games do you have?" Lucas asked eagerly.

Francine groaned and turned away. "I've had enough Onks versus whatever it was to last a lifetime."

"Orcs!" Fyo and Lucas yelled together.

"Oh, look, the ship's docked," Quinn said loudly. "Time to go!"

The airlock hatch opened, and the whole group crowded in. "Are you sure there's room for all of us?" Francine paused in the lobby. Sashelle sat beside her, ignoring the people.

"Squeeze in," Fyo called. "Plenty of space. The lock on the other side is big enough for deliveries."

Francine sighed and stepped in next to Marielle. Francine smiled. The former FSS agent smiled in return, a tiny quirk of her lips.

What's up with you and the Predator? Sashelle asked inside her head. Somehow, she could tell the caat was speaking only to her. She wasn't sure how she knew, but it was clear this was a private conversation.

"The predator?" Francine whispered at the caat. Sashelle looked at Marielle, then back at Francine. Francine looked away. A chuckle echoed through her head.

They dove through the zero-gravity connector one at a time, arriving in the now-open airlock of the freighter. Fyo flipped over Tony's head to the front of the group and pulled himself down by the handles set into the internal hatch. "Welcome to the *Eternal Void*. Shut the outer hatch, Francine."

Francine gave the hatch a shove, pushing herself into Marielle and Quinn. They laughed.

"Grab the handle, silly," Ellianne said.

Francine saluted the girl. "Yes, ma'am." She shut the hatch.

"Quarter gravity coming up in three, two, one, now," Fyo said.

They sank to the floor, and the inner hatch opened.

"Why did you name it the *Eternal Void*?" Quinn asked. "Not very cheerful."

"We didn't," Fyo said. "Just kept the original name. Trying to keep a low profile—maintain authenticity. She still transports ore when we don't need her."

The inner hatch revealed a long, narrow passageway. Unlike the freighter they'd taken to Lunesco, this ship's bulkheads were painted bright white, with excellent lighting. "*This* doesn't look authentic," Tony said.

"It doesn't fit the stereotype, but there are plenty of ships that look this good," Dusica said. "Considering the crew lives here full-time, it's only fair to make their living space as nice as possible."

"That's very egalitarian of you," Francine said in surprise.

"I'm not the spoiled Russosken the media sees," Dusica replied. "You, of all people, should know that."

"I do," Francine said softly. "I guess I've been gone long enough that I've forgotten the real you and bought into the myth. I'm sorry." She dropped her chin in apology.

Dusica nodded regally in response.

"Doesn't the love get you?" Fyo slapped his chest. "Right here?"

Dusica's lips quirked. Francine smacked him gently on the back of his head.

"Close the airlock so the staff can deliver our luggage," Dusica said. "Then show our guests to their quarters, Fyo. I need to check in with Captain Verdun."

"Yes, ma'am!" Fyo clicked his heels together and slapped his chest and arms in a complicated salute. "Come on, Lucas, help me with this." The two pushed the airlock closed, and Fyo showed the boy how to run the cycler.

"Now, to the staterooms!" Fyo waved his arm overhead in a circle and started off toward the stern of the ship, walking backward like a tour guide. "Follow me. Stay together, please! No pictures."

"He *has* been away from people way too long," Francine muttered.

Fyo took them up a ladder. They climbed through a hatch and went around the corner. Another clean, white passageway stretched the length of the ship. "This is my stateroom." He tapped on the first door on the right. "Dusica's is the last one on the left. The rest are open, so take your pick. We only have four guest cabins, so you'll have to share."

The door across from Fyo popped open, and Dareen stuck her head out. "Hi guys! Beat you here! Ellianne, you wanna share with me or stay with your mom?"

The girl looked at Quinn, then at Dareen. "I'm gonna stay with Dareen, okay? She won't make me go to bed if I don't want to."

Quinn chuckled. "Sure. But don't stay up too late." Ellianne cheered and threw herself at Dareen.

"I guess that means you're stuck with me," Tony said to Lucas. "Unless you'd prefer to stay with your mom?"

"Uh, no, thanks," Lucas said. "I'm too old to share a room with my mom."

"You can bunk with me," Fyo said. "I've got a whole suite, so there's way more room. Plus, I have—"

"Video games!" Lucas shouted.

"He's just like End." Dareen put a hand to her forehead as if the idea of video games gave her a headache. "Do they ever grow out of that stuff?"

"No," Fyo said.

"Do you want to share with me?" Francine glanced at Marielle as she opened the next cabin door. "It's only for a couple days."

"Sure," Marielle said with a careless shrug. "I can sleep anywhere."

"Is everyone here?" Dusica strode down the passageway, followed by a woman in coveralls carrying a box. "Before you get too comfortable, we need all electronics. Everything you brought aboard. Comtabs, games, tablets. Katya will bring them back after we scan them."

As she spoke, the crew woman stopped by each passenger, holding out the box. She gave Lucas a hard stare. "All of it. I know you have more than one."

"Geez," Lucas said. "Give me a minute." He put his comtab into the box, then pulled another device from his pocket. The woman narrowed her eyes. The boy sighed and put a third item into the container.

She turned to Fyo and jiggled the box. "Sir?"

"None of mine have been out of my possession—"

Dusica cut him off. "Come on, Fyo, you know the drill." She crossed her arms, foot tapping.

Fyo rolled his eyes and put a couple of devices in the box. "Take care of those, Katya." He gave her an outrageous wink.

"You know I will, sir." Katya grinned back.

Francine shook her head. Her brother still had a way with the ladies. She pulled out her own comtab and added it to the pile. "I have a tablet in my bag."

"We've already scanned the luggage," Dusica said. "Katya will bring your bags to your rooms when they're cleared."

Tony nodded in obvious approval as he deposited his comtab in the box. "Excellent discipline. I assume you don't need to have those active?"

"No, sir," Katya replied. "They should be turned on, but we can scan them in sleep mode."

Tony grimaced. "I might need to tweak a couple things. Let me know if you need my help with that one. Special model."

Katya glanced at the device as he placed it into the box and nodded. "I will."

"Dareen, your shuttle has been scanned and it's clean," Dusica announced. "Nice work."

"Thanks," Dareen said. "That's what happens when you don't let anyone else touch your stuff." She dropped her voice to a mutter. "And you can bet your last *matryoshka* doll that I'll scan it again when we leave you."

Francine bit back a grin.

"We'll jump in two hours," Dusica announced, looking at Tony. "I assume that gives you sufficient time?"

He nodded.

"Good." She turned toward the bow of the ship, Katya moving into formation behind her. "Then I'll see you all at lunch shortly after jump. Thank you for your cooperation." She swept away.

"I guess I need to go drink." Tony winked at the group. "Anyone care to join me?"

"There's a minibar in your room!" Fyo called. "Come on, Lucas, I'll show you my rig. It's awesome."

The boys—Francine couldn't help thinking of Fyo that way, and his recent behavior only reinforced that—disappeared into Fyo's stateroom. She nodded at Quinn and Tony. "See you at lunch."

CHAPTER 24

LIZ DOCKED the *Swan of the Night* at Xury Station hours behind schedule. "Damn comm systems."

"I told you I'd fix it," Maerk said.

"You *said* you fixed it after Lunesco." Liz ran her shutdown checklist, slapping buttons harder than strictly necessary. Maybe it would jiggle the loose wires together. "I told you this ship was a hunk of junk."

"Don't listen to her," Maerk whispered to the bulkhead.

Liz glared. He wasn't going to bring her around with his charming nonsense today. The shoddy comm system could have been disastrous for Dareen. "We need to have good comm. It's like life support. Two things you should never skimp on."

"I know," Maerk said. "I didn't skimp! This is a top-of-the-line Commonwealth number. And it's working fine."

"Then what's the problem?" Liz asked, sweetly, knowing the answer.

"It wasn't installed correctly," Maerk muttered. "Don't worry," he said, louder, as Liz stood and turned toward the airlock. "I've contracted with a professional to fix it."

Liz paused at the airlock hatch. "A real professional? Someone who's trained to work on Commonwealth equipment? Or some guy who claims he installed the speakers for a band that once played in the Commonwealth?"

"He's a Federation tech," Maerk admitted. "But he's the best we can get here. When we get back to N'Avon, I'll get it done right."

"You're damn right you will." Liz grabbed her jacket and stomped into the airlock. By the time the outer hatch hissed open, she'd calmed a bit. Dareen had sent a message saying she'd reached Tony and was safe. *No arms, no fowl*, as Maerk would say. But Liz didn't place any faith in domesticated birds and their lack of weapons. She intended to have a fully functional communication system before she left this station. No matter how much it cost. She'd make Maerk work it off.

The station hatch popped, and she swung into a narrow passageway. The switch to zero gravity lightened her mood, as always. She smiled as she pushed off the side of her ship and zipped to the far end of the tube. Grabbing a handle, she pulled her feet to the floor and engaged the magnets built into her shoes. Then she put her hand against the access panel and answered the questions.

"Nothing to declare. Delivering the attached items." She coded in her invoice number and waited for the light to turn green. The system confirmed cargo drones would accept the crates at the cargo deck of her ship, and then the screen displayed a speech bubble. She tapped the button.

"Passenger bound for Taniz Beta requests passage. Payment in escrow."

No shipments, just a passenger. Carrying people was a slim-margin business, but better than making the flight empty. And the shipment they'd brought to the research station paid well, so they could afford a lower-revenue leg. Maybe she could find a few smaller items. The researchers here must need things shipped out of the system from time to time.

She keyed in the request for a meeting. Not only did passengers use resources en route, but they required a more careful level of scrutiny before accepting the deal. On a ship as small as the *Swan*, Liz wouldn't take just anyone. Most transits took four to seven days, and she didn't have the patience to put up with stupid people that long.

Fortunately, she had time to kill while Maerk fixed the comm system, and she'd heard Xury sold a tolerable local ale. She added the local bar to the meeting request and sent it off. Then she posted an offer to ship items to Taniz Beta and systems in that direction, with contact at the bar.

The access panel digested her information, accepted her credentials, and requested payment for the advertisement. She tapped in the information. The inner lock popped open, and she stepped into the half-gravity of Xury Station.

The station walls were painted a sunny yellow, with full-spectrum lighting giving the place a late afternoon feeling. A couple of uniformed residents smiled and nodded at her as she passed. The nubby carpet gave her feet a pleasant massage through her thin-soled station booties. As she walked, virtual signs popped up indicating directions for administration, laboratories, restrooms, quarters and finally, the pub.

At the end of the passageway, she took a lift down two levels and stepped into a wide commercial concourse. Small shops and several restaurants occupied the outer edge of the circular courtyard. A large virtual fountain sprayed in the middle of the circle, and benches and tables lay scattered around the open space. Fine mist fell from overhead sprayers to add humidity and increase the feeling of authenticity.

An image of a foam-topped mug appeared to the left, so she followed the floating beverage to the "What's Your Xury Pub."

A smiling woman waved from behind a counter. "What can I get you?"

Liz blinked. "I expected an auto-pub. Uh, I'll have the local specialty."

"It's normally automated," the woman said. "But I had to tweak the brew, so you get a barkeep. One-time special deal. Was that pale or dark?"

"I'll try the dark." Liz flicked her comtab and sent payment to the pub. "What do you do when you aren't tweaking brews?"

"Microbiologist, of course. Yeasts are my specialty."

"You study yeasts out here? Do gas giants have a lot of yeast?"

"Not Xury itself, but dormant yeasts have been found on Seven." The woman laughed. "I'm not here as a scientist, though. I run the bakery, too. On sabbatical from the University of Romara's biology department. Studying Xury Seven helps pay the bills."

Liz shook her head. "You're on sabbatical from an academic posting and working in a bar and bakery."

"You got it. Most fun I've had in a long time. Here's your ale."

Liz accepted the mug and took a sip. Her eyes popped open. "This is really good! Your own or a station recipe?"

"I might have tweaked the station recipe," she replied with another laugh. "It was good before, don't get me wrong. But now..."

"It's amazing." Liz downed a satisfying gulp. "You might need to retire from that university job."

"Would if I could," she said. "But the pub and bakery belong to the station, not me. I barely make minimum wage maintaining the equipment. Maybe someday. Did you need anything else? Sandwich? How about a pretzel? Those *are* my own recipe and damn good, if I do say so myself."

"No, I'm good. I'm meeting a potential passenger here."

The woman's eyes focused over Liz's shoulder and an expression passed over her face so quickly, Liz wasn't sure what it was. Or if she'd really seen anything. The woman nodded toward the concourse. "Probably Amanda McLasten. I heard she was looking for a ride out-system."

Liz turned. A beautiful woman with long, dark hair and a flowing robe of silky material sat near the virtual fountain. She stood when she noticed the attention and walked toward them almost floating, her movements were so graceful. She stopped in front of Liz, smiling down at the smaller woman. "I'd know you anywhere. You must be Liz Marconi."

"How— Who told you that?" Liz stuttered.

"You look too much like Tony. He's only mentioned two female relatives besides Dareen. I can't imagine you're Lou."

"She's my mother," Liz admitted. "You must be Amanda."

"That's me." Amanda held up both hands. "But let's not talk about our mothers, okay? Let me buy you a drink, and we can discuss my travel plans."

"Deal." Liz finished her ale. "I'll have another one of these. And some of those pretzels."

Amanda flicked her comtab a couple of times and nodded at the bar. "Grab our drinks and find a table; I'll run to the bakery and get the pretzels."

Amanda met her at a small table far enough from the simulated fountain that it wasn't damp. "The mist is nice if you're only passing through but not great if you're sitting for any time. It gets cold." She placed a basket of thick, soft pretzels on the table. "It's odd that we didn't meet on Lunesco."

Liz shook her head. "Not that odd. I didn't set a foot on the dirt." She pressed her lips together. She'd thought about leaving the ship, but the local authorities might not have been happy with her actions. *They* had insisted on fair trials for the invaders.

"From what I heard, you weren't in any shape for socializing," Amanda nodded sympathetically. "Those Russosken are brutal."

"They were." Liz picked up a pretzel. "All the more reason to get rid of them." She sank her teeth into the warm bread and ripped off a bite.

"Shh," Amanda said, her voice low. "This station should be free from their influence, but this is still the Federation."

Liz nodded slightly and raised her voice. "These are really good!" She held up another piece of pretzel then popped it into her mouth. "Let's talk business. You need a ride to Taniz Beta? I think we can make room for you—but it depends on how much cargo you'll have."

Making a prospective client feel you had to go out of your way for them was a good negotiation technique.

"I travel light. I have some equipment being delivered, but I never travel *with* it. Safer that way. Plausible deniability. So, it's just me and my little bag." She held up a sparkly purse by one finger.

"That's all?" Liz looked at the other woman's clothing, hair, and makeup. "That's not big enough for a change of underwear."

"Never wear it. Takes up too much space." Amanda laughed. "Just kidding. You should see your face. I have two wheeled bags, but they're standard commercial size. How much will you charge me?"

They dickered for a few minutes, haggling over the cabin, cargo space, and food. "If I bring a case of wine to share, does that help?" Amanda asked.

"You should have led with that. I might have given you free passage if the wine was good enough."

They both laughed. By the time they'd finally settled on a fee, the beer and pretzels were gone. "Do you want to grab dinner?" Amanda asked. "Or whatever meal you're on?"

"I have to get back to the ship." Liz waved her comtab. "I've been ignoring my partner's texts for the last ten minutes, but he needs a part I can pick up over there." She nodded at an electronics kiosk across the concourse. "We should be ready to leave in the morning. See you about eight, local?"

"Deal." Amanda extended her hand. "See you in the morning."

CHAPTER 25

THE *ETERNAL VOID* eased into orbit around a purple-green planet a few days later. Various views of the system had appeared on screens in the dining room. Quinn, Tony, Francine, and Marielle sat at a long rectangular table, eating lunch.

"Do you know what system we're in?" Quinn asked.

"Not a clue," Tony said. "The comm shield on this ship is impressive."

"I've tried hacking it." Francine stacked pickles on her sandwich. "Whoever built it was *good*."

"Did you try?" Marielle asked Quinn.

"No," Quinn replied. "I figured I'm on thin ice here. Dusica's not going to kick Francine off the ship, but I have no doubt she'll dump me in a heartbeat if she feels I'm a risk. I took a look at the code and noodled around with a downloaded copy, but I haven't tried anything on the live system."

"Probably for the best," Tony said. "It doesn't pay to upset your hosts—unless it's really important."

Dareen, Fyo, and the kids exploded into the room. "Sandwiches again?" Fyo exclaimed.

"What do you usually eat on this ship?" Dareen asked.

"I've only flown on it twice," Fyo admitted. "On the way to Robinson's and this time. We had some really nice stuff on the way out."

"If you want the good stuff, you'll have to crash Dusi's stateroom," Francine said. "I saw a whole kitchen in there. Owner's suite."

"Good point." Fyo turned back to the door. "We always ate in there on the way out."

Dareen grabbed his arm. "I don't think she'd appreciate all of us showing up."

"Who cares?" Fyo said. "We'll be heading dirtside in an hour or so. She can survive that short an incursion."

"Or we can wait 'til we get down there." Dareen jerked her head at Ellianne and Lucas, who were happily loading their plates with chips, fruit, and cookies. "This is fine."

"Make a sandwich!" Quinn called out. She watched for a second, then turned to her tablemates. "They aren't making a sandwich."

"They wouldn't eat it if they did," Marielle said. "Better to not waste it. Lighten up, Mom. We're on an adventure."

"I guess," Quinn muttered. "But it seems like life has become more adventure than normal lately."

Tony grinned. "That's the Marconi magic. We turned out okay."

THE *MAGIC UNICORN* detached from the *Eternal Void* and dropped away from the larger ship. Dareen thanked the captain for his hospitality and set a course for Dusica's landing field on the night side of the planet. "They've got a state-of-the-art automated system. Which is good, since I hate landing somewhere new in the dark."

"Wouldn't expect anything less from Dusica." Quinn rode co-pilot. "She pays for the best."

"Did you get a look at that owner's suite? Wow. Fancy kitchen, high-tech everything. She even had a real shower in the head! The rest of the ship was so ordinary."

"Part of that was in case someone came aboard," Quinn reminded her. "It has to look ordinary to blend in. Some ships have extravagant owner's suites. Not usually ore haulers like that, but..."

The autopilot pinged, and they entered the atmosphere.

"You guys good back there?" Quinn asked through the intercom.

"Everything is green," Tony answered. In the background, Ellianne and Lucas argued over something.

"Sounds like you're having the kind of fun we had last week," Dareen laughed.

"It's all good," Tony replied. "They're letting off steam."

"Roger. We'll be landing soon." Dareen slid the comm screen to Quinn. "Contact the tower."

"On it. Tower—" She stumbled when she realized she didn't know the tower's name. "Uh, this is the *Magic Unicorn*, requesting permission to land."

"*Unicorn*, this is Argos Tower," a voice replied. "You are cleared to land on runway seven-two."

"Roger, Argos," Quinn said. "Runway seven-two." She flicked the mute button. "I'm not familiar with Argos, are you?"

Dareen shook her head. "Nope, but it's a big galaxy. He didn't seem surprised that you didn't know his designator."

"Maybe he's used to folks not knowing where they are."

"I don't think Dusica takes in *that* many visitors," Dareen replied. "And everyone else would know where they're going, but not who lives there."

"Good point." Quinn checked their vectors and instruments. "All green."

The younger woman flipped the intercom again. "We're touching down in ten, nine—"

The kids chimed in, counting down. On "mark," the wheels hit the runway, bouncing them down the kilometer-long strip.

"Small strip." Dareen's voice vibrated with the ship.

"Private?" Quinn squinted then zoomed in the external cams. "I only see one other craft. That's the shuttle that brought the others down." The sleek silver ship glowed under the spotlights. White-uniformed attendants swarmed it. Francine and her brother stood at the bottom of the steps, with Marielle a few steps above. "Who is that by Francine? The one wearing bright colors. And where's Dusica?"

Dareen shook her head. "We'll find out soon enough."

"*Unicorn*, Tower. Please proceed to the end of the runway and hold."

"Why?" Quinn asked, but the tower didn't answer.

"That's not really a question you're supposed to ask," Dareen said. "If they ask you to do something, it's for a good reason."

"Yeah, but there's no one here except Dusica," Quinn said. "If someone else is landing, they wouldn't have us hold at the end of the runway."

Dareen stopped the shuttle at the designated spot and started her landing checklist. "We can run through here." She pointed to a line on the screen. "The rest will have to wait until we park."

Quinn ignored her. "Tony, can you come up here for a minute?" she called. "Lucas, Ellianne, stay strapped in." She didn't wait for the expected complaint before clicking the off button.

The hatch at the rear of the cockpit opened and Tony stepped through.

"Dog that," Quinn said.

"Roger." Tony responded to her curt tone with efficiency. He shut and latched the hatch to cargo. "What's up?"

"I don't like any of this." Quinn zoomed the camera in on the small group of passengers grouped in the distance, but they had disappeared behind a ground vehicle.

"*Unicorn*, you're cleared to park," Argos Tower said. "Follow the landing lights." Green lighted streaked away from them toward the apron where the other shuttle sat.

"Maybe that's standard procedure here?" Tony asked. "Wait for passengers to clear the area? It kind of makes sense for a place with little traffic. Minimize danger to those unloading." He wrinkled his nose.

"Could be," Quinn agreed, "but something is bothering me. Dareen, Tony and I are going to check things out first. Don't start your shutdown until we give you the all-clear."

"If you say so." Dareen pushed the throttle for the taxi engines. "I trust your gut."

"And tell the kids to stay buckled up!" Tony went to the airlock and pulled out the gear Lou had added to both shuttles after Lunesco. He handed an ArmorCoat to Quinn. "Not stylish, but if you're worried, let's go full load."

She pulled the long coat over her shorts and t-shirt and slid a mini blaster into her pocket. "Give me one of those rifles, too. I've been practicing in the virtual range."

"Excellent." Tony donned his own gear and opened the airlock hatch. He stepped in, then leaned through to call to Dareen. "Stop fifty meters short and let us out there. Like we did on Varitas." He pulled the hatch shut and cycled the lock. He handed an earbud to Quinn. "Ready?"

Quinn slid the tiny electronic capsule into her ear canal, then held her weapon across her body. "Ready."

"Ready," Dareen's voice came through the tiny device. "Stopping in three, two, one, mark." The outer hatch popped.

Tony shoved it open and leaped over the steps as they unfolded from under the hatch. Quinn followed him down, landing in a crouch behind the shuttle's massive wheel. She swung her weapon around to aim toward the other shuttle.

"They're asking me what we're doing." Dareen's voice even and strong. "I gave them my silly girl act. Keeping the engines hot."

"Roger," Tony answered. "Close the hatch."

"You got it." The hatch clanged softly.

The ground vehicle beside the other shuttle lifted on a cushion of air and flowed toward them. "Can you see who's inside?" Quinn crouched in the shadow of the shuttle's massive wheel.

The transport settled to the ground beside the *Magic Unicorn* and eye-watering lights stabbed at them. The door opened. Francine leaned out, looking around. She made eye contact with Quinn behind the wheel. "I don't see anyone," Francine called. "I don't know—maybe something broke." Her voice sounded strained.

"Dareen, do not open the shuttle." Quinn bent lower. "Get down, Tony."

"They're telling us to come out," Dareen said at the same moment. "I said we have a slight malfunction with the airlock."

"You sure, Quinn?" Tony whispered.

"Francine saw me," Quinn replied. "She looked right at me when she said that. If that isn't a signal to hide, I don't know what is. But where?" The shuttle sat on the brightly-lit apron, surrounded by flat, open tarmac.

"We need a distraction, so we can get to that." Tony pointed at a meter-high shed about forty meters away. It looked like a well head or electrical stub.

Sashelle burst out from behind the tiny building. She streaked across the tarmac and flew into the air. Quinn stared, wondering how a creature without wings could jump that high. The caat landed on the windshield of the ground transport.

"Quinn, now!" Tony whispered harshly.

They ran.

"Dareen, go!" Tony called.

The shuttle's taxi engines whined. The caat roared like a wild animal three times her size. She leapt from the hovercraft to the tarmac and took off across the runway.

Quinn dropped beside Tony, behind the small building. "Now what?"

"We hide." Tony watched the shuttle turn at the end of the field, scattering gravel and burning rubber. "Dareen, get out of here. Back toward the jump point. Maybe the *Eternal Void* is still around. If not, try to negotiate a ride with another ship and get back to N'Avon. We'll try to get a message to Lou."

CHAPTER 26

THE WIDE AIRFIELD was surrounded by jungle. Quinn sucked in a deep breath of the thick, damp air, heavy with the scent of growing things. The ground vehicle had driven away after Dareen launched. She and Tony had crouched behind the shed for another ten minutes before running for the shrubs near the larger buildings. From there, they'd worked their way into the jungle.

Quinn followed Sashelle and Tony along a narrow path. She used her comtab as a light, but Sashelle didn't mind the darkness. "Have you ever been here before?"

Tony shook his head. "Nope. I'm not even sure where we are. I'm hoping this path goes somewhere useful."

"The tower controller said this was Argos. But I've never heard of a planet called that."

"Me neither. Must be a local name." He glanced over his shoulder. "The good news is this jungle gives us lots of cover."

"I hope there's nothing dangerous in here." She stepped over a vine laying across the path.

"Even in the Federation, only safe planets are colonized—or the safe parts. But shorts might not have been the best choice of apparel for tromping through a jungle."

"I didn't intend to tromp through a jungle." Quinn glanced down at her legs. "I intended to sit by a pool at Dusica's luxurious estate. Maybe even go for a dip."

"You have a swimsuit? I didn't pack any leisure wear for this trip."

Quinn laughed. "Neither did I, but the *Savoy One* had a pretty extensive wardrobe. Francine said we should help ourselves. Based on Fyo's description of his home, I did."

"I figured I could borrow something when we got here," Tony said. "Or we could go shopping. I suspect anywhere Dusica lives has ample commercial opportunities. Her shoes alone prove that."

"Too bad we didn't anticipate running for our lives." Quinn's laugh died. "At least I have the coat and a gun."

"I always prepare for that eventuality." Tony pulled a device out of his pocket. "But usually, my comtab works. Here, I've got nothing."

"Let me see that." Quinn stopped in a small clearing. "I had a refresher course while I was on N'Avon." She took the palm-sized box and sat on a boulder beside the path. Then she looked at the rock again, and the clearing around them. "Does this seem too manicured to you? I think we might be in a park."

"I guess that makes sense." Turned slowly, taking in the neat trees and grass. "We can't be far from civilization, since we just left a shuttle field."

Quinn pulled out her own comtab and pulled off the cover. "I have a card... There." She peeled a piece of plastic from the inside of the case and stuck it into Tony's device. She turned it off and on and adjusted the settings. "And...there. I think I've got a connection." She handed it back to Tony.

"Nice work!" He tapped and swiped the screen. "Gotcha. We're in Delian Park, on the edge of Argos. It's a city. This appears to be Taniz Beta."

"Now *that* I've heard of." Quinn rose. "Once Dareen figures out where we are, she should be able to go to Taniz Alpha and contact Liz. Or Lou."

Tony chuckled. "I was scheduled to come here after Robinson's World. They're anxious to get out from under the Russosken foot."

"Why would Dusica have her safehouse on a Russosken planet?" Quinn asked. "That seems dangerous."

"Hiding in plain sight? Or maybe she has resources here. It's a busy enough place. Someone like Fyo could hide in the crowd."

Can we get moving? Sashelle asked.

"Do you know where you're taking us?" Quinn asked.

Of course. The caat trotted away.

"After you." Tony bowed and gestured for her to lead.

FRANCINE MOVED onto the retractable steps and froze. A tall, artificially-blonde woman wearing layers of colorful, draped clothing and a fortune in jewels stood at the foot of the stairs.

"Faina, how nice to see you." Ludmila Nartalova, the *nachal'nik,* frowned. "And Fyotor. So nice to see you aren't dead."

Francine briefly debated running back into the shuttle. But if the *nachal'nik* were here, then the shuttle pilots would obey her. Doing otherwise would mean death. There was no escape. She raised her chin and slowly descended the steps. "*Voz'y Nachal'nik.* What a pleasure."

"Come, child, you used to call me *babushka,*" Nartalova said.

"That was before you killed my father and my brother." Francine worked hard to hide the tremor in her voice.

"Ah, but I obviously didn't kill your brother." Nartalova flicked her hand at Fyo. "So, you owe me an apology."

Francine flipped her hair over her shoulder as if she were strutting down a sidewalk in Rossiya City. "I don't owe you anything."

The *soldaty* behind Nartalova sucked in gasps.

Nartalova's eyes narrowed, but she didn't respond. "Fyotor, come say hello."

Fyo froze on the steps beside his sister. Francine took his arm and urged him down the steps. "Don't worry," she whispered. "I'll get us out of this." Fyo didn't even blink in response.

"And I see you brought a bodyguard." Nartalova's bright eyes glittered. Francine resisted the urge to look back at Marielle. "While I'm thrilled to see you finally learning some caution, it won't do you any good." She spoke over her shoulder. "Arrest the dark one."

"No!" Francine bit off the word almost before it escaped her lips.

The old woman smirked. "Never tip your hand, Faina." She tsked as the soldiers dragged Marielle down the steps. "Don't give your enemy anything to use against you. Dusica, so nice of you to bring them to me."

"What?" Fyo cried.

"She's lying!" Dusica rushed down the steps to grab Fyo's arm. "I didn't bring you to her, Fyo. You know I would never betray you."

"But we had a deal, Dusica," Nartalova said in a soft, faux whiny tone. "I told you I'd give you amnesty any time. All you had to do was bring Faina back. Fyotor is an added bonus."

Francine looked up the steps at her sister. "Tell me the truth."

"She offered, but I *never* agreed to it," Dusica said. "I—"

"Enough!" Nartalova said. "Get in the car. Your friends seem to think there's something going on here." She looked across the tarmac at the *Magic Unicorn* sitting at the end of the runway.

"We told them to wait, *Voz'y Nachal'nik*," the soldier behind her said. "You said you didn't want them to see this."

"Very good." Nartalova dusted her hands together. "Get them into the vehicle and call that shuttle over."

The shuttle taxied closer but stopped short. "What are they doing?" Nartalova demanded. "Take us over there. We need whoever is in that shuttle."

The vehicle lifted and slid forward, searchlights turning on to illuminate the spacecraft.

"Faina, tell your friends to come out," Nartalova said. "And don't try anything." She pulled a stunner out of her voluminous clothing and pointed it at Fyo.

With a wide-eyed glance at her sister and brother, Francine opened her door and stuck her head out. The airlock hatch of the *Unicorn* was shut, but something moved underneath. Francine squinted. There, in the shadow of the big tires, eyes blinked at her. Quinn. And there was Tony, behind the second set of wheels. *Sashelle*, she thought as clearly as possible. *If you're out there, now would be a good time for one of your last-minutes saves.*

"I don't see anyone," she told the *nachal'nik*. "I don't know—maybe they suspect something." She pulled her head in and started to close the door.

"Get them on the horn," the *nachal'nik* said to the driver. "Send the audio back here." She waved the weapon at Francine. "You will tell them to come out."

Francine held her hands up in surrender. The speaker crackled, then Dareen's voice came out, high-pitched and nervous. "I thought you wanted me to stop here!" she whined. "You keep changing your mind. I don't know what you want."

"Sashelle?" Francine said aloud, hoping to tip off Dareen. "This is Francie. Park your shuttle and come on out. I thought we were going to party by the pool?"

"Some idiot told me to wait," Dareen said. "Now he's telling me to move. If I wanted to be ordered around, I would have stayed at home. This is my shuttle, and I'm going to do what I want."

Nartalova glared at Francine and made a "keep talking" motion.

"Sashelle, chill," Francine said. "Ignore the idiots. This is my sister's airfield, so we can do whatever we want. And right now, I want to party. So, come on over and let's party!" She closed her eyes briefly, hoping Dareen would pick up on all the clues. She was a smart girl, and the two of them had never talked about partying, so...

Outside, something shrieked and landed on the vehicle's front window with an echoing thud. Huge paws pressed against the glass.

"What the—"

Francine turned a laugh into a gasp. Sashelle bared fang-like teeth at the driver and roared like a wild animal, then streaked away across the flight line. Every eye in the vehicle followed the caat—except Francine's. She watched the shuttle out of the corner of her eye and saw a flicker of movement as Tony and Quinn darted away.

Then the shuttle roared to life, launch engines firing. The blast heat washed over them, strong enough to reach them inside the climate-controlled cabin as the ship hurtled across the tarmac.

"What the hell is she doing?" a voice yelled through the comm. "Don't fire your launch engines on the apron!"

Francine bit her lip and shook her head as if disappointed. "I knew Sashelle was a mediocre pilot, but I had no idea she was so poorly trained." As if in reply, the shuttle turned and launched.

Don't take my name in vain. Sashelle's tone in her mind was dry.

Thanks for the assist, Francine thought back.

Predictably, the caat did not reply.

"Take us to the house," Nartalova growled at the driver. "Stupid girl."

"She's a bit of a wildcard," Dusica said.

"And tell the station to send someone after them," the old woman continued. "We must have a Russosken boarding party stationed here?"

Francine stared at Dusica, eyes wide. Dusica gave an infinitesimal headshake.

"Sorry, *Voz'y Nachal'nik*," the voice on the comm said. "We don't keep a boarding squad here. No use for them."

"I suggest you do something about that immediately," Nartalova said through clenched teeth. "Contact Rossiya and have them send a squad. If they launch now, they should be able to jump in before that *smut'yan* can find a way out of the system."

"Yes, *Voz'y Nachal'nik*," the voice said. "Immediately."

The hovercraft flew through a gate and onto a street. Regularly placed streetlights illuminated the industrial neighborhood, but all of the buildings were clean and well maintained. Trees grew in octagonal plots between each set of lights, and a walking path curved around them.

"This place is really tidy," Francine muttered to Fyo.

He didn't respond.

"The local government has strict appearance codes." Dusica's gaze darted to the *nachal'nik*, then to the driver.

"As it should be," Nartalova said. "An emphasis on conformity is useful in maintaining order. Surely you learned that as a child?"

"Of course, *Voz'y Nachal'nik*. Part of our education." Dusica stared out the window.

"We'll be there in five minutes, *Voz'y Nachal'nik*," the driver said.

Francine felt Dusica relax a notch. She glanced at Fyo, but he still looked terrified.

Sashelle, Francine thought, as clearly as she could. *Do you know where we're going?*

You're getting better at this, Sashelle answered. *It's about time. You're probably going to your littermate's house on the edge of the city.*

My littermate? Never mind. How do you know that? Francine thought. *Are you talking to Dusica, too?* An image of caat eyes narrowing in disgust intruded on her mind. So, no, then.

I've done some research, Sashelle finally answered. *Your littermate owns a house on the edge of town, and a larger estate farther out. I'm not sure the old* queen *knows about that one.*

Really? Francine's lips twitched at the venom in Sashelle's tone when she mentioned "the old queen." *How would she know about one and not the other?*

The driver works for your littermates. I believe they have a contingency plan for this situation.

How do you know? Francine asked again. *Can you hear what they're thinking?* The idea of the caat reading minds was slightly terrifying.

I will bring the Purveyor of Tuna and the Stealthy One, Sashelle said. *Do not despair.*

"Why are you making faces?" Dusica whispered in Francine's ear.

"Sorry. Just, uh, thinking." She glanced at Nartalova, but the old woman was watching the road. *The Stealthy One?* she thought. Sashelle didn't answer.

The neighborhood, which had transitioned to suburban dwellings while she'd been talking to Sashelle, thinned out. Houses were farther apart, separated by fences and landscaping. A high wall appeared on the right, cutting off the view. The hovercar turned into a driveway and slowed for an ornate gate. The wide metal panels slid apart as the vehicle approached, and they drove through.

"Nice," Francine said. "Very low-profile."

Dusica glared.

"Horrible neighborhood," Nartalova said. "But at least you keep the riffraff out."

The huge house sat well back from the road, protected by the wall. The car stopped under a wide porte cochère, and the driver leapt out. He opened the rear door and offered the *nachal'nik* his hand. The *soldaty* who had followed in a separate vehicle closed around the old woman and the car.

"Take that one to the cell." Nartalova pointed at Marielle in the front seat. "The rest, confine to their rooms." She turned and swept into the building.

"We don't have a cell," Dusica said in a low tone.

"I'm sure she had one installed for you," Francine replied. "She's very efficient when it comes to detaining people. We're lucky she didn't shoot Marielle outright." She tried to ignore the squeezing sensation in her chest.

"She probably decided she'd make a good hostage when she saw your reaction at the shuttle field." Dusica stepped out of the car.

Francine followed. "Hostages can be rescued. Dead is dead."

One of the *soldaty* pulled open the front door and yanked Marielle out, throwing her to the gravel-embedded driveway. Marielle stumbled and landed hard on her hands and knees. As she looked up, she gave Francine's the barest twitch of a wink.

The oaf who threw her down swung the butt of his rifle at

Marielle's skull. Her arm gave out and she fell face-first to the ground, the weapon flying harmlessly over her head. Francine clenched her jaw so she wouldn't smirk as they dragged the other woman away. Trust Marielle to underplay her capabilities while avoiding injury. She'd be okay for a little while.

CHAPTER 27

QUINN CLUNG to a branch in a tree outside Dusica's suburban home, fifteen meters from the ground, wondering how her life had come full circle. She hadn't climbed a tree since childhood, yet here she sat with Tony. From their vantage point, they could see over the wall. Strategically-placed foliage blocked much of the view, but both Francine and Dusica had their lights on and their drapes open. The two women paced inside their rooms in a synchronized display that would have been funny if they weren't captive.

"They're definitely sisters." Tony trained his scope on another window. "I haven't seen Fyo or Marielle yet, have you?"

The Sentinel is in the basement. Sashelle stretched across a lower branch. An image of Marielle accompanied the title.

"How do you know?" Quinn asked.

I tire of answering that question. Sashelle looked away.

"Sorry." Quinn pulled a face at Tony.

I saw that, Sashelle said.

"Of course you did," Quinn answered. "What's your plan?"

I got you here. Sashelle yawned. *The rest is up to you.*

"I think our best bet is to get Marielle out first," Tony said. "She's the most expendable, as far as the *nin-chuck* is concerned. And she'll be the most useful in a tight corner."

"Don't count the Zielinskys out as formidable partners." Quinn huffed a soft, humorless laugh. "And I think that's *nachal'nik*."

"I like *nin-chuck* better." He slid his scope into his pocket and climbed to a higher branch. "Or *nacho-lick*. Are there any basement windows, Sashelle?"

One near the door, to the tail-ward side.

"Tail-ward?" Quinn asked

Sashelle flicked her tail.

"The left." Quinn squinted that direction. "It looks like the ground slopes down to a door. That doesn't help much. I'm sure that door is guarded. Hey, are the lights on the right going dim?"

There's a cellar entrance on the whisker-side. The caat yawned again.

"Got it," Tony reported from above. "Slanted door in the ground. And yes, the light appears to be fading there. Does this remind you of anything?" He swung down to Quinn's level.

"Hadriana?" Quinn asked. "Casing the *old queen's* place? Nope, *bitch* is a better word for that old hag."

"Gretmar or the nacho-lick?" He slid down the trunk and jumped to the ground.

"Yes," Quinn said, following more slowly. They paused to grab their overcoats from the lowest branch. "These coats are super handy, with all the pre-filled pockets, but not great for climbing trees."

He moved the scope to the custom pocket inside the coat and slung his rifle over his shoulder. "Probably not ideal for daytime, either. I think it gets quite warm here."

"Then we'll have to make sure we get wherever we're going before sunrise." She glanced at the still-dark sky, then at the wall between them and the house. "Over?"

"Yup. This is the best place. That tree that should give us enough cover if anyone on the nin-chuck's team looks out. And the lights have dimmed here as well. Coincidence?"

"I don't believe in those. Trap?" Quinn frowned at the wall. "That looks like fun."

"I have string cable." He unspooled a length of twine-thin rope. "Maybe Dusica is helping us with the lights."

"How would she do that?"

"Hidden controls in her suite?" Tony ticked suggestions off on his fingers. "Pre-programmed rescue setting on the system? Duress signal to off-site staff? I'm surprised the nin-chuck risked bringing them to Dusica's house. But maybe she didn't have a lot of choice. Or she severely underestimated our Dusica. Over you go." He pointed at the wall.

"Should have grabbed that anti-grav lifter in the airlock." Quinn squinted at the rough stone wall. "But I think I can do this. Francine gave me some tips on climbing."

"You shinnied up that tree pretty fast." Tony nodded approvingly. "Anti-grav belts are great, if you don't have to wear them too long. Ironically, they're quite heavy when turned off. And bulky. Plus, short battery life. Here, I'll give you a boost."

She put her foot in his hand and pushed up as he lifted. Her fingers gripped the edge of a stone block, digging into the carefully-smoothed mortar. Her soft-soled boots flexed enough to give her traction as she scaled the wall. By the time she reached the top, her arms and legs burned, but she rolled onto the wide top in triumph.

"You okay?" Tony whispered through the earbud.

"I'm good. Toss the coats up." She sucked in a deep breath, then leaned down and snagged the first one with her fingertips. "Got it. Next."

Tony passed up the other coat. "Climb down. We don't want anyone to see you up there."

"Roger," Quinn replied. "Dropping the coats first. Oh, crap."

"What?"

Vicious barking answered his question.

Got it. Sashelle landed lightly near Quinn's head. She leapt down into the yard, growling at the dogs, and then took off across the yard. With a volley of noise, they thundered after her.

Quinn rolled off the top, hanging by her elbows for a second. She dug her toes into the wall again, then climbed down a few feet. Bits of mortar sifted down on top of her. A quick shake of her head cleared the dust, and she glanced down. Close enough to jump. "I'm down. Moving toward the trees on the whisker-side." She giggled softly at the terminology.

"Relative directions could be troublesome." Tony chuckled in her earbud. "I mean, who knows which way her whiskers are pointing now."

We use cardinal directions for absolute references, of course. The rhythm of Sashelle's words made it clear she was still running. *Spinward, anti, close polar, far polar.*

"Those sound cumbersome." Tony dropped beside Quinn.

"Only if you say them aloud," Quinn whispered. "It was pretty obvious what she meant."

Bent low, they ran across an open stretch of lawn, ducking into another copse of trees. Quinn handed one of the coats to Tony and shrugged into her own. "You see our target?"

"That slanted area beside the house." He leaned against a wide tree and pointed over his shoulder. "I'll send a drone."

"Pre-packed in these awesome coats?" Quinn laughed softly.

"Essential equipment." Tony nodded as he flipped the coat open and unsealed an internal pocket. "I only have two, so we have to be careful." He handed the tiny device to Quinn and tapped his comtab a few times.

The insect-sized device lifted off her hand and buzzed away into the night. They sat, shoulder to shoulder, behind the wide tree, peering at the tiny screen. Large cellar doors, the edges partially covered by grass, lay against the slanted earth at the house's foundation. Nothing moved. "Nothing to see here. Does that mean Nartalova's guys don't know about this entry, or it doesn't go anywhere useful?"

They think it's blocked. Sashelle sauntered up.

"Where are the dogs?" Quinn peered through the dark.

I might have opened a gate. The caat paced, seeming to look for the perfect place, then sat. *And then closed it again.*

"You let the dogs out?" Quinn chuckled. "Dusica might not be happy with that."

Not my problem. Sashelle raised a paw and licked it.

"How do you know they don't know about the cellar?" Tony stared at his screen, changing the view.

I asked the Ambassador. And I listened in.

"The ambass— You mean Francine?" Quinn asked.

Obviously.

"You listened in?" Tony repeated.

The caat's tail swished. *To the old queen's minions.*

"Good enough for me," Tony said. "Let's go."

CHAPTER 28

FRANCINE PACED ACROSS HER ROOM. Ten steps. The rooms in Dusica's house were large and luxuriously appointed, but with the door locked from the outside, it was still a cell. She turned and stomped back, staying close to the windows so Tony and Quinn would see her.

We're here, Sashelle said.

"Sashelle!" Francine clapped a hand over her mouth. She knew Dusica would have installed superb soundproofing in any house she bought, but no point in taking the chance of being overheard. "Where are you?" she whispered.

Open the window, the caat replied.

Francine squinted through the glass. With the lights on, it was hard to see anything beyond her own reflection, but she unlatched the lock and pushed the glass aside. Sashelle sat on the narrow ledge outside. "We must be five or six meters up!"

And? Sashelle put her paw against the force screen. Blue sparks danced around her fur, and she yanked her paw back. *Can you turn this off?*

"No need." Francine stuck her hand through. More blue flared around her arm as she did. "It only hurts bugs. And small rodents. You'll be fine."

The caat's ears went back and her fur stood out. *No, I won't. That field is dangerous to me.*

"How can you tell?"

Sashelle looked over the edge for a moment, then jumped into the black. *I'll come in with the Stealthy One and the Purveyor.*

"Where are they?" Francine asked. "What's the plan?"

But there was no reply.

⸻

SLANTED WOODEN DOORS protruded from the base of the house in the side yard. The high wall stood a few meters away, with bright light focused on the top. That left the narrow yard in shadow—perfect for sneaking in.

"I can't believe this is unguarded," Quinn whispered. "And that section of wall near the tree? An obvious blind spot."

"Dusica's really careful," Tony said. "If I were her, I'd have a preset in the security system that introduces failures in the event someone else takes over."

"You think she anticipated the nin-chuck taking them hostage?" Quinn asked. "And prepped a rescue setting on her security system?"

"If she's as smart as I think, yes." He leaned over to look at the old-fashioned lock on the doors. "I'll bet we would have set off all kinds of motion sensors normally. But she's on invasion mode, which deactivates certain areas to allow a rescue without alerting the captors."

"That's a whole level of paranoid I never want to visit."

"Leave it to the professionals." Tony inserted some tools into the lock and twisted. It clicked loudly. "We're in." He pulled the lock off and opened the slanted door. It swung wide on silent hinges, the overgrown grass folding neatly away. "See? This has been well maintained."

She climbed down a narrow wooden ladder. It looked flimsy but held her weight without a quiver. It ended about two meters down, and she stepped aside on the dirt floor. Tony followed her down and shut the door. The darkness closed in like a bag over the head. She fumbled in her pockets for a light she'd seen earlier.

Tony found his first. Red glowed beside her, lighting the low-ceilinged room enough to see any obstacles. The scent of damp and dust filled her nose, and she fought off a sneeze. Rows of shelves lined the small room, each filled with baskets, boxes, and bags. "Cold storage, like that cellar in Hadriana," Quinn whispered. "You called it. I still can't believe the *nachal'nik's* people didn't find this."

"They just got here," Tony replied. "They have four uncooperative prisoners. And maybe household staff with unknown loyalty. They probably secured Francine and the others, then checked her security system. They did a walk around the house to familiarize themselves with the layout and make sure the system was running properly."

"Why didn't they try the door?"

Tony shrugged. "They saw it, rattled the very-secure lock, and kept their fingers crossed. It's visible on the security cams—or was when they checked—so they're focusing their limited numbers on the prisoners. But we need to be careful. The nin-chuck's bodyguards aren't known for their stupidity."

Quinn looked around the room, then pointed. "I'm betting there's a door behind that shelf that leads to the rest of the house."

"Probably hidden from the other side, too." Tony strode forward and pulled on the shelf. It didn't move. "Look for a release."

"Where's Sashelle?"

The caat slid out of the shadows and stood by Quinn's leg.

"That's kind of creepy. When did you come in?" The caat ignored her, but Quinn felt a smug sense of satisfaction that definitely wasn't her own. She rolled her eyes and ran her hands along the underside of the shelves. "Here's a latch." She pulled on the bar tucked under the edge of the second shelf. The whole unit swiveled away from the wall in smooth silence, revealing a door.

"Get your stunner. They're quieter than the blast rifles." Tony eased the door ajar and slipped his drone through the gap. "Nothing." He scrubbed his hand through his hair. "Way too easy." He pulled the door open.

Sashelle sauntered in, moving fast without seeming to hurry. She prowled down a dark hallway and around a corner. *Another door here.*

"She's a good point guard." Tony followed her out.

Quinn brought up the rear, treading as softly as she could.

There are people. I hear two awake and one asleep.

"Asleep or unconscious?" Quinn whispered.

Could be either. Sashelle crouched by the doorjamb, her rear end wiggling as she dropped into attack mode. *I'll distract them.*

Tony raised an eyebrow at Quinn and grinned. "Excellent plan." He stowed the drone.

Quinn pointed her stunner at the door. Tony held up three fingers, counting down. On zero, he yanked the door open.

Sashelle burst through, yowling.

"What the—"

"Where did that come from?"

Something crashed.

Quinn stuck her head and her weapon around the doorframe, taking in the scene in a quick glance. Two large men seemed to fill the narrow hallway. One lunged after Sashelle as she streaked toward the stairs at the far end. The other swung toward the open door. Quinn shot him and he dropped. Tony took out the other.

"Where's the third person?" Tony hissed.

Sashelle jumped down the steps, landing solidly on the first man's stomach. She paced across his chest and face, then thumped to the floor and slunk toward a closed door.

Quinn crouched and rolled over one of the stunned guards. A

lanyard around his neck held a small, rectangular card. She yanked it off his neck and tossed it to Tony. "See if that works."

Tony snagged the lanyard and slapped the card against the access panel. The door clicked. He stepped back and nodded at the caat.

Sashelle washed her ear.

Tony pushed the door open and shined his red light into the windowless room. It was empty, except for the woman lying on the floor.

"Marielle!" Quinn whispered.

Tony hurried in and pressed his fingers against her neck. "She's—"

Marielle flipped over with Tony's arm clamped in her grip. In half a second, he lay face-down on the floor with the woman across his back.

"Marielle!" Quinn hissed, louder this time. "It's us!"

Marielle glanced at Quinn, then down at the man under her knees. "Oops." She stood and stepped away from him.

Tony rolled over, running his hand over his face. He blinked a couple times. "You're fast."

"Years of training," Marielle said.

"I thought you said she was asleep," Quinn whispered at Sashelle.

The caat's tail swished. *She was. Now she isn't.*

"Thanks. So helpful."

Marielle squinted at Quinn. "Who are you talking to? Is someone else out there?"

"Just the caat."

Marielle grimaced. "Riiiight."

"Quinn, secure those two and we'll bring them in here." Tony rose slowly, rubbing the back of his head. "Zip ties in the left lower pocket."

Quinn reached into her coat and pulled out the ties. She patted down the thug, removing a blaster and a knife. "Do you think we need to strip them?" With a grunt, she rolled him onto his stomach and secured his hands behind his back.

"If we're still here when they come around, we're toast." He helped her drag the second one into the cell. "We'll melt the lock. That'll slow them down. Marielle, here's a weapon. Do you have shoes?"

Marielle glanced at her bare feet and shook her head. "Maybe up there." She nodded at the steps. She took the weapons Quinn had removed from the unconscious man. The blaster strap went over her shoulder, then she shoved the knife into the larger guard's throat. Blood sprayed.

"Marielle!" Quinn's stomach heaved. She gritted her teeth.

"Eliminate the enemy," Marielle said. "Otherwise, they come after you."

Tony grabbed her arm before she reached the second man. "That's not how we're doing things!"

"Maybe not how *you're* doing things," Marielle said. "But I don't believe in leaving loose ends laying around." Before he could stop her, she swung around and fired her blaster into the second man's chest. The noise echoed through the tiny room and out into the hall.

"*Futz!* That was loud!" Quinn choked on the stench of burned flesh. She bolted for the door. "We need to move. Now."

Tony ran up the steps behind her, dragging Marielle with him.

They'd barely gotten halfway up when the door slammed open. Tony crouched, pulling Quinn down behind him.

Marielle stood on a lower step, aiming her blaster at the empty door. A head peeked around the corner, and Marielle fired. The *soldaty* dropped. Marielle leaped over Quinn and surged through the door, firing left and right.

"Clear," she called down the steps. "Move. Now. I hear more coming." She disappeared into the room.

They raced up the steps. Sashelle darted between them, streaking across the massive kitchen to a door. *This way.*

Quinn hurried after the caat, Tony on her heels. Marielle was nowhere in sight.

Sashelle pushed a door open with her head and slipped out. *Come.*

They followed, the door swinging to thump against them as they rammed through. Behind them, more rifle blasts. "She's alerted the whole damn house!" Tony growled.

Upstairs, the caat said. She raced across a huge dining room, darting between the chairs. Quinn and Tony followed around the end of the long table. At the far door, Quinn glanced back.

Marielle exploded into the room, flying across the polished table like a mug of beer sliding down a bar. She flipped to her feet without losing momentum and slammed into Quinn. "Move!"

They moved. Through the door into a wide hallway. Up a broad staircase, lit by a crystal chandelier. Everything blurred as Quinn focused on keeping her feet beneath her and the caat in sight. At the top of the steps, they raced down a long hallway.

Last three doors. Sashelle stopped suddenly in the middle of the hall. *GO!* She twisted around and raced back toward the stairs.

Quinn slapped the access card she'd taken from the guard against the door panel. The lock clicked. Without looking, she tossed the card across the hall to Tony. Sidestepping to present less of a target, she shoved the door open. "Francine? Fyo?"

"Coming!" Dusica called.

Quinn pressed a blaster into her hands and spun, not waiting to see if the other woman grabbed the weapon. She ran to the next door, reaching it just as Tony tossed the key to her. The door popped ajar and she shoved it open.

"RUN!" Francine screamed.

Quinn got a glimpse of the *nachal'nik* standing behind Francine, a blaster aimed over the younger woman's shoulder. Quinn lunged out of the way, taking Dusica down with her. The door hit the inside wall and bounced shut again. "GO!" Francine's voice cut off mid-yell.

"Out, now!" Tony yelled, pointing. "Follow Sashelle!"

They tore down the hallway on the heels of the caat. At the end, Sashelle swiped a tapestry with her claws, shredding it. Behind the hanging, a plain wooden door lay open, revealing stairs up and down. The caat went up.

"Really?" Quinn yelled after the animal. "Up?"

COME! The urgency in Sashelle's command left no room for doubt. Quinn bolted up the steps.

At the landing, she looked back. Tony, Dusica, and Fyo stormed into the stairwell and up the steps. Marielle stopped at the door, leaning around the jamb and firing down the hall. Quinn ran.

At the top of the steps, a door opened onto the roof. Quinn didn't know how Sashelle had opened it, but it stood wide, leading to a flat, open deck. A small hovercraft sat on the far side. Fyo raced past her, diving into the pilot's seat. Dusica pelted after him, taking the co-pilot's chair. Tony put a hand on Quinn's back, urging her into the back of the vehicle.

"No seats back here, so we'll have to hold on," Tony said. "Get down." He lay on his belly in the back of the vehicle, the door still open. As Marielle appeared at the door, Tony yelled, "I'll cover you!"

Marielle lunged to the side and sprinted around the edge of the roof. A helmet-clad head appeared in the doorway. Tony fired, and the helmet ducked. Quinn dropped to her stomach and yanked her blaster around. She peered through the rangefinder, setting the crosshairs in the center of the opening.

The hovercraft rose, jiggling a little. "Is everyone in?" Fyo hollered.

"NO!" Quinn yelled. "Marielle is over there."

The hovercraft lifted higher then swung sickeningly to the right. Quinn fought to keep her sights trained on the door as they swooped aside. Every time a helmet appeared, she squeezed off another blast. The craft dropped a bit, and then again more forcefully. Something fell across Quinn's legs.

"I'm in!" Marielle yelled. "Go!"

The vehicle sprang up, and they whooshed away.

CHAPTER 29

THE HOVERCRAFT PULLED up to a nondescript warehouse in the middle of an industrial neighborhood. Fyo got out and worked on opening the door.

"There are manual and electronic security measures," Dusica said. The others nodded, not bothering to respond. "We have to go back and get Francine." She rubbed her forehead as if trying to stave off a headache.

Fyo returned and eased the hovercraft through the now-open garage door.

"We will go back." Tony said. "But not this second. We need to contact Dareen, so we're ready to leave once we get her. Unless you have a shuttle that's uncompromised? And we need more weapons. And a plan."

"We have weapons." Fyo jumped out of the pilot's seat and hurried to the door. "Why do you think I brought you here? This safehouse has an armory. They all do."

"How many safehouses are there?" Tony followed Fyo across the garage.

"Do you have clothes here?" Quinn helped Marielle out of the rear of the craft. "And medical supplies? Marielle has minor injuries."

"We have a med pod." Fyo paused on the step. "And lots of clothes. There should be something to fit her."

Quinn stopped and looked around for Sashelle. "She was ahead of me on the stairs. I followed her to the roof. I don't know what happened after that."

"Who was?" Dusica asked.

"Sashelle," Quinn answered. "The caat."

"I'm sure she's fine," Marielle said. "Cats take care of themselves."

"She isn't just a cat," Quinn said, but Marielle shook her head and pushed through the far door.

It looked like a standard breakroom—utilitarian chairs and a table in one corner, dingy couch in another. Kitchen appliances took up one wall and a small window over the sink looked out into a parking lot. The sunrise bathed the small, barren space with pink light.

"Where are the weapons?" Tony opened a cupboard.

"Not in the kitchen." Fyo scoffed.

Tony pulled out a glass and filled it with water. "I didn't think so." Taking the glass, he followed Fyo out of the room, Marielle on their heels.

"Quinn, there should be food in the cupboards. Shelf-stable stuff," Dusica said. "I haven't eaten in hours. I'm going find Marielle some shoes." Without waiting for a reply, she followed the men out of the kitchen.

Quinn dug out food and spread it on the counter, then she made herself a sandwich. Before she finished, the others returned. Tony, Fyo, and Marielle bristled with weapons.

Dusica followed a few minutes later with an armful of things. She tossed the pile on the couch. "Go get changed," she told Marielle.

The dark-haired woman glanced at the couch then back at Dusica. They locked eyes for a few seconds, then Marielle nodded. "Hold my gun." She shoved a huge weapon at Dusica and stalked across the room, scooped up the clothing, and disappeared into the bathroom.

Quinn bit her lip to keep from laughing.

Dusica glared after Marielle, then carefully leaned the weapon in the corner and went to the sink to wash her hands. She muttered something about women who preferred guns to shoes.

"What is that thing?" Quinn pointed at the enormous tube-like device.

"Portable anti-aircraft rocket," Fyo said around a mouthful of something. "Heavy as hell, so it's not always worth the effort. If you're on foot, for example. But we've got the hovercraft."

"We can't use that again," Tony said. "They'll be watching for it. No way your nin-chuck's team didn't get a look at it. In fact, did you check for tracking? If they saw it before we ran, they'll have tagged it."

"We have a second vehicle here," Dusica said. "But we weren't tracked. It was scanned as Fyo drove it into this garage. Plus, the door to the roof hadn't been opened."

"How do you know?" Quinn asked.

"Because there would have been a smoking crater in the top of the stairs and a fog of *soldaty* ash clouding the hallway," Marielle said as she returned in clean, black clothing. She tossed a flowered blouse on a chair, shaking her head. She sat and pulled on the shoes Dusica had dropped by the couch.

Dusica glanced at her, eyes narrowed. "Who did you pay for that information?"

"I recognize the system." Marielle raised both hands in defense. "High-end security for wealthy private citizens. I'm sure you have tweaks I wouldn't know about, but when you're protecting a home, even the multi-thousand credit systems start with an off-the-shelf plan. Then you add the frills, some more lethal than others. If you don't mind maiming or killing the bad guys." She gave Tony a mock-glare.

He held up his hands. "I don't mind killing the bad guys when they're shooting at me. It was the noise I objected to. And the fact that the bad guys were tied up and unconscious. Plus, that extraction would have been a lot smoother if they hadn't known we were there."

"They knew you were there when the first guy went down," Dusica said. "Biometric monitoring is standard in *soldaty* uniforms. But I don't care about that. I want to get my sister back before the *nachal'nik* kills her."

"She won't kill her," Tony said.

"You don't know the *nachal'nik* if you think that." Dusica folded her arms over her chest.

Tony smiled and shook his head. "I know her well enough to know she won't throw away the only leverage she has. She has something we want, and we have something she wants. She'll offer a trade."

"What do we have that she wants?" Dusica asked.

Tony looked at Fyo. "Him."

CHAPTER 30

EVERYONE STARED at Tony in confusion. He hid a grin at their expressions. Looking at Fyo, it was obvious to him, but the others didn't see the resemblance.

"Why would she want him?" Dusica said. "She tried to have him killed. She's not going to trade Faina for him."

"She wants him now because she knows who he is," Tony said. "And she's thrilled she didn't succeed in eliminating him all those years ago."

"What are you talking about?" Fyo asked. "I'm the same guy I was four years ago when she firebombed our car. I'm shocked she didn't have her *soldaty* blast me the moment we landed."

"Exactly." Tony pointed at the younger man. "She didn't have you killed outright or hauled away to make an example of you. She locked you up in a luxurious estate, with your sisters as collateral for good behavior. She probably plans to take you back to Rossiya City."

"But why?" Quinn asked. "What's different?"

"She knows who Fyo *really* is." He watched Dusica closely. Did her eye twitch? She was probably an excellent poker player.

Marielle was also watching Dusica. "She knows, too. Whatever this secret is, Dusica knows. Has known for a long time."

"I believe you're correct." Tony nodded at Marielle. He turned to Fyo. "You are the *nachal'nik*'s grandson."

Dusica laughed tightly. "Outsiders are always confused by our families. *My* father's *half-brother* was the *nachal'nik*'s son, but Fyo has a different father." She glanced at Fyo. "Don't listen to Tony, he's confused."

"No, I'm not." Tony locked his gaze on Fyo. "You are the *nachal'nik*'s grandson. Your father was Matvei Nartalov, deceased son of the current *nachal'nik*. You really are the fairytale princess."

"No, you're wrong," Dusica said shrilly. "Matvei died before Fyo was born. Our mother was with my father, Taras, when Faina and I were young. Then she married Roman, Fyo's father."

"True. But Roman wasn't Fyo's father," Tony said. "Your mother conceived Fyo via artificial means, using a long-frozen sample. Fyo is the posthumous child of Matvei Nartalov. I believe your father and mother planned it, so they could wrest the Russosken from Nartalova's grip. Why the Russosken are so bent on having a hereditary ruler, I don't know, but your parents decided to create one. Fyo."

"My parents didn't speak to each other for a decade," Dusica said. "They didn't plan anything together. And then he died in that stupid rebellion."

"That stupid rebellion, in which he enlisted his ex-wife's new husband and her son?" Tony asked, pointing at Fyo. "Or that stupid rebellion that he organized to bring the *nachal'nik*'s grandson to power. Which makes more sense?"

"If he was going to claim Fyo was the new *nachal'nik*," Quinn said slowly, "wouldn't he have advertised it that way? Hey, everybody, here's the heir to the throne. Let's get rid of the old queen. Why hide it?"

"I'm sure he intended to advertise it that way." Tony nodded. "That's how I figured it out. There were whispers. He told his most trusted supporters who Fyo was. They rallied their troops and rebelled. And got put down by Nartalova's superior numbers before the word got out. They didn't tell the lower levels who he was. Only the generals."

"And those generals were all executed," Quinn said.

"You'd think they would have told me if that were the case," Fyo said.

"They didn't want you getting any ideas before the deal was done and Dusica's parents were firmly in control. Plus, you were only seventeen." Tony spun around to pin Dusica with a stare. "Right?"

Dusica dropped onto the couch. "Yes. You're right. You figured it out. Huzzah."

"What?!" Fyo yelped. "He's right? I'm that witch's grandson?"

"Of course you are." Dusica threw up her hands in disbelief. "Have you ever looked in a mirror? You look just like her! The older she gets, the more obvious it is." She shook her head. "But you're still my little brother, and I don't care about the Russosken. I care about you."

"Did she know?" Fyo demanded. "The old witch, did she know who I was when she had our car firebombed?"

"I don't think so," Dusica said. "Tony got that part right—only the highest levels of the rebellion knew who you were."

"If she had known, she wouldn't have killed you," Tony said. "She might have imprisoned you, but she's going to need a successor. That's why she wants you now."

"How did she find out he was still alive?" Dusica asked.

Tony shrugged. "Maybe she got lucky? I wasn't there when she first saw him. Did she look like she expected him?"

Dusica closed her eyes for a long moment, then shook her head. "No... Maybe. It's hard to say. She's an excellent poker player. I *think* she was surprised to see he was alive. And maybe happy? Because she already knew who he was. She must have learned about his parentage between the rebellion and now. There was a really bad period a couple years ago when she was in a foul mood all of the time. Maybe she'd learned that she'd had her own heir eliminated?"

"Doesn't really matter, does it?" Tony shrugged and picked up his sandwich. "We can be sure she knows now, and she's going to want him back. I hope that's the key to keeping Francine alive long enough to get her out. But if my plans are proceeding on schedule, the *nachal'nik* is going to be too busy to worry about any of this before long."

Dusica's eyes narrowed. "What plans?"

Tony smiled. "The new rebellion."

MAERK LEFT Liz in command of the final approach to Taniz Beta and went to check on their passenger. Amanda sat at the table in the main compartment with electronics spread out across the surface.

"What's all that?" Maerk asked.

Amanda eyed him for a moment. "It's my rebellion tracking gear."

Maerk laughed, then stopped. "Oh, you're serious."

"Deadly."

Cold dripped down Maerk's spine. He knew—theoretically—that Amanda and Tony had been "spreading the rebellion" as they traveled, but the idea that people would start shooting soon left him uneasy. "Is it safe to land on Taniz Beta?"

"Safe is a relative term." Amanda rocked a hand back and forth. "For now, you're unlikely to get killed by a stray energy beam, if that's what you're wondering. But it's going to get hot down there. Soon."

"Then why are you going?"

"Oh, I'm not," Amanda said. "I'm staying here."

"You're scheduled to leave the ship as soon as we land," Maerk said. "We check in with Taniz Beta Prime, then we drop to the dirt. You leave, we pick up our new cargo—already bought and paid for—and head back out." He made appropriate landing motions with his hands as he spoke.

"That was the plan," Amanda agreed pleasantly. "It isn't anymore."

"Have you talked to Liz about this?"

"I'm talking to you." A mini blaster appeared on the table beside her piles of equipment.

Or maybe it had been there before and Maerk hadn't noticed it. He glanced at the gun, then at her hand a few centimeters away. "Are you threatening me? On my own ship? Because it's been done before, and we've taken precautions to make sure it doesn't happen again." Thank Saint Drausinus they'd spent the credits. He hadn't thought they'd need to use the system so soon.

Amanda stood, hands held out from her sides, and stepped away from the table. "I'm not threatening you. I am giving you the benefit of my inside information. Offering a new, lucrative contract. And suggesting your cooperation would be appreciated by not only me, but by your cousin Tony."

"How about you stop threatening or suggesting in flowery words and tell me what the hell you want?" Maerk crossed his arms over his chest, trying to look intimidating.

"I want to stay in orbit around Taniz Beta, in this ship, because it's convenient." She shrugged one shoulder. "My stuff is already here. *Things* are going to start happening. Soon. This would be a good place to monitor those things. And I will pay you for the hospitality."

"You want us to stay in orbit and provide you with a mobile monitoring station," Maerk said.

"Exactly." Amanda smiled. "The pieces are all in play. My sources report the *nachal'nik*—the leader of the Russosken—is here. An unexpected bonus. We thought we'd have to hunt her down after this is all over, but I have operatives on Taniz Beta. We can decapitate the Russosken as soon as the first attacks take place, and it will just be a matter of mopping up."

"I thought the Russosken was more autonomous than that," Maerk said. "Petrov seemed to do his own thing. Even if his boss had been taken out, he would have been a formidable enemy."

"I'm not saying it's going to be easy," Amanda said. "We've spent months—years, really—putting all the pieces into the best position. Each planet will have to do their part. But that's already set up. Taking—"

"Maerk!" Liz's yell cut over Amanda's smooth words.

He backed toward the hatch to the cockpit, keeping his eyes on Amanda. "What?"

"We need to make a little detour."

Amanda started toward him, leaving the blaster on the table. "What kind of detour?"

Maerk put his arm across the opening, stopping Amanda from entering the small space. "Explain," he called over his shoulder.

"I got a message from Dareen." Liz's voice sounded clipped. She was worried. "She's here. With Quinn's kids. Alone."

CHAPTER 31

MAERK FORGOT about Amanda and spun into the cockpit. "What? How? When?"

Liz threw the message onscreen. Dareen stared out at them with Lucas beside her and Ellianne in the jump seat behind. All three looked both excited and scared.

"We came here with Dusica, Francine's sister," Dareen said. "She didn't tell us where we were going, but she had this swanky yacht. When we got here, Tony and Quinn rode to the surface with us, and Francine and Fyo went with Dusica."

"Fyo?" Amanda peered around Maerk's shoulder. Liz shushed her.

"When we landed, something seemed off," Dareen continued her report. "Tony and Quinn loaded for bear and jumped out short of the parking place. Like Tony does, when he doesn't want to be noticed. Then they told me to take off and find someplace to hide. I launched and used Tony's specialized comm gear to learn where we were. Dusica's ship and landing strip were blocking our navigation and comms because she didn't want us to know where her safehouse is. Long story. Anyway, we headed for Taniz Alpha.

"We have enough supplies for a few days, possibly a week, if necessary. I also have untraceable credits so we can dock at Taniz Alpha. I won't do that until we have to. Hopefully, you'll get this message before I have to. Or Tony and Quinn will have me come pick them up. Or something. We'll be fine." She smiled a broad, fake smile at the camera, and at the kids. "Dareen out."

"If Fyo is still alive, we need to get down there and help Tony," Amanda said before Maerk could get his thoughts together.

"Who is Fyo?" Liz threw up a hand. "Never mind. Don't care. I'm setting a course for Taniz Alpha to retrieve the kids."

"Wait," Amanda said. "Fyo is the Russosken leader's grandson. She eliminated him four years ago—long story. But if he's still alive, and here, and she knows it... This could change everything." She turned and hurried out of the cockpit. "Please don't change course yet!" she called over her shoulder. "Tony might need our help."

Maerk glanced through the hatch. Amanda threw herself down in her chair and started swiping and flicking madly at her comm gear. "She doesn't want to go to the planet. Or at least, she didn't want to a few minutes ago."

"Don't really care what she wants," Liz said. "Dareen is out here on her own. I'm going to help her."

Maerk put a hand on his ex-wife's shoulder. "Dareen is fine." He pointed at the timestamp on the frozen video. "She only sent that a few hours ago. Give her a call. She should be close enough for direct comms. Then we can figure out what's best with that one." He jabbed a thumb over his shoulder. "She was making some interesting demands a few minutes ago."

Liz froze for a second, then looked up. "What do you mean?"

He explained Amanda's proposal. "Tony might need us to extract him if things get as hot as she implied. And it sounds like now she might want to go dirtside after all."

"Well, I need a decision." Liz raised her voice to reach the lounge. "We'll be in Prime's sphere of control in about ten minutes. I need to know if I'm requesting permission to dock, land, or orbit."

Amanda hurried back into the cockpit. "Look, things are set to blow. We've got operations set up on fourteen different planets—due to kick off tonight. We don't have anything on Taniz Beta. It's a minor world as far as the Russosken are concerned, so there aren't a lot of *soldaty* here. But it has excellent comms, so we decided it would be a good location to use for command and control.

"Our operations are intended to be as independent as possible. Simple formula, really: take down the local Russosken leadership. If you decapitate an organization like this, it falls apart. The Russosken don't take good enough care of their rank and file to generate loyalty in most of them. They'd rather go home to their spouse and kids. And many of them are conscripts. They'll bolt the minute they get a chance if their leader is gone or confused." She yanked on her thick braid, thinking.

"The *nachal'nik* is here, and so is her grandson. This is the best possible opportunity to take out the leadership for the whole thing. I want to go to the planet. If you can't take me there, drop me at the station. I'm sure there are shuttles from Prime to the surface on a regular schedule." She looked from one to the other. "Our original deal was a dirtside drop, but if you can get me to Prime, you'll still get your full payment. Just help me get there."

"If Tony's there, we need to check in with him." Liz glanced at Maerk. "You're right, Dareen will be fine. I'll send her a message to contact Lou if she doesn't hear from us in the next three days. That gives us plenty of time to drop Amanda and find Tony. Are we still headed for Mederdra Field? Prime is signaling." She pointed to a light that had started blinking red.

"Yes," Amanda said. "Mederdra Field. Thanks."

DUSICA, Fyo, Marielle, and Quinn gathered around the table in the breakroom. Cups and plates lay forgotten as they peered at a map projected above the flat surface. A pile of napkins with notes scribbled on them lay in front of Tony's empty chair. Quinn riffled through them, looking for something useful. They mostly appeared to be doodles.

"They will have locked the external doors," Dusica said. "Now that they know the cellar can access the house." She glared at Quinn.

"Number one," Quinn said coldly, "we don't know that they know that. They know we came in through the basement, but we made sure the access to the cellar was closed. And number two, would you have preferred we left you there?"

"You should have had a better plan," Dusica said, her voice raised. "So we didn't have to leave her—"

"*We* should have come up with a better plan?" Quinn snarled. "You brought us here to your 'safehouse.' You're the one with the local contacts."

"Stop." Anger was clear in Marielle's soft voice. The others stopped mid-argument and stared at her. "What's done is done. We're all tired and worried. Let's come up with a plan to get Francine out of there."

"If they're still there," Fyo said morosely. "How do we know the old witch didn't take her off-planet?"

"They're still there," Quinn said without thinking. Sashelle would tell her if Francine was moved. She wasn't sure *how* she knew the caat could reach her this far away, but she was certain.

Maybe because I made it known to you, Sashelle said. *You aren't that far away.*

"How do you know?" Dusica demanded.

"We have someone watching the house." Quinn wished she'd kept her mouth shut.

"Who?" Dusica glared at her. "You said you don't have any local contacts. How do we know your informant hasn't sold us out?"

Quinn snorted. "I can guarantee she hasn't sold us out."

Fyo's brows furled. "When did this person contact you?"

Quinn held up a hand to ward off questions. "She'll let me know if anyone leaves your estate. That's all you need to know." She sure as hell wasn't going to tell them her contact was a caat. And she wasn't one hundred percent sure Sashelle would contact her if the *nachal'nik* left the estate *without* Francine. A ghost of a chuckle echoed in her head.

The door opened, and Tony strode in from the parking lot. "We've got help on the way. Liz and Maerk are landing at Mederdra Field in about twenty minutes." He glanced at Quinn. "Liz said Dareen and the kids got away safe. They're on their way to Taniz Alpha. Amanda is with Liz and Maerk, though. She's very interested in 'meeting' the *nachal'nik*. How many people will that hovercraft carry?"

"It was built for four," Fyo said. "But we modified it to make it faster and to carry cargo. It has jump seats in the back for eight adults."

"Perfect." Tony rubbed his hands together. "You two up front, three of us plus Liz, Maerk and Amanda in the back. And Francine, after we free her. Still room for our agent." He winked at Quinn. "How long will it take to get to Mederdra? That's not where we landed."

"It is. Mederdra is a cargo field that uses the same runway as Argos." Dusica stared at Tony for a few seconds. "Faina told me about Liz and Maerk. Who is this Amanda person?"

"She's working on breaking the Russosken grip on this sector of the Federation." Tony smiled. "And she said things are going to get hot tonight."

"She will help me get my sister back?"

"Yes," Tony replied patiently. "I told you, she wants to meet the *nachal'nik*. Since they're in the same place..."

"She wants to meet the *nachal'nik*?" Fyo asked. "Is that a euphemism for 'kill'? Because I get first dibs. She tried to kill me once. Paybacks are a bitch."

"No one gets dibs in a war," Tony said coldly.

Behind him, Marielle grunted in agreement. "If you get the shot, you take it. You don't hold off for someone with a grudge. This isn't a game."

Fyo huffed out a sigh and rolled his eyes. "Fine. Let's go."

As they gathered their weapons and moved to the garage, Quinn grabbed Tony's arm. "You sure he'd be a better *nachal'nik?*"

Tony's lip curled on one side. "Better, no. But definitely not worse. At least not in the short run. I'm counting on Francine to keep him in line long-term."

"Have you met Francine?" Quinn murmured. "Long-term doesn't appear to be her strong suit."

In the back of the hangar-like garage, Fyo pushed aside a huge door. Another hovercraft lay there, similar in design to the first, but this one was painted white with a bland corporate logo on the side. They climbed into the rear compartment after Fyo showed them how to open the hidden jump seats. They strapped in and slid the doors shut. Fyo drove again, with Dusica in the co-pilot's seat.

"It's about ten minutes from here," Dusica said, before closing the door between the two compartments.

"I don't like being in the back," Marielle muttered. "No windows, and how do we know they're really taking us to the field? Maybe they're going to try to cut a deal with the *nachal'nik* by handing us over."

"Since Fyo is the one the nin-chuck wants, I doubt they'd be able to cut a deal," Tony said.

"No, but they could sell us out to the local Russosken leader and take off," Marielle suggested. "The two of them have been in hiding together for a long time. Maybe they'd be willing to leave Francine behind rather than risk their own safety."

"I heard that," Dusica's voice said through the intercom. "And while the idea makes my blood boil, I can see how you might come to that conclusion. I assure you, my sister is my top priority."

"What if you have to choose between Fyo and Francine?" Marielle asked.

There was silence. "I won't let that happen," Dusica said. "Oh, and by the way, I *am* the local Russosken leader."

CHAPTER 32

TONY RAISED his brows at Quinn. It made sense that Dusica ran this planet. "That could be a problem. I don't know what Amanda's got planned for the local rebellion, but the plans on other planets have involved taking out the leaders."

"I'm not worried," Dusica said. "I treat my people very well. They will not betray me."

Was there a faint tremor in her voice? "I hope you're right," Tony said. "We'll see what Amanda says soon enough."

"ETA is five minutes," Fyo said. "We aren't going to trade them, are we?" His low question came through the intercom loud and clear. It went dead with a snap.

"I guess we'll have to trust," Tony said. "Any word from our 'local agent'?"

"She's been quiet," Quinn said. "Speaking of agents, Amanda must have a local contact."

"I'm not sure. We didn't have time for details."

They rode in silence for a while. The vehicle stopped a couple of times, then the intercom snapped on again. "We're here. I see a ship that matches your description," Dusica said. "It's buttoned up tight. Someone should go meet them."

"Quinn, give Liz a call," Tony said. "I'm getting out so they can see we aren't under duress." He didn't mention the family duress protocols—neither Marielle nor the Zielinskys needed to know.

Marielle unclipped her harness and lifted her massive weapon. She dropped to her belly, nose near the door. "I'll cover you. Quinn, watch that side."

He was out before Quinn reached the floor. The door slid almost shut, with the nose of Marielle's anti-aircraft rocket protruding through the gap. A click and metallic scraping accompanied Quinn opening the far side. Tony crouched beside the hovercraft's skirt, scanning the field.

The *Swan* stood about fifty meters away. When he was confident they weren't being watched, he stood. With his back to the vehicle, he made the hand signals Liz would recognize.

"Nothing moving on this side," Quinn whispered through the earbud he still wore. "Liz says we should come closer."

He hooked his fingers into the handle and pulled the door farther open. Marielle patted the floor next to her head, and he sat there, holding the strap from one of the empty jump seats.

The craft hissed across the tarmac, stopping a few meters from the *Swan's* hatch. It popped open as they arrived, and Maerk peeked out. "Is it safe?" he called in a stage whisper.

Tony rolled his eyes. Maerk was hopeless at stealth. "Safe enough. We're coming in."

"Should someone stay with the vehicle?" Quinn asked.

"I'm sure Liz has the cams watching. And I'll put up a drone. Give me a minute." Tony pulled out his bug-sized flying camera as the others climbed down from the craft. "Quinn, make the intros, will you?"

"Sure." She led the others to the hatch, and they disappeared inside.

Tony put his drone on a pre-programmed observation orbit, then set the second one on a larger flight plan around the entire field.

Once he was happy with their reporting, he followed the rest into the airlock.

Liz waited for him there. She squeezed him in a tight bear hug, then pulled back and punched him in the arm. Hard. It was her traditional greeting after he'd been out on a mission. Her way of saying, "I missed you, you jerk. You should be more careful."

Tony grinned and ruffled her hair.

She slapped his hand away. "Treat your elders with more respect, punk."

"Yes, Auntie Liz."

"Ugh, don't call me auntie." She cycled the inner door, and they hurried into the lounge.

"What's the sitrep?" Tony asked as soon as he reached the table. The others had gathered there, and Maerk brought over a bottle of water and glasses.

"Nice to see you too, Tony." Amanda fluttered her eyelashes with a flirtatious smile.

"Nice to be seen." Tony smirked. "Sitrep?"

Amanda huffed a disappointed sigh and flicked her comtab. A star map hovered over the coffee table, and they all turned to look. "The planets in blue are under Russosken control. Red planets are pure Federation. The oscillating glow indicates worlds that will be launching operations in a few hours." She looked at the time on the screen. "Strike that. The first attack will be in one hour, on Sendarine, and then they'll spread across this area." She waved at the projection, and the blue planets faded to green in a wave across the display.

"Isn't that Lunesco?" Quinn asked, pointing at one of the green dots.

"Yes," Amanda said. "Green means they're on our side. The *nachal'nik* has a force headed that direction, which was what prompted the launch of this operation. They jumped into the system yesterday. We timed it for when they are far enough from the jump beacons to create a significant delay in their ability to return to

Rossiya. We had assumed the *nachal'nik* would be there. Now that we know she's here, we expect that force to come this way as soon as they twig to the attacks."

"They could continue to Lunesco, though?" Quinn asked.

"They could," Amanda agreed. "But we beefed up Doug's system, so he should be able to handle most of them. Auntie B will have to mop up anything that gets through, but she's more than capable. I'm not worried about them. I am concerned about here." Amanda pointed at the ground.

"Once word of the operation gets out, we believe the *nachal'nik* will recall the forces she sent to Lunesco. But she'll bring them here, because she's here. I'm shocked she left Rossiya during the 'Lunesco Reprimand.' That's what they call it." She looked at Dusica. "What will happen if they come to Taniz Beta?"

Dusica's eyes went wide, and she froze. Expressions of surprise, anger, and fear passed swiftly over her face before her jaw hardened. "Up until today, she would have used me as liaison between my forces and hers. They would have set up a security perimeter around the planet. Her team would have control over the planetary defense forces. Now?" She shook her head. "I don't know. She'll probably try to put Anatoly Serinsky in charge of the local forces." Her lip curled. "He's her primary enforcer, and he's an animal."

"How will your people respond?" Amanda's gaze locked on Dusica's face.

"If I can get a message to them, they will subvert her command," Dusica said. "I imagine she's told them I'm injured, and she's taking control until I'm recovered. If they think she's being helpful, not taking over..."

"Will she bother?" Fyo asked. "In my experience, she prefers to brag about her successes. Won't she rant about what a disappointment you have been and how she's swooped in to pick up the pieces and save the day?"

"That sounds like her," Tony put in.

"Surely she's smart enough to hide her cards." Marielle's deep voice was skeptical. "Staying on top of the Russosken must require some finesse."

Fyo laughed. "You aren't very familiar with us, are you? Bragging about conquests is a Russosken ritual. Every coup ever ends with the winner broadcasting their success."

"*Ends* that way," Tony said. "They still use subterfuge in the middle. Don't assume they're careless or stupid. Based on my few seconds of contact with her, and *years* of research, I think she'll do exactly what Dusica said—claim to be helping. Easiest way of taking control. When it's all over, and they've won, she'll execute anyone who wasn't on her side. Including anyone loyal to Dusica."

Dusica nodded in agreement.

"What happens if we eliminate her early on?" Amanda said. "Say, before she even knows about the rest of the operation?"

"If that was easy to do, someone would have already done it," Quinn said.

"I didn't say it would be easy," Amanda said.

"We have a couple advantages," Tony said with a sly smile. "We have her grandson. And the commander of the local forces is on our side." He nodded at Dusica. "Let's draw up a plan to make use of those resources."

QUINN GOT up and stretched her back. They'd been planning for hours and she needed a break. She poured herself another glass of water and paced around the outer edge of the room. Tony, Dusica, and Amanda still had their heads close together, discussing details.

"We should probably move the hovercraft," Fyo said from the couch. He'd been flicking through local screens since the beginning. "It's been sitting out there all this time for anyone to see."

Liz shrugged. "We frequently have trucks parked near us. If anyone's looking, they'll assume you're making a delivery. The company name is vague enough you could be anything. Food delivery, equipment repair, clothing designer."

Fyo laughed and struck a pose. "I do have a flair for fashion. But I still think I should move it. I could take it back to the warehouse."

"How would you get back here?" Liz shook her head. "We'll need it later for transport. I'll open up the cargo hold, and you can drive it inside. Make sure no one is watching when you do."

"Good idea." Quinn picked up Tony's comtab. "There's no activity at this end of the field." She widened the view from the drones. "Now's as good a time as any. With the cargo ramp facing the fence, you should be protected from casual observation." She dropped the device gently on the coffee table.

Fyo grinned and grabbed his jacket. "See you in a few."

"Liz!" Tony called. "Can you look at this?"

"Sure. Gimme a sec." She turned to Quinn. "Open the hold for Fyo, will you? Big red button at the back. You can't miss it."

Quinn laughed. "I've helped you load cargo before. I think I know how to open the ramp." She set her glass on the counter and made her way to the back of the ship. The heavy hatch clanged shut, and she stopped to dog it. With the way things were going, it didn't hurt to take extra care.

She hurried across the empty hold and found the control panel near the ramp. It wasn't really a red button, but she'd operated the ramp several times, and it still responded to her handprint. The massive door groaned as the seal released, then ratcheted down in a click-and-thump rhythm. When it reached level, she stepped out and rode the door to the ground.

Waves of damp heat washed over her. The air was sweet and heavy with earthy and floral scents. It was late afternoon, and the sun shone into her eyes, glinting off the white stripes painted on the tarmac. Thick foliage pushed against the force fence guarding the boundary of the shuttle field. Movement caught her eye, and she swung around. A small, hairy animal swung from one of the twisted trees before disappearing behind the leaves.

The hovercraft hummed as it rose from the ground. Quinn stepped off the ramp and walked to the side of the ship to wave at Fyo. "Bring it in!"

Fyo waved back, then spun the craft until it faced away from the ship. What was the boy doing? When he started to pull away, Quinn swore. She knew he was up to something, and it would likely get them all killed. She launched herself at the craft, pushing her legs as fast as she could. She managed to get her fingers into the half-open rear door. With a heave and a scream, she hurled herself into the departing vehicle.

CHAPTER 33

"WHAT THE HELL ARE YOU DOING?" Quinn demanded as she yanked open the door to the front of the hovercraft. "This is no time for joyriding around the field!"

With a growl, Fyo darted a glare over his shoulder. "What are you doing here? Get out!"

"I will not." Quinn threw herself into the co-pilot's seat. "Where are you going?"

"To get Faina!" Fyo pulled up to the automated gate and waited for it to open.

"What?" Quinn reached over and pressed the power button. "Are you crazy?"

The hovercraft sank to the road.

"What are you doing?"

"I'm stopping you from getting killed," Quinn said. "Or getting your sister killed. Those experts back there are making detailed plans to retrieve your sister. What makes you think you can do better on your own? If you want to save her, go back there and help them."

"They don't want my help," Fyo said. "They treat me like a child."

Quinn's nose wrinkled. They had ignored almost everything Fyo had said. Eventually, he'd given up and wandered away to play with the video screen. "I know. They don't listen to me, either. They're the experts."

"Yeah, but I've lived here all my—" A horn cut him off. "There's someone behind us. We're blocking the gate."

Quinn gestured for him to pull forward. "Let's find somewhere to talk. How about that parking lot?"

Fyo powered up the hovercraft, drove it into a shopping center, and parked across three slots.

"Really?" Quinn said. "You're one of those people?"

"I don't want anyone scratching my paint," Fyo said defiantly.

"Because you care about the paint on a carpet cleaning hovercraft?"

"Yes," Fyo said sullenly. "No. But there's no one here."

"True enough." She looked around the empty lot. "That restaurant looks pretty busy. Is it any good?"

Fyo's eyes lit up. "That's Marcelo's. Excellent food."

"Great, I'm starved." Quinn opened her door. "Let's get dinner. Then we can talk."

They placed an enormous order at the to-go window and waited in the bar. Quinn had a fizzy fruit drink, while Fyo had a beer. She waited until he'd drunk about half of it and shoveled most of a plate of appetizers into his mouth. "What was your plan?"

"I dunno," Fyo said. "I thought if I could find Sergei Wernerov—he's Dusi's chief of staff—I could get him to help me. Maybe warn him about the stuff that's going on and break Faina out."

"This Sergei is loyal to your sister?"

"Yeah, he'd do anything for her. He was a friend of her dad's. For some reason, he thinks the car bomb was his fault. He's the only one who knows I'm Fyotor. Everyone else calls me Lev. They think I'm—Actually, I'm not sure who they think I am. A friend of Dusi's? But Sergei knows I'm Fyo, and he's sworn to protect me."

"Do you think he knows about your real parentage?"

Fyo's lips twisted. "I suppose he must know. He and Dusi's dad were close. Yeah, I guess so."

"Does Sergei live on the estate? Do you think the nin-chuck would have hurt him?"

Fyo's lips twitched at the mispronunciation, and he laughed. "Sergei lives on the *real* estate. That place the *nachal'nik* took us is Dusi's townhome. The estate is about twenty klicks that way." He pointed toward the shuttle field.

"Would she have called him into town?" Quinn asked. If she did, the man was probably dead already.

"If she knows about him," Fyo said. "Dusi has all kinds of contingency plans. The staff at the townhouse know if anyone but her shows up, they're to implement one of those plans. Most of them include sending a warning to Sergei then cutting off all communications with the estate. Plus the rescue protocols." He grinned. "That's why it was so easy for you and Tony to break in."

Quinn huffed out a surprised breath. "That's exactly what Tony said. That man is too smart." Her comtab pinged. She held it up. "The food is ready. Let's take it back to the ship. There's enough for everyone, and they probably won't have noticed we're gone," she lied. Tony had texted her a few minutes after they arrived at the restaurant, but she told him not to worry. "You can tell them about your plan to contact Sergei and we'll go from there, okay?"

"I guess I was hangry." He chugged the end of his beer and set the bottle on the table. "You drive. I'll eat. If there's any left, I'll share." He grabbed the bags of food and followed her out the door.

THERE WAS plenty of food left; Quinn had ordered enough for an army. She and Fyo spread the offerings across the kitchen counter and set a stack of plates and cutlery at one end, then they both filled plates and moved to the couch.

"I can't believe you have room for more." Quinn eyed the huge heap of food on Fyo's plate.

"Excellent metabolism." Fyo patted his belly.

"Thanks for this." Tony hefted his own massive serving and sat in the armchair near Fyo. "It occurs to me you might have valuable information."

Fyo shot a glare at Quinn. She shook her head and raised her eyebrows. "Didn't say a word." Of course, she'd texted Tony, but that didn't count as saying words, did it?

"Maybe Sergei could help." Fyo said.

"Who's Sergei?" Tony skewered a piece of meat.

"He's no one important," Dusica said quickly.

Fyo glanced at his sister, then back at Quinn. She made a face and a "go-on" motion with her hands. "Sergei runs the estate. He knows everyone. If anything happens to Dusica, he's the second-in-command."

He said it without emotion, as if the chain of command was academic. Quinn wondered if he ever felt slighted that he wasn't second.

"Fyo!" Dusica hissed.

"What?" Fyo demanded. "These people are helping us rescue our sister from our own clan. They deserve to know about any assets that could be helpful. You think sending them in blind is a better plan?"

"They aren't blind!" Dusica snarled. "They knew everything they needed to know about the townhouse, the staff, and the *nachal'nik's* local support. They don't need to know all our secrets!"

"Why not?" Fyo dropped his plate on a side table with a loud crack. "They're risking everything for us. Or is the estate your backup plan? If everything falls apart, you'll leave them here to fight the *nachal'nik,* and we'll hide away on the estate?"

Dusica's face went pale.

"That's it, isn't it?" Fyo leapt to his feet and advanced on his sister. "You were keeping an ace in the hole."

"I have been protecting you your whole life!" Dusica met him in the center of the room. "You have no idea how much work has gone into creating a safe place for you. Someplace no one else can find you. And now you're spilling to these outsiders?" She switched languages and spit out a torrent of unrecognizable syllables.

"My translation program doesn't recognize this language," Tony said in surprise. He pulled out his comtab and tapped it. "Nope, nothing. Remarkable." He put it away and went back to eating.

"You don't seem too worried about Dusica's secrets," Quinn said.

He shrugged, ignoring the raging argument continuing above their heads. "We knew she was holding back—that she had another bolt-hole. I didn't think it was pertinent."

"And we knew she'd abandon us if things got too hot." Amanda dropped onto the arm of Tony's chair as if she owned it. "We included that in our calculations."

"But what about this Sergei guy?" Quinn turned in her seat so she could keep an eye on the screaming siblings. Maerk sat at one end of the table, watching them avidly, while Liz continued to work her way through her plate without a blink.

"What's his role?" Tony asked. "What can he do for us?"

"Fyo said he's in charge of Dusica's estate," Quinn said. "He's her second-in-command, but the *nachal'nik* doesn't know anything about him. I suppose he can provide sanctuary if things go bad."

"Sergei?" Amanda's eyes unfocused, then her head shook. "I don't know anything about him, either. That's really odd. I thought I had a good catalog of all the Russosken leadership."

"I don't know that he's technically Russosken." Quinn picked at her remaining food. "At least, not Russosken leadership. Dusica has her own, separate network. I'm sure there's some overlap, but the chain of command would be distinct."

Amanda nodded. "That's excellent. We'll leave Sergei out of this for now. Once we've finished the coup, he might be our ticket to rebuilding."

Dusica screamed something, and Fyo fell silent. The siblings glared at each other for a few seconds, bodies tense, before Fyo slumped and whispered something to his sister. Her face crumpled and she threw herself at him.

After a brief hug, Dusica stepped back, her face blank, and turned to face the others. "I apologize for that outburst."

Fyo made a half-bow in their direction. "I, too."

Tony turned to look at the pair. "Can this Sergei help us get Francine out of the nin-chuck's hands?"

Dusica and Fyo exchanged a look, then both shook their heads. "He can give us a place to hide afterwards," Fyo said. "But he can't help with the raid."

"Fair enough." Tony held out Fyo's nearly-full plate. "Dusica, eat. Fyo, take a look at the plans on the table and tell me what you think. I'm going to finish my dinner."

CHAPTER 34

AS DUSK FELL on the shuttle field, the hovercraft eased out of the *Swan's* cargo hold. It closed behind them, and they whisked across the tarmac, giving a wide berth to a ship unloading across the way. Quinn sat in back of the cargo area with Tony. Marielle and Amanda rode near door to the cab; Fyo drove and Dusica rode shotgun. The door between the front and rear compartments remained open, and Quinn shifted so she could peer through the windshield.

Beside her, Tony stiffened, then relaxed. He bumped his shoulder against hers. "You worried?"

"I'm not a professional extraction specialist, so yeah." Quinn leaned against his muscular arm. "But I have faith in your plans and your spectacular luck."

"Luck is ninety percent planning."

Did his cheek brush against her hair, or was that the movement of the vehicle? Quinn didn't care at the moment. She was too keyed up in anticipation. She glanced around the space, but Marielle and Amanda were both engrossed in their comtabs. She settled more comfortably against Tony. "Do you believe in coincidence?"

"Yes and no," he said. "I like to think everything is part of a bigger plan."

"So, fate?"

"No, not that either." Tony scratched his nose. "I think there's an order—maybe it's God, maybe it's the universe—they're kind of the same thing. But we have free will, so we can mess up the order. In my experience, messing with the natural order is a bad long-term choice, regardless of how attractive it looks at the moment."

"Some people might argue taking down the leader of an organization that has existed for centuries is going against the natural order."

"We're not taking her down, we're making a substitution," Tony said. "I don't think the universe cares who's in charge. If we leave a void, then chaos steps in. But if we transition to something else—some other form of order—then we're in good shape."

Marielle snorted. "I say we take out the bad guys and let the universe fend for itself."

Amanda nodded, looking up from her device. "You and me both, sister. Looks like we're here."

As they unbuckled, Tony ran a comm check. When everyone in the vehicle had replied, he flicked his external link. "Liz?"

"I'm here." Her voice came through the earbuds as if she was in the same room, rather than klicks away in the ship. "We're ready for a fast departure, if necessary."

"The bike is fully charged and I'm in place," Maerk said from a few streets away. "Ready with the distraction. I wish we were with you instead of hiding here."

"I wish Fyo was back on the ship," Dusica muttered.

Fyo glared.

"What?" Dusica snapped. "I've been keeping you safe my whole life."

"You keep saying that," Fyo complained, "but I've only been 'dead' for four years. Before that, you never paid any attention to me at all."

"Don't you know anything about the Russosken?" Dusica sounded as if she was proud that he didn't. "Never let anyone else know your weak point. You're mine. You always have been."

Marielle groaned. "Isn't that sweet? Can we please get to work? I have a friend to save. I thought she was one of your weak points, too?"

"If she was, I wouldn't tell you," Dusica muttered. "Weren't you listening?"

"Enough." Tony swung his weapon off his shoulder and made eye contact with each of them as he said their names. "Fyo, you're with Quinn. You'll take control of the surveillance system. Dusica, you're with me. Our goal is to get Francine as soon as we clear the way. Amanda, you're in the truck. Join up with Marielle when we get inside. Let's go." He slid the door open. In silence, they jumped out of the vehicle. Amanda moved to the cab of the vehicle and drove away. Tony led the others along a wide alley with a wall on one side and well-manicured jungle on the other.

Took you long enough, Sashelle said inside Quinn's head.

"We needed a plan," Quinn said. "You were welcome to join us."

I was watching. Her eyes glinted as she paced along at Quinn's side.

"Are you bigger?" Quinn asked. Sashelle was huge by housecat standards, but tonight, she seemed even larger. The top of her ears twitched near Quinn's hip, and Quinn was not a short woman.

Predictably, the caat didn't answer.

"I see your friend is back," Marielle whispered through the comm. "Is she your 'watcher'?"

Quinn stumbled. "You think the caat is an agent?"

"I've heard of stranger things," Marielle said. "A trained working animal with a camera could provide excellent surveillance."

Sashelle hissed.

"It's not quite like that," Quinn said. "Sashelle is much more independent."

Marielle gave her a thoughtful glance, then looked at the caat again in silence.

Tony flung up a hand, and they stopped in the shadow of a huge tree. "The house is just ahead. Amanda, you ready?"

"Let's do this."

The hovercraft hissed toward them from the other end of the alley. At the back of Dusica's house, it stopped. Dusica pressed her comtab, and the gate opened. The vehicle pulled through and the gate clanged shut, bouncing a little from the force. The hovercraft drove on.

Watching her comtab, Dusica counted down. "Three, two, one, now!" Together, they raced to the gate and pulled it open far enough to slip between the open jaws. Inside the compound, they melted into the bushes.

"Housekeeping is always a risk," Marielle muttered to Quinn where they crouched in the bushes. "Especially when you take over someone else's house."

"You've done this a lot?" Quinn watched the hovercraft pull up to the door on the "tail-ward" side of the house. A purring chuckle slipped through her mind.

"I'm not usually on the attacking end," Marielle replied. "But I've secured enough residences to know you always check housekeeping. They have keys for everything and show up at inconvenient times." Her teeth glinted in the failing light. "Luckily for us, the *nachal'nik*'s boys aren't as experienced as we are."

"They're used to moving into already-secure buildings," Dusica agreed. "But don't forget—as soon as the first armored *soldaty* goes down, the others will know something is up. Biometric monitoring is standard."

"Good reminder, but keep the rest of the chatter down," Tony said. "Let's go."

They made their way across the large back yard, stopping beneath the rear windows. The hovercraft door opened and Amanda got out, wearing a SwifKlens uniform. As she pulled out a hover cart, the door of the house slammed open and three uniformed *Russosken* spilled out to surround Amanda.

"Halt!"

Amanda spun around, her eyes wide. "Who are you?"

"Hands up!" one of the *soldaty* yelled. "Against the car." A second one grabbed Amanda's arm and spun her around, slamming her against the vehicle.

"Ow!" Amanda yelled. "Let me go! I'm going to file a complaint!"

A tooth-rattling boom rumbled through the neighborhood. Down the alley, the empty shed Dusica had identified exploded in flames right on time. Marielle took aim.

"What the—" the leader started to yell. He slumped to the ground. The other two collapsed in quick succession.

Marielle smiled at Quinn over her weapon, her eyes cold and feral.

Quinn shivered.

"Go!" Tony hissed through the earbuds. "We're on the clock!"

Amanda leaned into the hovercraft and hit the auto-return button. The vehicle rose and slid away toward the gate. Marielle stalked into the house, moving as gracefully as Sashelle, close on her heels. Quinn followed them carefully, not wanting to be the one who alerted the enemy. They padded up the stairs with Tony, Dusica, Amanda, and Fyo bringing up the rear.

At the top, Marielle froze. She held up two fingers and gestured to the right.

Two people coming from the living room, Sashelle told Quinn.

Quinn narrowed her eyes at the caat. *I know what the signals mean*, she thought as clearly as possible.

Sashelle's tail twitched.

The door whisked open, followed by two pops and two thuds.

"Remember, don't shoot anyone not in uniform," Dusica whispered through the comm system. "The civilians are loyal to me."

Marielle nodded curtly and ghosted through the kitchen door. Something thudded. "Clear."

Leaving the others in the kitchen, Fyo led Quinn down a back hall past several plain wooden doors. At the third one, he stopped and pointed. Quinn put her back against the wall beside the door and held up three fingers. Fyo copied her stance on the far side, his hand hovering over the access panel.

She counted down. Three. Two. One.

When the last finger went down, Fyo pressed his palm to the panel. The door whooshed open, and Quinn darted in, crouching low, weapon aimed.

Dim light greeted them. An ancient-looking man sat in a chair pushed away from the bank of computer monitors that lit up the far wall. His hands were already rising before Quinn brought the weapon around to point at him.

"Don't shoot," the old man said. "I'm not touching anything."

"Wilfrud, it's me." Fyo crossed to the old man's side. "Are you okay? Did they hurt you?"

"Lev!" Wilfrud cried.

Quinn and Fyo shushed him.

"Sorry," the old man whispered. "I'm so happy to see you. Is that really *Ledi* Faina up there with the *nachal'nik*?" He pointed at the screens.

Quinn kept her eyes on the old man, but he didn't so much as twitch.

"Yes, that's her," Fyo said. "We're coming to get her out."

"The *nachal'nik* has a dozen *soldaty* with her," Wilfrud said. "Four are assassins—including Anatoly Serinsky. The rest are regular *soldaty*. In fact, a couple are new recruits. She wasn't expecting any trouble."

"She's down by four," Quinn replied with a laugh. "But I don't know which four. How do you know what their specialties are?"

The old man laughed. "I looked them up. This system has access to the highest level of Russosken databases. You got one of the assassins. Good work."

She glanced at Fyo.

His eyebrows rose. "Dusi *is* a member of the ruling party, so she has access to sensitive information. Why didn't the *nachal'nik* replace you when they took the house? And where's Serinsky?"

"He's with her." Wilfrud grinned. "She left me in control of surveillance because I've been feeding her information for years. She thinks I work for her."

"You've been doing what?" Fyo's voice amped up, and Quinn shushed him.

"He's a double agent," she said. "Or triple. I assume Dusica knows what you've been doing?"

"Of course," Wilfrud said. "My loyalty to *Ledi* Dusica is unquestionable."

"I'm questioning it," Fyo retorted.

"I'm not a hundred percent sold, either," Quinn said.

"Fine, not *unquestionable*," Wilfrud grumbled. "But I am loyal to her. Anything I do for the *nachal'nik*, I have done at *Ledi* Dusica's behest or with her full knowledge and backing."

Quinn went to the computer and started swiping screens to find the ones she needed. "Two guards on the main stairs," she told the rest of the team. "One on the back. Which ones are the assassins?"

Wilfrud looked at the screen, then pulled a folded piece of paper from his pocket. He consulted it and pointed at the screen. "That one. Serinsky and the other one are in the suite with her. They are very dangerous."

"So are we." She relayed the information to the others.

"Going up the back stairs now," Tony answered.

"We've got the front," Marielle said. "I'll take care of the assassin."

"Roger." Quinn nudged Fyo. "Time to go. You can chat later." She plugged a data-card into the computer system. "This will let you talk to me, Wilfrud. Tell me if anything changes. Anything at all."

"Yes, ma'am," Wilfrud replied. "Keep *Ledi* Dusica safe."

"I'll do my best." She nodded at the old man and headed out the door.

CHAPTER 35

FRANCINE SAT in a plush chair in the corner of a well-appointed office. The seat cushion was deep enough that getting out of it could be difficult with her arms tied together. Difficult, but not impossible. She leaned against the thickly-padded back, enjoying the feel of the silky pile against her arms and legs.

She still wore the clothes she'd arrived in—a short skirt and sleeveless top. Not the best apparel for running or fighting, but it allowed freedom of movement, so she wouldn't complain. She'd kicked off the high-heeled sandals hours ago, both because they had rubbed her toes raw and because running would be easier barefoot. When one had been captured, being prepared to assist in the rescue was one's first priority.

She chuckled internally at the tone her thoughts had taken. Being in these surroundings brought back all the old habits: the diction trained into her by her mother, the impulse to keep all entrances within view, and petrifying fear of the *nachal'nik*. But she wouldn't let that stop her. She'd fought her way to freedom once before; she'd do it again.

A deep boom rumbled through the house, shaking it. "Was that an explosion?"

The other occupant of the room, the *nachal'nik*, ignored her. The old woman swiped the display projected above the desk, paging through screen after screen.

That was a bomb, Sashelle said. *Fire is consuming a small building nearby. Humans are brutal. When caats fight, we do it honorably, one-on-one. Not blanket attacks on wide swathes of the innocent population.*

Francine bit back an almost hysterical laugh. *You're right, humans are barbaric. Especially on Russosken-controlled planets. I thought Dusica said the locals love her.*

I suspect the locals know the old queen is here. Sashelle stalked into view on the ledge outside the window. *The Purveyor and the Stealthy One are here, too. With your littermates, the Sentinel, and another.*

A vision of Amanda McLasten appeared in her mind. "Great." She glanced at Nartalova, but the old woman didn't pay her any attention. *What's the plan?*

They have entered the house and will take out all opposition, Sashelle answered with an almost audible shrug.

Time to get ready to leave, then. Moving slowly to avoid attracting the *nachal'nik's* attention, Francine slid to the front of her seat. They hadn't bothered securing her legs, since the *nachal'nik* was lethal in her own right and her guards were just outside the door. Francine measured the distance between herself and the old woman's scrawny neck. Two steps, possibly three. Nartalova was in excellent shape for her age, but she was still well into her eighth decade. The question was whether Francine could silence her before she alerted the guards.

She stretched her arms and legs slowly, making sure nothing was asleep. She needed all her limbs in working order. *You coming inside?* she asked the caat.

The humans have everything under control. And the blue fire is still on the windows. I shall wait here and observe.

Francine chuckled.

"You find something amusing, Faina?" Nartalova asked.

"No." Francine belligerently neglected to add the expected title. Being in the *nachal'nik's* presence might return her to a childlike state of nervousness, so she'd take her wins where she could get them.

"No what?" the *nachal'nik* called her bluff.

"No, you old witch." The words tumbled out of her mouth before she could stop them.

"What did you call me?" Nartalova stood and stalked across the room.

"Old witch. Or do you prefer skanky bitch?" Francine's heart pounded in her chest. Why were these words coming out of her mouth? She'd seen the *nachal'nik* kill for lesser insults. She wouldn't hesitate to eliminate Francine.

Except she already had. Maybe she was worth more alive than dead now? But she didn't want to test that theory.

"You will apologize for that remark," Nartalova said. "Now."

"Not gonna happen." The response still surprised her, but she didn't fight it. If her inner bad-ass was coming out to play, maybe she should trust it.

It's not your inner bad-ass, idiot, Sashelle said. *It's me. You should definitely trust.*

Francine's lips curled up. The caat hadn't steered her wrong yet.

Nartalova jammed her sharp nails into Francine's thick blonde hair and dragged her head upward. Francine drove her feet against the floor, surging to her feet. Catching the *nachal'nik* off balance, she slammed her head under the old woman's chin, forcing her head back. She followed that by slamming her bound hands into the witch's gut.

Nartalova stumbled away, screaming for help. It came out as a gargled moan, but it was enough. The door burst open and *soldaty* poured into the room.

"Lock her in the dungeon!" the old woman croaked.

Dungeon? Despite the danger, Francine's lips twitched. The old woman thought she lived in a fairy tale.

"I don't recommend the basement, *Voz'y Nachal'nik.*" The highest-ranking soldier spread his hands as if apologizing for contradicting his ruler. "There is unrest in this neighborhood. I've sent two of my men to check it out, and I don't want to spread the rest thinner than necessary."

He considers a building exploding to be unrest? Francine marveled.

"Fine. Just get her out of my sight!" Nartalova commanded. "And find out what the hell is going on. Taniz Beta has always been the least of my worries. Even I must admit Dusica has been an excellent steward of this world. The eruption of violence now—when I am here—is troubling."

The men bowed and one of them grabbed Francine's arm. She planted her feet, resisting when he dragged her toward the door. He spun and slapped her, his reinforced gauntlet splitting the skin on her cheekbone.

Friends are coming, Sashelle said. *Do not fear.*

The senior guard jerked, his face invisible behind his helmet's mirrored faceplate. He took a step back, pulling Francine with him. "*Voz'y Nachal'nik,* I regret to inform you—our security has been breached."

Francine glanced at the window, but the glowing eyes were gone.

TONY STOOD at the bottom of the back stairs, back against the wall. Dusica waited on the other side of the door, hand on the knob. Tony counted down with his fingers, and she yanked.

And nearly fell down when it didn't budge. "Damn door," Dusica muttered. "Gotta remember to fix this." She twisted the knob the other direction and pulled again. The door swung forcefully, narrowly missing her nose.

Tony darted around the jamb, blaster aimed up the stairs. The *soldaty* fired at him, and he ducked behind the door. "Full riot gear," he muttered to Dusica. "Too bad Francine's lockup trick won't work here."

Dusica gave him a questioning look, but he waved it off. He pulled a concussion grenade off his belt and tossed it up the stairs. Dusica slammed the door shut.

Boom.

Before they could open the door again, it burst into flames. "*Shirtazh*! They're using flame throwers! Those *shirtazh smut'yan* are using flamethrowers IN MY HOUSE!" Dusica lunged forward, jammed the muzzle of her blaster through the burning hole in the door, and held down the trigger. A stream of energy poured up the stairs.

"Ow!" She flung the weapon away and dove for cover.

"They overheat if you do that," Tony said.

"You think? Did I get him?"

A pair of bolts slammed through the hole in the door, burning the wallpaper across the hall.

"Nope," Tony said. "Marielle, what's your status?"

"Kinda busy," Marielle gasped through the comm channel. "Call back later!"

"Quinn! Where are you?" Tony called.

"With Amanda and Marielle," Quinn answered. "She took out one of the guys on the stairs, but one is still firing, and he's got backup. Fyo should be coming your direction. Wilfrud says the police are en route to the neighborhood."

Tony stuck his gun through the hole and pulled the trigger a couple times. "What will the police do?"

Dusica lifted her nose. "Whatever I tell them to do."

"You sure about that?" Amanda asked through the comm. "You thought all these folks were loyal to you, but they're blowing up the neighbors' houses."

"No, that was Maerk," Tony reminded her.

"Great!" Dusica groaned. "Maybe you should call off your goons."

"You were in on the planning, Dusi," Fyo said. "You knew they'd be creating distractions."

"Distractions are one thing! Blowing up the neighbors' property is something else."

"What kind of Russosken are you?" Amanda asked. "Don't you guys break people's stuff for a living?"

"They've blasted a hole in my door!" Dusica wailed. "They've singed my wallpaper! I don't want them destroying the whole thing!"

"Plus, I'd like to get out alive," Marielle answered. "Front stairs are clear. Hey, where's the caat going?"

No one answered. More blasts rained down the back stairs. The wall opposite the door burst into flame. Dusica screamed in frustration. Fyo thundered down the hall,

Tony ducked out, popped off a couple of shots up the steps, and flung himself out of range again. "Where *is* the caat going?"

An ear-splitting shriek echoed down the stairs and something heavy fell, bouncing down the steps and rattling the remains of the door. The fragments shuddered and crumbled into a burning heap, with an armored *soldaty* lying in the middle of the pile.

Don't sit there washing yourselves, Sashelle said inside Tony's head. *There is prey to be toyed with.*

Tony darted a look into the stairwell, but it was empty. He blasted the light fixture at the top, throwing the space into shadow, then jerked his head at Dusica. They leapt over the prone man, taking the steps two at a time.

At the top, they stopped to check the upper hallway. Blaster fire rained down on him and he ducked. "Two guarding the third door on the right," Tony whispered through the comm. "That means two more inside with Francine and the nin-chuck. We're at the top of the back stairs."

"We're just around the corner," Marielle answered.

"These guys are expecting us," Tony said. "Full riot gear, and they've set up a barricade in front of the door. We can go in firing everything we have, but they've got the gear to weather it."

"Can you reach the last door on your left without getting caught in the fire?" Fyo asked.

"If you lay down cover, I think we can," Marielle answered.

"Good. That room has a bathroom with a connecting door to the next room," Fyo told them. "If you get in there, we can burn through the wall into the suite they're guarding. I'm coming to help."

"What?!" Dusica shrieked. "That bathroom has vintage fixtures!"

The soldiers by the door, alerted by her cry, started firing at them. Tony ducked. "Dusica, shut up. It's come down to your house or your sister. Which is it?"

Dusica heaved a dramatic sigh. "Faina, of course."

"Russosken are very dramatic," Fyo said, his words broken by panting gasps. The thumping of his feet as he ran added punctuation. "We wail and moan about everything. It's our way of dealing with grief."

"Not a great trait during a sneak attack," Marielle growled. "If you're coming, get your sorry butt up here."

"Almost there," Fyo said. "And you're one to talk. You went crazy down there. Tony, draw their fire."

Tony and Dusica lay on the steps, peeking over the threshold, blasting the Russosken barricade with their rifle fire. Tony got a lucky shot, hitting the closer guard in the helmet, which would temporarily blind him. The other guard turned to target them while his partner was down. Marielle, Quinn, Amanda, and Fyo snuck across the corridor behind the defenders and through a door.

"We're in," Fyo reported. "Keep 'em busy."

CHAPTER 36

THE *SOLDATY* FORCED Francine into the sitting room. She kicked and twisted, until one of the men slammed his rifle butt against her head. Her vision went gray, and her legs gave out.

Ambassador. Sashelle's voice cut through the fog. *Your pride is nearly here.*

"My what?" Francine peeled her eyes open. She lay on Dusica's expensive Rossiya silk carpet with something dripping down her forehead. She turned her head the barest bit to the right and saw drops of blood on the yellow-and-blue rug. "Dusi's gonna kill me."

Your pride, Sashelle insisted. An image of Dusica, Fyo, Tony, Quinn, and Marielle intruded on her fogged mind. *They are in the next room. You need to be ready.*

Francine groaned. "Great timing."

Another explosion boomed through the house, rattling the hideous china figurines in the heavy wood display case. Francine pushed herself up to her hands and knees.

An armored *soldaty* stood by the window, peering out. At Francine's movement, he swiveled toward her, weapon pointed between her eyes.

"Don't shoot," Francine croaked. "I won't do anything."

"If you hadn't bitten me, I might be inclined to believe you."

Had she bitten him? "That was a stupid idea. Don't know what I was thinking. It's not like you have a lot of skin showing. Where did I bite you?"

He didn't reply

Dominant wrist. Sashelle's tone oozed satisfaction.

"Are you taking over my mind? I didn't want to say all those things."

"What are you talking about?" the *soldaty* asked.

I wanted you out of that room. Poking the old queen seemed an expedient method. Plus, she was pissing me off.

"Expedient?" Francine spit out the words. "You could have gotten me killed."

I didn't.

"What are you talking about?" The *soldaty* sounded rattled.

Francine grinned and pushed up to a sitting position. "What's the plan?"

They will be coming through that wall in a couple minutes.

"How?" She touched her temple, but the cut seemed to have stopped bleeding. Based on the blotch on the carpet, Rossiya silk was nicely absorbent.

"Who are you talking to?" The *soldaty* stalked across the room toward her. "You were scanned for comm gear."

She gave him her best evil grin. "Voices in my head." For good measure, she crossed her eyes then rolled them back, so he'd see only the whites.

Duck!

Francine dropped her head to her knees. Something heavy swooshed over her. She caught a glimpse of the *soldaty*'s rifle butt swishing away. She twisted and rolled, coming to her feet and closing with him before he could reverse the weapon. She grabbed the rifle, and they grappled for a few seconds. With the whine of his power armor, he shoved, pushing her into a wall.

She released the weapon and dropped to her knees before he got the gun against her throat. The wall behind her back vibrated. Was it warm? *Oh, futz.* Sashelle had said they'd be coming *through*. She dove between the *soldaty's* legs, sliding across the floor toward the center of the room.

The *soldaty* spun and put his foot on her back. "Freeze. Or I shoot."

Francine turned her head slowly, peering up from the corner of her eye. With the helmet on and the faceplate set to opaque, it was impossible to see his expression, but his voice carried a hint of bluff. "If you were allowed to shoot me, you would have already."

Before he could answer, a gout of flame burst from the wall and enveloped his head.

"WE'RE IN!" Quinn told Tony as Marielle shoved her weapon through the still-burning wall.

Marielle's rifle whined and barked three times. On the other side of the wall, something thudded to the ground.

"How do you know you didn't hit Faina?" Fyo yelled.

"I look before I shoot," Marielle said sarcastically. "It's called aiming."

Fyo peered at the small opening in the wall. "How could you see through there? You can only see a tiny part of the room."

"I saw a *soldaty* helmet." As Marielle spoke, she pushed Fyo aside and kicked through the lower part of the weakened wall. "He's not dead, though, so let's get in there." She threw her shoulder against the remains and burst through. "Francine?"

Quinn followed Marielle through the gap, her gun held at the ready. Amanda rushed in behind her, clearing the other side of the room. Marielle stood over the *soldaty*, who had started pushing to his feet. He glanced at her and dropped to his belly, hands spread wide.

Probably terrified of Marielle, Quinn thought.

"Watch him," Marielle told Quinn. "If he so much as twitches, shoot him again."

Quinn trained her rifle on the prone man.

Watch the— Sashelle's comment cut off.

The door to the hall burst open. Keeping her weapon pointed at the target, Quinn leapt over him in an effort to meet the new threat without exposing herself to the closer one.

She needn't have worried. Amanda, Fyo, and Marielle fired in quick succession. Three point-blank hits to the helmet appeared to be the magic number—the *soldaty* sank to the ground. A second one darted back into the corridor.

Weapons whined, and bolts of energy flashed past the open door—Tony, keeping the other *soldaty* pinned down outside.

Fyo dropped to his knees beside his sister. "Are you okay?" His hand hovered over her bloody temple.

She batted his hand away. "I'm fine. Thanks for the spectacular rescue. Dusi's going to kill you, though." She pointed at the ravaged wall.

"How many is that?" Quinn asked.

"How many of the assassins?" Marielle stalked to the stunned man in the doorway. His armor appeared to have been fried, but he moved a little. Marielle brandished her knife. "Still three to go." With brutal efficiency, she jammed her blade into the man's neck. Dark red blood pulsed around the blade. She yanked it out and turned toward Quinn. "Two, now, if you count the one in the hall."

"You don't need to kill this one. He's just a soldier, not one of the assassins. And he's not moving, are you?" Quinn poked Francine's former captor with her rifle. "Take off your helmet."

The man didn't move.

"Take off your helmet, or I'll let her kill you," Quinn said. "Slowly."

The *soldaty* raised his hands to his head and carefully unlatched the helmet. "Don't shoot." Still on his stomach, he pulled off the smoke-stained bowl and let it roll to the side, exposing his short blond hair.

He was young, probably no more than twenty. Like most *soldaty*. Young and expendable. Quinn gritted her teeth. "If you move, I will shoot you. If you attempt to contact anyone else, I will shoot you."

"Quinn, we don't have time for this," Marielle snarled. "If you won't take him out, I will."

"We don't have time?" Quinn asked. "What's your rush? We've got Francine. That was the goal, remember? And the nin-chuck only has one protector remaining. If you don't count the one in the hall. How's it going, Tony?"

"I can do this all night," he replied. "But I'd prefer not to. Can someone get the drop on this guy?"

Marielle heaved a sigh. "I have to do everything around here." She glared at the others and pointed to Quinn's captive. "Watch him. Don't let the queen of mercy here get blindsided." She stomped to the door. "Keep him busy, Tony."

Almost faster than Quinn's brain could process, Marielle leaned out and fired three long blasts. Then silence.

"That was easy," Fyo said, "Now what?"

"Now we finish the job." Amanda pointed to the office door.

"Be careful." Quinn jumped when Wilfrud's voice came through the comm. She'd forgotten the old man was there. "The one with her is Anatoly Serinsky. He's a very dangerous assassin." Quinn relayed the message to the others.

"It had to be Serinsky," Fyo said. "The Demon of Rossiya."

Quinn nudged the *soldaty* captive with her rifle again. "What's your name?"

He glared up at her, his cheek still pressed firmly to the carpet.

"Name," Quinn snapped.

"Aleksei."

"Who do you belong to, Aleksei? The *nachal'nik*? Or the Russosken?"

The young man looked confused. "That's the same thing."

"No, it isn't." Fyo stepped to Quinn's shoulder. "Are you loyal to that woman, personally, or to the Russosken—the people?"

The *soldaty* stared up at Fyo, twisting his neck to get a better look. "Who are you? You look like her."

"This is Fyotor Nartalov, rightful heir of the Russosken," Quinn said. "The *nachal'nik* attempted to assassinate her own grandson, but he is alive. He wants freedom and prosperity for all Russosken. What do you want?"

She stepped back and allowed the boy to roll over and sit up. "I want to be free," he whispered. "All hail Fyotor!"

"Give me your helmet." Quinn nodded to Fyo. "Cover me."

Fyo swung his blaster around to point it at the boy sitting on the carpet. Quinn took his soot-covered helmet and reached inside. She yanked out the foam padding around the chin and snapped the microphone module out of the casing. "Now he can't talk to Serinsky. Put that back on."

The boy took the helmet and sealed it over his head. Quinn pulled the powerpack from the boy's blaster, snapped a cover over the internal connections rendering it useless, and slapped the battery back into place. She handed the rifle to the boy. "You've taken me and Francine—" She gestured for the other woman to rise. "—prisoner. Take us in there."

"They won't trust him," Tony hissed through the comm. "They have biometrics. They'll know his helmet was breached."

"Doesn't matter," Quinn said. "We just need enough doubt to get in. Then Marielle will take out Serinsky and we'll grab the nin-chuck. Coup complete."

"It can't be that easy," Marielle said. "It never is."

"Sashelle," Quinn called softly. "Where are you?"

Here.

Quinn looked around the room, then spotted Sashelle sitting near Francine's feet. "When did you—Did anyone see the caat come in?"

Everyone, even Aleksei, shook their heads.

Predictably, the caat did not elaborate.

"You're no help *here*; we need eyes in there." Quinn pointed to the inner room. "Tony, can you get a drone inside?"

"Would it matter if I could?" Tony asked. "You can't think they're still in there. I'm sure they ran as soon as we burned through that wall."

"They would have," Dusica said. "Except that room is the saferoom. This door is the only way in or out. The bad news is, it's heavily defended. The good news is, they're definitely still in there."

"But there's a window," Francine said. "What kind of saferoom has a window?"

"A window with a military-grade defense shield and internal, isolated sixty-hour power source," Dusica replied.

"No wonder Sashelle didn't want to come inside," Francine muttered. "But I put my hand out the window!"

"Yeah," Dusica said. "There's a standard bug screen. The force shield gets turned on when we go into lockdown mode."

"When did that happen?" Tony asked. "Shouldn't it have been impossible to get this far if the house was in lockdown?"

An alarm started blaring. The walls rumbled, pictures and shelves shaking. A grinding sounded, and bright blue sparks danced across the doors and window.

"I guess it happened now," Fyo said.

CHAPTER 37

QUINN ACTIVATED HER COMM CHANNEL. "Wilfrud, are you there?"

Static buzzed in her ear. She tried again. "Wilfrud?"

"Any luck?" Tony asked.

"Nope." Quinn dropped onto the chaise lounge. "Now what?"

"The walls to that room are all shielded?" Tony asked.

Dusica nodded. "All the walls, windows, ceiling, floor. Like a big cage."

"Controlled from where?" Tony asked.

"In there, of course."

Marielle crossed to the window and peered out. "Could they have snuck out the window and activated the saferoom remotely after they left? Or on a countdown?" She pulled her weapon off her shoulder and aimed it out the window.

"I—uh, maybe? Why do you ask?"

"Because there are two people fleeing across your front lawn." She snapped the safety off and aimed the weapon.

"Don't shoot!" Tony cried. "That force shield will ricochet the pulse faster than—"

"No, it won't," Dusica yelled as Fyo, Tony, Amanda, and Quinn bolted for the door. "Take the shot!"

They thundered down the stairs, the sound of Marielle's blasts punctuating the night.

"You got him!" Francine's voice carried over the thump of their footsteps.

Sashelle streaked by, leaping down the front staircase in two massive jumps. She pulled up short at the front door, tail lashing. *Hurry up, humans!*

Tony reached the bottom seconds later and threw the door open. Sashelle disappeared into the dark. Fyo stormed past, Quinn and Amanda hurtling down the front steps behind him.

Across the lawn, a dim lump near the front gate started to rise. Serinsky heaved himself to his feet and stumbled away, his scorched armor glinting in the street lamps. The others gave chase. Tony got a shot off, taking him down again. Amanda leapt onto the fallen man and pressed the muzzle of her rifle to the weak joint between the helmet and the body armor. "Don't even try it."

Tony raced up and slapped a device to the man's power armor. "Clear!" Amanda jumped away, and lightning sparked over the man's body in a bright net. "Armor is dead," Tony said with satisfaction. "Zip ties, Amanda."

Quinn didn't slow down. Tony and Amanda were more than capable of taking care of one Russosken assassin in nonfunctional armor. She chased after Fyo. He sprinted around a corner and stopped so suddenly that she slammed into his back.

Ten meters ahead, the *nachal'nik* stood in the middle of the sidewalk, breathing heavily. She held a pistol to Maerk's head.

"*Futz!*" Quinn cried, her blaster pointed at the old woman.

Nartalova glared at Quinn "Don't come one step closer."

"Or what, *Babushka?*" Fyo snarled. "You'll kill an innocent bystander?"

"In a heartbeat." The old woman's her gun shifted, pointing at

Fyo. "Or maybe I'll kill you first. Since you're supposed to be dead anyway."

"You *shirtazh smut'ya!*" Fyo took another step, and the *nachal'nik* fired a shot over his head. Fyo froze.

"You're surprised the bloodthirsty leader of the galaxy's most violent clan is willing to kill her rival? You've been hiding too long." Shaking her head at his naiveté, Quinn turned to the old woman. "Nartalova, there's nowhere for you to go. Shooting anyone else will only make this worse for you."

"I have resources you know nothing about," the old woman called. "I have legions waiting to race to my rescue. I can snap my fingers—" She paused, as if realizing her hands were full with the gun and Maerk's arm. "They'll come. They'll save me and if need be, avenge me."

Something moved in the shadows. Quinn kept talking, hoping to distract the old woman. "But they aren't here. We took out all your *soldaty.* Half of them didn't want to be here, anyway. What have you done to make them loyal to you? You rule through fear. Do you really think they wouldn't rather take their chances with your successor?" She jerked her head at Fyo. Maybe that wasn't a great idea. She didn't want to push the old woman into shooting Fyo. "And don't get any stupid ideas about killing him. Dusica and Fran—Faina will step in."

She hissed at Fyo. "Get behind me!"

"I'm not hiding behind a woman any longer," Fyo said proudly. "I've hid behind Dusi too long. Now I'm standing on my own."

A blaster whined and spat. Maerk jerked to the side just in time and the bolt of energy sliced the air between Fyo and Quinn.

"*Futz!*" Fyo cried.

"Run, little boy, or I'll fry your liver!" Nartalova yelled. Her hand shook.

A ferocious roar split the air, and Sashelle burst out of the shadows, claws extended. With a shriek, she launched herself at the *nachal'nik,* taking her to the ground. The old woman's hand was ripped from Maerk's arm. The blaster fired, the bolt flying far over Quinn's head. Nartalova hit the ground, and her head cracked against the sidewalk.

The caat rode the woman down, then sprang off and stalked a few steps away. There, she sat and groomed herself.

Quinn and Fyo stared at the *nachal'nik* lying on the ground in a growing pool of blood. Maerk stumbled away and heaved into a nearby bush.

Tony found them a few moments later, still unmoving.

Sashelle's tail twitched. *What's for dinner?*

THE LOCAL POLICE arrived to investigate multiple reports of shots fired and buildings burning. "This is most unusual." The officer made notes in his comtab and took vid. "You have no idea what caused this damage?"

Standing in the alley behind her house, Dusica gazed at the smoldering hulk of her neighbor's shed. "I heard the blasts and saw the flames. Wilfrud and Maerk put out the fires." She glanced at the two men, leaning against a large tree. "You didn't see anything unusual, did you?"

Both men shook their heads. Quinn was glad Maerk stayed in the shadows. The greenish tinge to his face might have tipped off the officer.

"Thank you for your assistance, madam." The officer clicked his comtab off. "The other neighbors thought they heard weapons discharge? Just before that shed exploded."

"Uh..." Tony glanced up and down the alley conspiratorially. "The guy next door hides his stash in there. From his partner." He mimed chugging a drink. "It's a bit of a sore spot in their relationship, so... That stuff makes a hell of a noise when it explodes. Don't ask me how I know."

"How do you know, sir?" the officer asked, deadpan.

Tony shrugged. "Back in college...long time ago."

The other man nodded. "I understand. We don't want to get involved in a domestic disagreement unless one of the parties is in danger. I don't suppose..." He glanced at Dusica.

"No," Tony and Dusica said in unison.

"Very good." The officer tapped his comtab and stuck it into his belt pouch. "Thank you for your assistance, sir, ma'am." He nodded to Wilfrud and Maerk and returned to his vehicle.

"You'd better make a big donation to the policemen's ball," Tony said.

Dusica gave him a confused look, which he waved off.

"Now what?" Quinn asked when they returned to the house.

"Have you heard anything from out in the 'verse, Amanda?" Tony waved at the ceiling as they entered the dining room.

They sat around the huge table, ignoring the smells of smoke and ozone. Sashelle curled up on a big pillow in the corner, having downed two cans of tuna while they waited for the police to arrive.

Amanda projected her star map above the table. "Good news all the way around. We'll have to get a mop-up crew out to Varitas. Their attempt didn't go over as well as we'd hoped."

"I'm not surprised," Tony replied. "They definitely felt like more of a *talking* than *doing* group. You aren't going, are you?"

"Hell no," Amanda replied. "I don't go anywhere I'm not welcome. I'm not proud of being a tax agent, but I don't need to get discriminated against over it."

Tony turned to Dusica. "What are you hearing from the Russosken, Dusica?"

"A couple clans have requested guidance. I've told them the *nachal'nik* will get back to them as soon as possible. Handle things locally as they see fit, but with the current circumstances, staying under the radar would be preferred. Hopefully fear of the locals will keep them from trying to get revenge. Most of the clans have been decimated. Fyo's going to have his work cut out for him."

Fyo sat at the head of the table, steadily making his way through a fifth of Taniz Wiskee. When they all glanced his direction, he waved the bottle regally and burped.

"We'll get him in shape," Francine said.

"We?" Quinn asked.

"I'm going to stay with Fyo and Dusi, to help them consolidate whatever's left of the Russosken. Marielle's going to take care of security for us. She's already got one recruit."

She grinned at Aleksei, matching Fyo drink for drink. Disposing of his former comrades' bodies had been his task. A reminder of what could happen to those who crossed Dusica and Fyo.

They'd disposed of all but Nartalova's body. Hers went into a stasis chamber so they could prove her rule had rightfully devolved to Fyo.

"Those two are going to have a really bad morning," Quinn said. "I hope you have some strong anti-hangover meds."

"They'll be fine," Dusica grumbled. "They'll probably feel better than me in the morning. Hardheaded boys."

"Tha's your nin-chuck you're talkin' abou'." Fyo hiccupped loudly.

"Show some respec'," Aleksei muttered to his glass. He downed another shot, then laid his head on the table. "All hail the nin-chuck."

Amanda stretched her back, arching and thrusting her chest toward Tony. "Now what?" She glanced at Quinn. "What's next for you?"

"I need to figure out what Reggie is up to," Quinn said. "And make sure he doesn't get another hook into the kids. He doesn't want them. I'm sure he's doing it for Gretmar. Can't have the neighbors talking about who's raising her grandchildren." She rolled her eyes. "Luckily, Dareen and Liz are keeping them safe for now."

Amanda turned to Tony. "How about you? You still in?"

"I'm going to wait and see where the dust settles," Tony replied. "If we've really succeeded in loosening the grip of the Russosken, then the Federation is next. I'm going to start with Andretti and work my way up." He grinned.

Marielle raised an eyebrow at Quinn. "You gonna let him gather all the glory?"

"I'm going to help, of course." Quinn smiled. "I'm not big on revenge, but if I happen to get a bit while trying to make the world a better place, I'm all for it."

FIND out if Tony and Quinn can make the galaxy a better place in *Krimson Flare*.

AUTHOR NOTES

September 4, 2023

Thank you for reading the third book in the *Krimson Empire*.

The rebellion is under way! Quinn has finally dedicated herself to helping, rather than just floating along in Tony's wake. We've learned a lot more about Francine and her powerful family. The Russosken are broken—it's time to take on the Federation. That's coming—in book 4.

I first wrote this book in March and April, 2020, in the heat of the pandemic. It's kind of weird to read my notes from that original book, as I talk about my daughter spending time at the elk ranch. It's a ranch on the edge of town that ran elk when we first moved here. It's been cattle for over a decade now, but everyone still calls it the Elk Ranch. Anyway, the teens would drive out there and park on the 20-foot-wide verge then hang out in their individual cars, so they were "socially distanced." I'm sure there was some cheating going on, but we're rural enough that we weren't hit too hard.

I mentioned in the first two books my gratitude to Craig Martelle who originally published this series. I'd also like to thank his beta team. They read everything Craig publishes and are a fantastic resource. They offered suggestions when I got stuck, and nudged me

AUTHOR NOTES

in various directions when they thought a small tweak would make the story more enjoyable. They're also really great at picking out inconsistencies and plot holes! Without them, this series wouldn't have been as strong.

Thanks to James Caplan, Kelly O'Donnell, John Ashmore, and especially to Mickey Cocker, who has hyper-jumped to the great library in the sky. We miss you, Mickey!

Thanks so much to my amazing Kickstarter backers. I've listed your names on the next page. Without you, this relaunch would have been so much harder!

I'll be republishing the entire series soon, distributing it through Amazon, Kobo, Barnes and Noble, Apple Books, Google Play and all of the other retailers. I also plan to make the books available for sale on my website. If you know anyone who'd like a copy of the series, please send them to juliahuni.com. And if you enjoy hopeful science fiction with heart and humor, check out my other series.

You can find me all over the inter webs.

Email: julia@juliahuni.com
Amazon https://www.amazon.com/stores/author/B07FMNHLK3
Bookbub https://www.bookbub.com/authors/julia-huni
Facebook https://www.facebook.com/Julia.Huni.Author/
Instagram https://www.instagram.com/Julia.Huni.Author/

If you'd like to keep up to date on what's going on with my writing, sign up here. Plus, you can download a short story about Sashelle.

ALSO BY JULIA HUNI

Space Janitor Series:
The Vacuum of Space
The Dust of Kaku
The Trouble with Tinsel
Orbital Operations
Glitter in the Stars
Sweeping S'Ride
Triana Moore, Space Janitor (the complete series)

Tales of a Former Space Janitor
The Rings of Grissom
Planetary Spin Cycle
Waxing the Moon of Lewei
Tales of a Former Space Janitor (books 1-3)
Changing the Speed of Light Bulbs
Sun Spot Remover

Friends of a Former Space Janitor
Dark Quasar Rising
Dark Quasar Ignites

The Phoenix and Katie Li
Luna City Limited

Colonial Explorer Corps Series:
The Earth Concurrence

The Grissom Contention

The Saha Declination

CEC: *The Academy Years* (books 1-3)

The Darenti Paradox

Recycled World Series:

Recycled World

Reduced World

Krimson Empire:

Krimson Run

Krimson Spark

Krimson Surge

Krimson Flare

Julia also writes earth-bound romantic comedy that won't steam your glasses under the not-so-secret pen name Lia Huni

FOR MORE INFORMATION

Use this QR code to stay up-to-date on all my publishing, and get access to my free bonus stores:

Printed in Great Britain
by Amazon